"WHY DON'T YOU TELL US, MS. MIDNIGHT, WHY YOU WERE AT CASTLEBERRY'S?"

"I was there to sell hats. I'd heard..."

"Whatsa matter, Midnight Millinery's not doing so good?"

"The shop is doing quite well, thank you. I heard that Doreen Sands was on a buying frenzy, big orders, high prices."

"So you thought you'd cash in? Whaddya do, stick them with your inferior stuff, seconds and near misses?"

"Of course not. I sell only the highest quality. Here, let me show you."

I got out two hatboxes, opened the first and took out three berets and showed them to Detective Turner. "See, nothing inferior about these hats."

He opened t  ide. "Uh oh," he

BARBARA JAYE WILSON

CAPPED OFF

A BRENDA MIDNIGHT MYSTERY

AVON

TWILIGHT

This is a work of fiction. Names, characters, places, and incidents either are products of the author's imagination or are used fictitiously. Any resemblance to actual events, locales, organizations, or persons, living or dead, is entirely coincidental and beyond the intent of either the author or the publisher.

AVON BOOKS, INC.
1350 Avenue of the Americas
New York, New York 10019

Copyright © 1999 by Barbara Jaye Wilson
Inside cover author photo by Gene Daly
Published by arrangement with the author
Library of Congress Catalog Card Number: 99-94791
ISBN: 0-380-80355-0
www.avonbooks.com/twilight

First Avon Twilight Printing: August 1999

AVON TWILIGHT TRADEMARK REG. U.S. PAT. OFF. AND IN OTHER COUNTRIES, MARCA REGISTRADA, HECHO EN U.S.A.

Printed in the U.S.A.

WCD   10 9 8 7 6 5 4 3 2 1

*Dedicated to X-Dot Potato,
the best little dog*

ACKNOVLEDGMENTS

I would like to thank the milliners of the past, present, and future for inspiration and all those hats.

New York milliners are fully supportive of one another. The way we figure,
it's a really big city, and it's got plenty of heads
to go around. We all do what we can to keep the inhab-
itants well-hatted.

History has demonstrated that the competition comes
not from the milliner up the avenue or across town, but
from the horrific specter of bare-headedness. Any time
any one of us makes a sale and sends a stylish customer
out into the world with a good hat on her head, milliners
throughout the city benefit.

So great is the spirit of milliner cooperation, that one
Sunday last summer when I spotted hundreds of antique
hat blocks for a few dollars each at the Twenty-sixth
Street flea market, the first thing I did—after securing a
couple of dozen for myself—was to drop a quarter into a
pay phone and punch in Fuzzy's cellular number.

She picked up on the first ring. "Have no fear, Fuzzy
here," she said in her foghorn-like voice.

"Where are you?" I asked. With her cellular phone, I
never knew for sure.

"Home at the loft."

She didn't stay home long. While I was still filling her
in on all the whos, whats, wheres, and whens about the
hat blocks, she grabbed her laptop computer, ran out of
her building, and hailed an uptown-headed cab. After we
hung up she called, faxed, or e-mailed every milliner in

the tristate area—all from the back seat of the cab. She managed to get a brief message up on her web page before she arrived at Twenty-sixth and Sixth.

That Fuzzy was a cyber dynamo.

I didn't stick around the flea market to see her. I was already late for a blind date at a trendy new restaurant a block or so north of the Flatiron District. This all happened one of those times my sometime boyfriend Johnny Verlane and I were on the outs. Somebody had fixed me up with the friend of a friend's friend, some guy who used to play guitar in some band I might have seen some time. He was waiting in the bar when I arrived, halfway through Bloody Mary number two.

The restaurant was noted for its dramatically high vaulted ceilings, extremely bright decor, and a wait staff made up of black-clad, sunken-cheeked models and aspiring actors. The ridiculously expensive leaden pancakes came with artificial maple syrup served in a plastic container that stuck to the hot pink one hundred percent polyester tablecloth. The coffee was weak, the omelets dry, the guitar player turned out to be a jerk and a half, and the date was a big fat flop.

Once again I told myself never again.

On my way home I stopped back by the flea market. The dazed vendor didn't know what hit him. "All of a sudden," he told me, "a swarm of frenzied women swooped down on my booth and wiped out my entire inventory of hat blocks. Who were they anyway?"

"Milliners," I said.

Three months later Fuzzy called me with the latest millinery news flash. "Brenda," she said, "you better pack up some sample hats and get your size-four butt over to Castleberry's. Doreen Sands is buying like it's going out of style, spending like crazy, big bucks, big orders. You do know Doreen, don't you?"

"Only by reputation."

And what a reputation. Doreen Sands was known as the best millinery buyer in all of New York City, which pretty much equaled the whole country. Milliners like to gripe about millinery buyers, but everybody agreed that Doreen Sands was the absolute tops. She had exquisite taste, and was known to be honest and fair in her dealings. Through intelligent promotion she had done a lot to expand millinery awareness. It was quite a coup when upstart Castleberry's made her an offer she couldn't refuse and pried her loose from a prestigious position in a long-established uptown store.

"You don't need an appointment," said Fuzzy. "All you've got to do is pop by the buying offices on audition day and wait your turn. What could be easier?"

"Thanks, but I don't think so," I said.

My Greenwich Village hat store, Midnight Millinery, struggled. In order to keep the landlord happy, I sometimes wholesaled to boutiques. To maintain my artistic integrity, I stayed away from department stores and the large orders they frequently placed. And Fuzzy knew it.

"Don't be like that," she said. "I'm not talking couture here. Whip up something special. You can still give it that Brenda Midnight flair, but keep it simple. Surely you can come up with a couple of styles that don't take a week to make."

Easy enough for Fuzzy to say. Her hats were way high on concept, way low on the hand stitches, plain old way out. She'd once glued a yard of chartreuse belting ribbon to an old Ramones album cover, tied it on her head, and started a fad.

"I'll think about it," I said. "Thanks for the tip."

"Very funny," said Fuzzy. She knew quite well that a tip is a top of a hat. "If you go, tell Doreen Sands I sent you."

Instead of resisting, I met Fuzzy's challenge head on. That very day I designed a unique gravity-defying beret that didn't take forever to make, and didn't suffer too awfully much from machine work. From that basic hat, I devised several shape variations, and chose fabric in a fashion-forward fall palette.

A week later, I was ready. I got out my two hard case travel hatboxes and packed up the new samples, threw in a couple of little hatlettes from last season, and—in a burst of optimism—my order book. Then I headed over to Castleberry's vast department store on Sixth Avenue.

Castleberry's. A seven-story-high, block-long department store. Not what anybody would expect plopped down into the heart of charming, bohemian, Greenwich Village. When the plans to build were first announced, the idea didn't sit at all well with the bongo-thumping poets, tie-dyed hippies, safety-pinned pink-haired punks, yupped-up stockbrokers, and assorted radicals, painters, writers, singers, dancers, designers, and actors who lived in the neighborhood.

It doesn't take much to get Greenwich Villagers up in arms—they'll protest at the drop of a hat—but knocking down a gritty neighborhood bar where abstract expressionists used to brawl, a candy store that still made honest-to-god genuine New York egg creams, and a world-famous pizza joint to make way for a department store got everybody more riled than usual.

Groups sprang up to do battle, coalitions formed, factions broke off, and infighting began. They marched, sat-in, signed petitions, and wrote letters to current officeholders as well as anybody running for anything anytime in the foreseeable future.

None of it did any good.

Inch by inch, girder by girder, brick piled atop brick, the structure that was to become Castleberry's rose. During the year-long construction, Sixth Avenue turned into a disaster zone. Gigantic cranes dangled heavy stuff overhead, lines of churning cement trucks double-parked, and for several months crossing the avenue was next to impossible.

Once the building was up and the store had a hoopla-filled grand opening complete with a parade of baby elephants in silly costumes, a very strange thing happened. The denizens of Greenwich Village awoke one day to the realization that their wishes had come true. With Castleberry's department store in the neighborhood, nobody ever had to go above Fourteenth Street anymore, not even to buy sheets. Now, whenever villagers congregated outside the store, it was to line up for a twenty percent off early bird sale.

I circumvented such a line of eager shoppers when I arrived a few minutes before ten lugging my two hatboxes. My instructions were to go to the service entrance on the side of the building. Fuzzy was right. I didn't need an appointment. When I called the buying office, an efficient voice mail system told me to show up on any first Wednesday of the month and wait my turn. I figured it would be a long, possibly humiliating wait, so I brought along a tailoring book to pass the time. If nothing else, maybe I would finally master bound buttonholes.

A guard in a dark green, gold-trimmed Castleberry's uniform stood in front of the service entrance. I told him my business. He pushed open the door and pointed me toward an elevator. "Take it to the top floor and follow the signs to the buying offices," he said, "and don't forget to sign in."

The swift-moving studio-apartment-sized freight elevator deposited me on the seventh floor. Buying offices were to the right; credit department, return window, and employee lounge were all to the left.

I stood outside for a moment or two to adjust my skirt and get up my nerve, then entered the buying office reception area. The place was already jam-packed with designers, plus all the stuff they hoped to sell. I maneuvered around big black cases, wheeled trunks, and bulging garment bags to get over to the desk where a bored receptionist in a fitted blue suit greeted me with a sigh. "What do you have?"

"Millinery," I said.

She scratched her head with a professionally manicured fingernail and gave me a blank look.

"Hats," I explained, hoisting the hatboxes so she could see. "You know, like berets."

"Oh yeah, right. Hats. That's cool. I like hats. My boyfriend says I have a hat face."

Every woman has a hat face. All she has to do is find

the right hat, or else wear the wrong hat the right way. I didn't want to get into heavy-duty millinery theory with the receptionist, so I mumbled something about her good cheekbones and added my name to the bottom of a very long sheet of paper.

All the seats and much of the standing room had already been taken. I found a piece of wall to lean up against, put my hatboxes down, and soaked up the unpleasant atmosphere. Nervous designers eyed each other jealously. Shoes tapped on the tile floor, and fingernails drummed on any available surface. I seemed to be the only milliner, at least I was the only person in the room with hatboxes. I hoped that meant the wait wouldn't be as long as the sign-in sheet indicated.

Think again.

I opened up one of my hatboxes, took out the tailoring book, and puzzled over the step-by-step illustrated instructions for bound buttonholes. Every so often the receptionist called out a name and one of the waiting designers would drag a garment bag through a set of metal doors that led to the individual buyer's offices.

After an hour of concentrating on the tailoring book, I began to get antsy, looked up and saw that the crowd had thinned out enough to free up some chairs. I sat down in one, put my feet up on my hatboxes, leaned back in the molded plastic chair, and thought about my presentation.

In all, I'd brought two variations of three basic berets in six different fabrications. That was a lot of hats. Not too many, I hoped. I didn't want to confuse the issue. I wouldn't show the hatlettes to Doreen unless it seemed appropriate. I loved them—tiny wisps, more idea than hat—but some buyers didn't go for them at all. Any of the designs would be possible to make in the big numbers Fuzzy had hinted at and still maintain a vestige of my artistic integrity.

I did some rough calculations. If Doreen Sands ordered two dozen of each beret and gave me a decent delivery date I'd be okay, three dozen and I'd have to cheat and sew in the head-size bands by machine. Four dozen I didn't want to think about. If the hats got displayed in one of the big windows facing Sixth Avenue . . .

I was busy daydreaming and counting my hats before they were sold when all of a sudden I noticed a distinct change in the atmosphere. The remaining designers stopped tapping and drumming. There was a commotion outside in the hallway. No sooner had I realized something was happening than a green-uniformed Castleberry's security man burst through the door, sprinted across the waiting room over to the inner double doors, which he held open for the two EMS workers who charged in behind him. Behind the EMS workers came two uniformed cops.

One of the cops, a petite, blond-ponytailed female, planted herself in front of the outer door, folded her arms, and announced to everyone in the waiting room, ''None of you even think about leaving.''

2

Take a roomful of nervous, competitive designers impatient to get on with it already, add some kind of as-yet-undefined, but obviously major problem, stick a pipsqueak lady cop with a rotten attitude by the door, have her tell everybody they can't leave, and you've got what is known as a real bad New York experience.

To keep from fully experiencing it myself, I returned to the tailoring book. To hell with bound buttonholes; instead I decided to read up on the importance of proper interfacing—much easier to understand in the chaos, and of potentially greater use in millinery. However, with all the bad vibes shooting around that room, it was hard to concentrate, even on interfacing.

The designers grumbled and cursed their rotten luck, each other, and Castleberry's for allowing such a thing—whatever the hell it was—to happen.

After a few minutes one designer got fed up with the situation. He stood, slung his garment bag over his shoulder, and boldly approached the lady cop.

"You can't keep me here against my will," he snipped.

The lady cop cleared her throat. "Sit your ass back down. I, and only I, will let you know if and when you can leave."

"Do you have any idea who I am?" asked the designer.

The lady cop shrugged.

I didn't recognize him either. If he were the big deal

8

he pretended to be, he wouldn't have to show up to wait his turn on audition day. He'd have his own showroom and buyers would go to him.

"I'll have you know that I have friends in high places," he boasted. "Very, very high places. And you'll be very, very, very sorry you ever messed with me."

He was poised to say something else when the outer doors flew open. The lady cop stepped out of the way and in marched two men side by side. One was black, the other white. The designers must have noticed the mens' fine custom-made suits and expensive shoes and perhaps thought they were department store bigwigs.

I knew different.

Turner and McKinley.

Oh boy. I scrunched down in my chair and propped up the tailoring book in front of my face.

Too late.

Turner had already spotted me from across the room. "Not you again," he said, not sounding any too happy about the fact.

"Geeze," added his partner McKinley. "If it isn't Brenda Midnight, our very own neighborhood milliner."

I forced a smile. "How nice to see you, detectives."

Turner and McKinley were more Johnny Verlane's friends than mine. Back when Johnny was a struggling actor and his now top-rated *Tod Trueman, Urban Detective* television show was just another pilot, Johnny's agent called in a couple of favors and arranged for Turner and McKinley to give Johnny lessons in how to walk and talk and drive like a cop. In return, Johnny told them the name of his tailor, gave them occasional entertainment freebies, and saw to it that they got invited to glitzy show biz parties.

My relationship with the two detectives could best be described as shaky. I'd done them a couple of favors which they never fully appreciated and they'd done the same for me.

For a moment there in the waiting room, none of the three of us said a word. I looked from one scowling de-

tective to the other. I could feel the electricity in the air
as our brains sputtered and churned, calculating who currently owed whom what.

I guess the detectives came up on the deficit side.
Turner refreshed his frown and told me I was free to go
home. Actually what he said was, "Get out of my face,
Ms. Midnight." He seemed crankier than usual. Johnny
had mentioned that the detective and his long-time girlfriend had recently broken up. I figured that was why.

McKinley was no worse than his usual grouchy self.
"We do know where to find you, Ms. Midnight. We'll
deal with you later."

I closed the tailoring book, slipped it into one of the
hatboxes, and got up to leave. It was an uncomfortable
situation. I felt the icy stares of each and every designer
who was still stuck in the waiting room. The receptionist
sneered. Even the lady uniformed cop gave me a strange
look as she shoved the door open for me.

It is all who you know.

Clearly, something very bad had happened at Castleberry's. With homicide detectives Turner and McKinley
on the scene, it was pretty clear what, if not exactly to
whom. I had a hunch about that, and it did not make me
happy.

I exited the same way I'd come in, down in the freight
elevator and out the side service entrance. The guard I'd
seen on my way in was still on duty, a worried look on
his face. I was afraid he'd stop me, and ask where the
hell I thought I was going. Fortunately he was more focused on the street where a news van had double-parked,
blocking what I knew to be Turner and McKinley's
unmarked vehicle.

A photogenic anchorman eased himself out of the van
and casually shook his sandy-colored razor-cut hairstyle
into place.

I got out of there.

I stopped by the apartment to pick up my little dog, Jackhammer. Together we headed over to the shop, a tiny

storefront on nearby West Fourth Street. From outside, I heard my telephone ring. As I struggled to roll open the gates and unlock the door, my answering machine took the call. When I finally got inside, Fuzzy's voice boomed out of the speaker. "Did you hear about—"

I put down the hatboxes and picked up the phone. "I not only heard," I said, "I was *there*. In the flesh, hats in hand, so to speak."

"There? Where?"

"Castleberry's of course. Isn't that what you're calling about?"

"No. Do tell. What happened at Castleberry's?"

"Well," I said, "the other day after you called, I made up some berets with Doreen Sands in mind. I took them over to Castleberry's this morning, but before I got in to see her, there was a big commotion. Whatever happened must have been pretty bad. EMS showed up, then the cops. I got sent home because—well, just because."

Tempting as it was to tell Fuzzy all the details, it seemed wise to hold off a bit. I didn't want her jumping to any conclusions. She'd have it up on her web page in two minutes. "So, what was it you called about?" I asked.

"Bodies," she said. "Another bankruptcy auction. They've got oodles of plush felt bodies and hoods, good colors, a veritable hat blocker's paradise."

Jackhammer ran around the periphery of the shop, sniffing, making sure all was in order, then curled up on the bed he'd made by piling up scavenged fabric scraps.

I put the hatboxes under the counter and tuned in an all-news radio station. After twenty minutes of traffic updates about a wreck and subsequent snarl at the Holland Tunnel, there was no mention of Castleberry's. I changed to a talk station, where every caller sounded completely and totally insane. Much more of that and I'd be afraid to walk outside ever again. I shut the radio off, fully confident that sooner or later, Turner and McKinley would come by as promised and give me what was sure to be bad news.

Meanwhile, I had work to do, a new design to perfect. The basic shape was good, strong, and sculptural, but something was not quite right. The problem was, I couldn't figure out what.

That afternoon Turner and McKinley showed up and confirmed my hunch. Doreen Sands, millinery buyer extraordinaire, had been murdered, shot dead.

"That's what I thought," I said.

"And just why did you think that, Ms. Midnight?" asked Turner, his voice dripping sarcasm.

"Big hint: Two crack homicide detectives on the scene."

"Not that," said McKinley. "How'd you know who the victim was?"

"Educated guess," I said. "Doreen Sands is the millinery buyer. I signed up to show her some hats. None of the other designers had hatboxes, so it seemed likely I was the only one to see her. Even accounting for the requisite power trip, she kept me waiting an awfully long time. She must have already been dead when I showed up."

Before he got carted off to jail for reasons no one in my family would ever divulge, my great-great uncle made farm chairs, the kind with woven-cane bottoms, from trees that grew on his farm. Industrious, he produced hundreds. Those that didn't sell, got passed down. Everybody in the family has at least two sitting around somewhere.

My two chairs were stationed at Midnight Millinery to the left of the storage room. McKinley picked up one of them, spun it around, and sat in it backwards. Tipping it dangerously far forward, he said mockingly, "She musta already been dead." He looked at Turner. "Right pard?"

"Yep," said Turner. "She musta been." He turned to me. "What we want to hear from you, Ms. Midnight, is not about who musta been dead or when or how they musta got that way. We have sophisticated scientific methods to determine that. What we want to hear from you is the insider stuff."

"What insider stuff?"

"Designer dirt. Like, for instance, the power trip you mentioned. Give us the lowdown on that."

Turner was talking "we" but McKinley had tuned out of the conversation. He got up and carried the farm chair over to the light of the window and pretended to examine the caning. If I was interpreting correctly, it was his turn to play good cop.

"The power trip is no big deal," I explained. "Department store buyers have power over designers. To make sure nobody forgets that fact, they make us wait. In general, the bigger the buyer, the bigger the store, the smaller the designer, the longer the wait. This is hardly unique to hat making. I bet the same kinda stuff happens at the precinct. Right?"

"Difference is," Turner huffed, "nobody got offed at the precinct this morning. Why don't you tell us what you were doing at Castleberry's?"

"I was there to sell some hats."

"Whatsa matter, Midnight Millinery's not doing so good?"

"The shop is doing quite well, thank you, but it never hurts to diversify. I heard that Doreen Sands was on a buying frenzy, big orders, high prices."

"Where did you hear that?"

"Uh . . . through the millinery grapevine." I could see no reason to specifically name Fuzzy.

"No kidding. A millinery grapevine?"

"It's real," I said.

"If you say so. Through this millinery grapevine, you hear you can make a killing, and decide to cash in. Is that right, Ms. Midnight?"

I let his killing reference slide. "A good solid order in a high profile store is not cashing in. I frequently sell wholesale."

"You mean you stick other stores with your inferior stuff, seconds, and near misses?"

"I most certainly do not. All my hats are top quality, no matter where they're sold. I have my reputation to protect."

"Come on, Ms. Midnight, you can level with me.

Doesn't your top quality vary depending on what you can get away with?''

I didn't understand Turner's attitude. While the detectives and I often didn't see eye-to-eye, they'd always raved about my hats. Now Turner was insulting me. What did that have to do with murder? His line of questioning was really starting to make me mad. "All right," I said. "Guess I'll have to show you."

I retrieved my travel hatboxes from beneath the counter and put them on top of my blocking table. I opened one, lifted out a cotton velvet beret, and took it over to show Turner. "I challenge you to find anything inferior about this hat."

As Turner looked at the hat his frown deepened.

"I'll admit," I said, "this style is relatively easy to make. If necessary I can use a machine." I babbled on about artistic integrity to Turner. I don't think he got it.

McKinley, meanwhile, put down the farm chair and wandered over to the blocking table. He opened up the second hatbox and peeked inside. "Uh oh," he said.

There was something intriguingly ominous about the way he said it.

Turner and I went over to the blocking table and looked down into the hatbox. Nestled amid the tissue paper, half hidden by a midnight blue beret and one of the tiny hatlettes, was the glint of gunmetal.

3

Thrump.

McKinley's head slammed into the roof of the vehicle. He yelled at Turner. "Hey! Watch out, okay."

Turner, who had hit fourteen potholes on the way from Midnight Millinery to the precinct, swerved and missed the next one he'd set his sights on.

I didn't know whether to chalk it up to Turner's general bad mood brought on by his recent breakup, or if he was upset about the gun in my hatbox.

I know I sure as hell was.

Still in shock, I sank way down in the back seat, pulled my hat brim low, and tried to figure out what had happened and what it all meant. The what had happened part had me stumped. What it all meant though, was easy enough to determine. I was in a heap of big trouble.

It took me a while to get up enough nerve to ask if I was under arrest.

Turner grunted. McKinley smirked.

It seemed likely. I mean, I'd been at the scene of the crime, and not long after a gun had turned up in my hatbox. If I were Turner and McKinley I would arrest me. However, I would also inform me that I was arrested and read me my rights.

"Well, am I?" I asked again.

No answer.

When Turner finally spoke, it was a complete change

of subject. "So," he said, "how's Johnny?"

I had no idea what Turner was up to, but I played along anyway. "Fine," I said. "Johnny's just fine and dandy."

"You two on-again or off-again?" asked McKinley.

"Neither," I said.

Johnny and I had advanced to a new plateau. I no longer referred to him as my ex-boyfriend—with emphasis on the ex part—but I didn't refer to him as my boyfriend either.

The detectives waited for me to elaborate, but it was too abstract to explain. Turner and McKinley were more into the concrete.

At last I said, "Johnny is writing a book."

McKinley spun his head around and looked directly at me. "Since when can Johnny write? He's a fine actor . . . but."

I knew exactly what McKinley meant by that but. "It will be an as-told-to," I said.

"That's different," said McKinley. "Who is he as-tolding it to?"

"That all depends," I said, "on whether he does a fitness book or a cookbook. I hear it could go either way. Lemmy Crenshaw is still hashing out the details."

I shouldn't have mentioned Lemmy.

Not so long before, in a situation I'm sorry to say was a little bit my fault, Turner and McKinley had mistakenly come to believe that Lemmy had murdered a feather salesman. Thanks to my hard work, the true killer had been exposed. The detectives and Lemmy still held onto infantile grudges. And now, I'd reminded them, which would make them even more angry.

Turner pulled into the precinct drive, let McKinley and me out of the car, and then drove off to find a place to park. McKinley ushered me up the stairs and into the tiny grim cubicle the two detectives shared. He slammed the two hatboxes down on his desk.

"Sit," he said, jutting his chin at an ugly green folding chair in front of his desk.

The hot seat. I couldn't get comfortable. The chair

frame cut off my circulation, the back slats dug into my spine, and whenever I twitched the chair squeaked. An effective discomfort detector, the detectives used the chair as their personal unofficial low-tech polygraph machine.

I had no reason to lie. At least I didn't think I did.

Turner came in, rounded his big oak desk, and sat in a comfortable nonsqueaking upholstered executive swivel chair. He picked up a ballpoint pen and tapped out a rhythm on his in/out box.

McKinley stood in front of me, hands on hips. "All right, Ms. Midnight," he said, "you've got a hell of a lot of explaining to do."

That was not a question, so I kept my mouth shut. I crossed my legs. The chair squeaked.

"How'd the gun get in your hatbox?"

That was a question, so I answered to the best of my ability. "I don't know." Twitch. Squeak. It was difficult to keep a shred of dignity in that chair.

McKinley bent down and brought his face so close I could smell his breath mints. "Did the gun materialize out of thin air?"

Of course he was being sarcastic, but actually, that possibility had occurred to me. It seemed as likely as any other explanation. "Is it the murder weapon?" I asked.

Turner stopped tapping so that he could fully concentrate on glaring at me. "Allow me to clarify," he said. "We're the cops. That means we're the ones who get to ask the questions. You're the milliner, who was not only at the scene of the crime, but who left said scene of said crime with a gun, which could well be the murder weapon. That means you're the one who has to answer the questions."

He resumed tapping.

That was clear enough. I did some answering.

No, I had not left the hatboxes unattended. No, I had not seen anyone put the gun in the hatbox. No, I had not dozed off. No, no, no.

"You sure about that, Ms. Midnight?"

"Positive."

"Think hard, Ms. Midnight. Were your eyes always on both hatboxes?"

"Yes."

"You were never distracted, not even for one second?"

"Well, I was reading a tailoring book, but the boxes were right next to me the whole time. When I sat down, I propped my feet on them. Nobody came near either box. I'm sure."

"Was the room crowded?"

"At first it was, but then . . ."

We went round and round for a long time, making absolutely no progress, until finally the detectives stopped asking. Except for the chair, which squeaked every time I drew breath, the room was silent. After a while, I foolishly risked another question of my own. "Is it okay if I go now?"

Turner sighed as if the weight of the world had dropped directly on his shoulders. To my great surprise and relief he said, "You may."

For the moment at least, I definitely was not under arrest. I leaped out of the hot seat. "When do I get my hats back?"

Turner shook his head. "The stuff's not even at the lab yet. How the hell would I know when it's coming back?"

McKinley had a more helpful attitude, but no facts. "In time, Ms. Midnight, you'll get your hats back in time."

On my way out, Turner said, as I knew he must, "Don't you be sticking your nose into this one. Leave the police work to us."

"Don't worry," I said. And I meant it.

How come you can never find a pay phone when you need one?

Actually, several pay phones were taking up valuable sidewalk space in the neighborhood right around the precinct. None of them worked. Finally, in front of the fruit store on Hudson Street, I found a phone with a dial tone. I dropped in my money and called Johnny. "Okay if I drop by?"

"Sure," he said. "Do me a favor and pick up some

bay leaves on the way. My lentil stew is kinda one-dimensional.''

I figured that meant he was doing the cookbook.

I had to hand it to Johnny: he was refreshingly unaffected by his *Tod Trueman, Urban Detective* fame and the fact that females of all ages swooned at the sight of his smoky gray eyes, high cheekbones, and full head of thick black hair. He was still the same guy I'd met not long after he'd landed his first role, a spot in a twenty-second aftershave commercial.

We were both squeezed into his tiny avocado-colored, wedge-shaped kitchen, me on a high stool by the window which looked out over a shaftway, him in front of the stove stirring a large stainless steel pot of lentils with a big, awkward kitchen utensil that looked like it weighed a ton. Not knowing much about cooking gear, I conjectured it was some kind of specialized lentil spoon.

I handed him the bay leaves.

''Thanks.'' He tore the package open, sniffed the contents, then dropped several bay leaves into the stew.

I was bursting to tell him about Doreen Sands getting killed and the gun in my hatbox, but thought it best to ease him into the story gently. He had a tendency to worry about me. I didn't want him to get too upset. ''You'll never guess who I ran into today?''

Johnny looked up from the lentils and smiled. ''Turner and McKinley.''

So much for easing him into it. ''How'd you know?''

''McKinley called not long after you. He made some small talk, then out of the blue, mentioned that his sister makes a mouth-watering sweet potato pie. Then Turner got on the line and said that *his* sister is an aerobics instructor who has developed a new method that guarantees weight loss. They don't call me *Tod Trueman, Urban Detective* for nothing. I quickly deduced that Turner and McKinley must have heard about my book. When I asked how, your name popped up.''

''What did they say about me?''

''Only that I should warn you about messing around in

police business, which leads me to believe you're up to something. Again.''

While Johnny worked on the stew, adding ingredients and stirring vigorously, I filled him in. "Turner and McKinley put me in the hot seat," I said. "It was awful." I felt guilty as soon as those words were out of my mouth. How could I be fretting and complaining and feeling sorry for myself. Doreen Sands was dead.

"You really don't know how the gun got into your hatbox?"

"Not a clue," I said.

Johnny shrugged. Then, as per his instructions, he warned me not to mess around in police business.

"But the gun—"

"Brenda," he said sternly. "You know what'll happen if—"

"It already happened. Like it or not, I'm in deep trouble. That gun in my hatbox makes it look like I killed Doreen Sands. Either that, or in cahoots with whomever did. If I weren't personally acquainted with Turner and McKinley, they'd have arrested me. I'd be locked up right this minute."

"Don't be silly, Brenda. They couldn't possibly think you had anything to do with murder. Once the gun gets to the lab, and your fingerprints aren't on it, you'll be officially in the clear."

Oh right. Fingerprints. Johnny had a good point. I felt a little better.

"Did you know Doreen Sands?" he asked.

"By reputation. I never met her."

"So leave it alone. As usual, Turner and McKinley are right."

I admitted that maybe, just maybe, they were. This time.

Johnny continued to stir the lentils. He gained speed and became extremely animated. He flung the specialized lentil spoon over his head in a figure eight pattern, hopped up and down on one foot, and after a little kick, switched to the other foot. Then, balancing himself against the stove, he did six deep knee bends.

"What the hell are you doing?"

"Knee bends."

"I can see that. Why?"

"Lemmy had a brainstorm. He wants me to combine the cookbook with the fitness book. The high concept, he says, is to work out and cook at the same time. I thought I'd experiment with the idea."

I experimented with the idea of finding more normal friends. I could move to a town where everybody looked the same and dressed the same and acted the same and thought the same. Of course, nobody in such a town would be caught dead in a hat, so they wouldn't buy hats, and I'd be forced to do the same as everybody else, something like type or word process or desktop publish or whatever they called it these days. As quickly as the thought entered my head, it evaporated.

I went back to Midnight Millinery and played a rousing game of Catch the Squeaky Toy with Jackhammer. I let him win. Afterwards, he dragged the toy over to his bed, curled up, and conked out.

All alone, I let down my guard. I was truly upset about Doreen Sands. Dead Doreen Sands. I didn't have to know her to like her and respect her and to wish she hadn't been killed. Besides, I felt like I knew her. She was, after all, a hat person.

Then there was the alarming fact that somebody had somehow managed to sneak what would probably turn out to be the murder weapon into my hatbox without my knowing it. Who wouldn't be upset?

Once again, I went over everything I could remember from the time I left Midnight Millinery with the hatboxes until the time I returned. Once again, I drew a blank. The thin air theory had a lot going for it.

4

"How could you not notice a gun in your hatbox? A gun is considerably heavier than a hat, no?" Elizabeth suppressed a yawn. She had on her ratty old pink and white chenille bathrobe and yellow rubber flip-flops. Her long silvery hair hung down free, though it still showed bumps from the singular braid she often wore. Obviously, she'd been asleep when I pounded on her door.

I was lucky to catch her at home at all. For a woman in her seventies, she'd been keeping mighty odd hours. It's not like I intentionally kept track, but Jackhammer is very protective of his territory. He raises a fuss whenever anybody—friend or foe—dares to tread in our end of the building, so I could hardly help but notice the comings and goings of my across-the-hall neighbor.

"Well yes," I said, answering her question. "Guns definitely outweigh hats."

Unfortunately, I spoke from experience. You wouldn't think it to look at me, but there'd been a couple of extreme situations in my millinery career when I'd actually had to hold a gun. Each time I'd been terrified, and the last thing in the world I'd been concerned about was the weight of the gun. Nevertheless, the guns-to-hats weight ratio was pretty much a no-brainer.

"However," I continued, "I wouldn't necessarily have noticed the extra weight. I took my hard case travel hatboxes to Castleberry's because they look more professional. Those boxes are heavy enough all by themselves. Besides the hats, I had my order book in one box and a six-hundred-page tailoring book in the other.''

"Six hundred pages on tailoring?''

"Lots of pictures.''

"Well, then, that explains it,'' said Elizabeth.

"It explains why I didn't notice the additional weight, but not how the gun got in the box in the first place,'' I said. "That's driving me nuts. I've been over everything again and again trying to figure out exactly how that could have happened.''

"It's no mystery,'' said Elizabeth. "You possess a fiercely creative mind. It wandered in search of new data, and while it was elsewhere, somebody—presumably the killer—sneaked the gun into your hatbox.''

I shook my head. "No. I was alert the entire time. I knew exactly what was going on in that waiting room.''

"Didn't you look at the tailoring book?''

"Well, yes. That's when Turner and McKinley think it must have happened, but I know better. Neither bound buttonholes nor interfacing are so enthralling that I'd miss somebody putting a gun into my hatbox. That's kind of a big deal. Besides, when I was sitting, my feet were on the boxes.''

"You underestimate the ability of the creative mind to concentrate. Think how the time flies when you're working on a brand-new design. Hours seem like minutes, minutes like seconds.''

"I still say I would have noticed.''

Elizabeth yawned. This time she made no effort to hide it.

"I better go,'' I said. "I can see you're pooped.''

"Sorry,'' she said. "I stayed up most of the night.''

I was itching to know what she'd stayed up to do, but she didn't volunteer any information, and I was too polite to ask. Come to think of it, she hadn't brought out any of the notorious cookies she was always concocting from the most unlikely ingredients. She never failed to offer a treat from her latest batch. Something was most definitely up.

Jackhammer zigzagged in front of me checking out rocks on the sidewalk. A couple of quick sniffs and test licks satisfied him that none were edible. We turned into the newspaper store. I kept him on a short leash so he couldn't forage in the candy and cookie display that fronted the counter.

The man behind the counter kept an eagle eye on Jackhammer. "Long time, no see," he said to me. "I can't remember the last time you were in here."

Neither could I. To buy the paper seemed a big waste of money when I could get it a day or two late from a neat stack in the compactor room at the end of my hall. Today however, I needed fresh news, so I gathered up the *Times*, two tabloids, and gave the man my money.

"You make hats, don't you?" he asked.

"Yes."

"Thought so. I bet you know the buyer lady who got offed at that fancy department store over on Sixth Avenue. That's pretty funny don't you think, a buyer buying the farm like that? She bought it, all right, bought it big time."

No, I didn't think it was funny. Not at all. I could hardly blame the counter man for saying it though. He had only mimicked the tabloids. Two of the local dailies had vomited up identical insensitive headlines. BUYER BUYS FARM in bold two-inch-high type. The *Times* stuck the story in the back of the Metro Section under the kinder and gentler heading DEPARTMENT STORE MERCHANDISER SLAIN.

I read every word of every story and was relieved to find no mention of me, or Midnight Millinery, or that the probable murder weapon had been found in a hatbox. For that, I owed Turner and McKinley. The *Times* quoted Turner as saying, "This one looks like murder." Aside from that he had no comment, although a confidential police source disclosed the investigation had turned up no known motive. The source then posited the tragedy was a random robbery gone bad.

That comment prompted a sidebar in one of the tabs questioning IS ANYBODY SAFE ANYWHERE ANYMORE?

BOUTIQUE AND DEPARTMENT STORE CRIME WAVE. The
story told of a rash of boutique robberies and a mugging
the month before in the intimate apparel section of a major
department store. No surprise to me. Boutiques are sitting
ducks and department stores have more nooks, crannies,
blind spots, and dark corners than any New York street.
Take such a venue, add cash-and-credit-card-carrying
shoppers, and it had to happen some time. The paper
copped out of divulging store names.

I'd hoped to learn more about Doreen Sands, but there
was nothing of significance in any of the news stories and
very little in the obit. Age: thirty-five. Hometown: Chi-
cago. Funeral: Saturday.

I studied my hat production schedule. Even after dropping
everything to design the special line for Castleberry's—a
collection now stashed somewhere at the Sixth Precinct—
I was caught up on my regular work. The dark truth behind this was the fact that a while back I'd missed a season and had fallen so far behind, that I was actually ahead
and wound up in the luxurious position of designing next
fall's hats this fall, a whole year before I'd be selling
them. It was much more natural than designing six to nine
months out of season as I'd been attempting to do ever
since opening Midnight Millinery.

In order to maintain this advantageous timing position,
I had to get cracking, so I got out my design head block,
tore off a length of pattern paper, and started to work.

Elizabeth was right. I was certainly capable of intense
concentration. Working was far better than worrying. Not
that I didn't worry some. I'd have felt a whole lot better
if Turner and McKinley had called with news that the lab
had found fingerprints on the gun which led them to arrest
the killer, who'd made a tearful confession, and I could
pick up my hatboxes at my convenience. But the phone
didn't ring.

A little after noon Fuzzy rocketed into Midnight Millinery. She was not quite five feet tall, and gloriously fat,
with a tangle of bright red hair down to where her waist

would have been if she'd had one. Tipped dangerously
far over her freckled forehead was a new hat made out of
a cereal box selectively sprayed with gold paint so that
some of the original graphics showed through—quirky
type and a picture of extruded cereal nuggets afloat in a
bowlful of milk, and topped with disks of sliced banana.
Fuzzy had glue-gunned tiny plastic bananas all over the
box, which emphasized the theme while adding texture.

"What brings you to the Village?" I asked.

"Just passing by," she announced. "I thought I'd
check out the competition." Her loud raspy yuks filled
the room and sent Jackhammer scurrying into the storage
room.

Fuzzy didn't fool me for a minute. Her hats enjoyed a
unique position in the millinery universe; there simply
was no competition. She'd come by to snoop, to see what
I knew about the Doreen Sands murder.

Playing along with her ruse, I got out some new pro-
totypes. She oohed and aahed at the appropriate times,
then said, "Show me the hats you made for Doreen
Sands. I'm dying to see what you came up with."

I couldn't tell her those hats were at the precinct without explaining why, so I hemmed and hawed and finally
said I'd left them with a friend of a friend, which was
actually the truth since Johnny was friends with Turner
and McKinley.

"What the hell for?" she boomed.

"Photos," I said. That too, may well have been true.
The cops no doubt did photograph evidence, and much as
I hated to think of them that way, my hats were evidence.

Fuzzy let the subject drop. "How about lunch?" she
said. "We need to talk about your part in my show."

"Show? What show? You never told me about any
show."

"That's why we should go to lunch."

No matter what the season, or how bright the sun, inside
Angie's it was always midnight in winter, jazz on the
jukebox. Tommy, the bartender and probable owner, nodded as Fuzzy and I passed through the bar on our way to

the back room. I patted my canvas bag and smiled. Tommy winked. The bag wiggled.

My deal with Tommy: Jackhammer was welcome as long as I pretended to sneak him in. That way, if an undercover restaurant inspector happened to be on the premises, Tommy wouldn't get busted for allowing a dog in a dining establishment. To my knowledge there had never been an inspector at Angie's either under- or over-cover since prohibition.

Fuzzy scoped out the dimly lit back room. "Groovy dive."

I slid into my favorite booth. Sometimes, when the sun was in the exact right position in the sky, and enough light filtered its way through the grime- and grease-encrusted window, and I held my head just so, I could make out the heart Johnny had carved into the table with our initials inside. Not today though.

I ordered my usual grilled cheese and a glass of red wine from Raphael the waiter. He eyed the canvas bag and asked, "Our special little burger ball for Jackhammer?"

I nodded. Jackhammer climbed out of the bag.

Fuzzy ordered Angie's world-famous cheeseburger and a dark beer. Raphael scurried off.

"About my show," Fuzzy said. "It's gonna be like a multimedia rant all about hats. You'll never guess who I got to do the lights."

"I don't know, who?"

"Your friend Chuck Riley."

"Chuck?" Since when did Fuzzy know Chuck?

"None other. I ran into him online in a chatroom full of lighting technicians. I was searching for somebody who could do lasers, strobes, all the seventies disco crap, with some updated swirling sixties psychedelia thrown in. Chuck said it would be a piece of cake. He was also willing to work for free. When I told him I made hats, he asked if I knew you."

Chuck hadn't breathed a word of this to me.

Raphael dropped off our food. Jackhammer downed his burger ball in one gulp. We humans were more restrained.

Fuzzy told me about her show. "Lights, action, and cameras. Everybody who is anybody in the media will be present, plus a multitude of milliners, and, of course, you. I'm either gonna call it New Millinery for a New Millennium or Milliners Milling Around the Millennium."

"Catchy," I said.

"So you'll do it?"

"I don't know," I said. "I can't act."

"Who said you had to act? All you've got to do is show up in a sexy black catsuit with your most fantastic hat on your head and walk among the audience while I recite a hat rant through a phase-shifting device."

"Oh."

"Come on, Brenda."

It sounded awful. However, in my experience, the more terrible Fuzzy's events sounded, the better they turned out. I figured I had nothing to lose. "Okay," I said, "I'll do it."

"Great. I knew I could count on you, Brenda. Seven o'clock the Tuesday after next. Be there or be—"

"You've got to be kidding. That's not nearly enough time."

"Of course it is. It's exactly enough time. I'm after spontaneity. If I wanted studied, stupid, and dull, I would have told you weeks ago. So, we've got that settled, right?"

I opened my mouth to protest, but she cut me off.

"You know Brenda, this cheeseburger is absolutely scrumptious." She rubbed the last morsel around a coagulated pool of ketchup. "Angie's is gonna get discovered."

"I'm afraid Angie's already got discovered," I said. "It makes all the best 'Best Of' lists. It's quiet this time of day, but just try to get in around dinner time or on weekends."

"Bridge and tunnel crowd?"

"Yep."

Raphael came back. "More drinks?"

We both opted for coffee.

"Who else's arm did you twist?" I asked.

"You mean who else has agreed to be in my extravaganza? I put up a list on my web page. Each day I add
new names. Go look. Also, as a service to the millinery
community, I've got a new feature, sort of a bad customer
alert. Call it an early warning system. I list all the shop-
lifters, check bouncers, wackos, and pains in the ass, with
photos if possible. Check it out, and if you've got anyone
special to add, let me know."

"Neat idea," I said.

"I'm full of them," she said. She pulled a big bright
plastic watch out of her purse. "Gotta go twist some more
arms."

I signaled Raphael for the check.

On the way out of Angie's, Fuzzy said, "We can talk
more about my show at Doreen's funeral."

Oh. The funeral. Boy, did I not want to go to that funeral. Ever since I read the obit, I'd been debating whether
to go or not. On the one hand, I didn't know Doreen
Sands. On the other hand, she was a great millinery per-
sonage to whom I should show respect. And on still yet
another hand, there was always the remote possibility that
the killer would show up. It was a cliché, but hey, stranger
things had happened. I might recognize someone from
Castleberry's waiting room, someone who'd left before
the cops arrived, someone who might have put the gun in
my hatbox. If so, I could help Turner and McKinley
match up fingerprints from the gun to a real live killer. I
owed them that much for keeping my name out of the
paper.

"See you at the funeral," I said.

"The hats are sure to be fabulous."

5

So, Chuck was doing Fuzzy's lighting, and he'd kept me in the dark.

I felt lousy, betrayed. It was like the time in eighth grade when my best friend from school joined the Belup's Creek Lanes teen bowling league and ended up on a team with my best friend from the neighborhood. All of a sudden I wasn't anybody's best friend anymore.

Putting aside hurt feelings, I supposed it would do Chuck good to get out of his computer-filled, boarded-up East Village storefront. Except to see Elizabeth, or pick up a slice of pizza, he rarely ventured out into the non-digital, nonelectronic world. Lately he'd been keeping even more to himself. I figured it had something to do with the huge crush he had on Elizabeth, who very graciously pretended not to notice. I too pretended not to notice, although I tried to let Chuck know without actually verbalizing that if he ever wanted to talk, I'd listen.

I wondered if Chuck and Fuzzy had more than a working relationship. They both had red hair and an interest in technology. And, unlike Chuck and Elizabeth, Chuck and Fuzzy were of the same approximate generation.

Instead of allowing my imagination to run hog wild, I decided to call Chuck, drop some big hints, and see how he reacted. Besides, I needed his help to get to Fuzzy's web page.

*   *   *

"My computer's broken," I said.

"Last time I visited Midnight Millinery your computer was unplugged," said Chuck. "Give it some juice. That ought to do the trick."

"It's not that easy," I said. "A couple of months ago during an intense production crunch I needed more work space, so I unplugged all the components and shoved the whole mess under the counter. I forgot what plugs in where."

Chuck sighed. "And I suppose you expect me to come over and put all the pieces back together."

"Would you? That'd be great."

"Tell me, Brenda, why, all of a sudden, do you give a flying electron about the computer you never use?"

"I got this hankering to surf the web, cruise the information superhighway."

Chuck groaned. "We don't call it *that* any more."

"Okay, how's this: I need to access Fuzzy's web page."

"Oh yeah, that's right, you know Fuzzy, don't you? She's one amazing dame. She talked me into doing the lights for some show."

"I know. I'm in the show."

"Cool."

"So, will you fix my computer?"

Ten minutes after Chuck clomped into Midnight Millinery, he had me up, running, and online.

"See?" he said. "Piece of cake."

"Easy for you to say."

Seeing him in person, I realized that Chuck's hair really wasn't very much like Fuzzy's. His was carrot-colored; hers more a blue-red. And, despite Fuzzy's name, Chuck's hair was far fuzzier, dry and bushy, a genuine fire hazard. Fuzzy's tendrils clumped together in soft ringlets.

Underneath that fuzzball Chuck looked awful, paler and greener than usual. Maybe skinnier too. It was hard to tell due to his new mode of attire, baggy red and yellow plaid trousers.

"Nice pajamas," I commented, wondering what he'd

done with his wardrobe of ripped jeans. Worn denim made good hats.

"Like my earring?" he asked.

"Not bad," I said, examining the object that dangled from his lobe. "What exactly is it?"

"Two fifty-six-K SIMM chip," he said, as if I knew what that meant. "You can have some if you want. I've got a whole bunch. Technologywise they're like eight and a half steps beyond useless. Maybe you could stick them on your hats."

"No thanks. I'm not into surface embellishment."

"I bet you knew that millinery buyer who got whacked over at Castleberry's?"

"Not really." Another technical truth that wasn't very truthful. I'd resolved not to say a word to Chuck about the murder until I found out what the deal was between him and Fuzzy. If I told him that I'd been at Castleberry's, he'd finagle the entire story out of me, including the part about the gun in my hatbox, and if he told Fuzzy, it'd be up on her web page, and I'd never live it down.

To steer clear of that subject, I made the mistake of asking Chuck if he'd seen Elizabeth recently.

"Look, I don't wanta talk about Elizabeth, okay."

Later, long after Chuck had stormed out, I went online all by myself. After a few false attempts, I somehow managed to find my way to Fuzzy's web page, where I was greeted with a barrage of sound and pictures, a millinery wonderland.

Animated hats danced around, leading the way to the various areas chock full of millinery lore, gossip, style-spotting reports, ads from supply houses, and news of Fuzzy's upcoming show. I was happy to see lots of familiar names on the list of confirmed attendees. I was beginning to look forward to the event.

Most of the information was available to anyone who happened to click on by, but Fuzzy was too careful to allow random cyber-wanderers into the bad customer zone. It appeared in a Milliners Only area. To gain access I had to answer three tough millinery questions. The first

two—one about banding ribbon, one about head size—
were technical. The last question referred to an obscure
story about the legendary milliner, Lilly Daché. I took a
wild guess and typed in "horny toad" which must have
been correct because the bad customer warning page began to appear on my monitor.

Pixel-by-pixel, low-resolution security camera images
displayed the so-called bad customers—two alleged shop-
lifters who, according to reports posted by milliners, often
worked as a team; one alleged check bouncer; and one
alleged detail-obsessed, all around pain-in-the-ass. I'd had
customers like her before, demanding women who expect
a hat not only to make them gorgeous, but also to protect
them from the sun, the rain, and to solve all their men,
money, health, and job-related problems. When it doesn't
quite work out that way, when the hat fails to do the trick,
when reality strikes, the milliner gets the blame.

Fuzzy's web page worked its magic on me. I got fired up
about her show and inspired to design a new hat specifically for the occasion. I had a vague idea about elegant
curves swirling upward, started sketching, and let my
mind wander.

Unfortunately, my wandering mind got into trouble.
Before I knew it, I was fretting about that gun again,
wondering how it got in my hatbox. Then, a truly awful
thought hit me. I closed my sketchbook and called
Johnny.

"Remember what you said about fingerprints on the
gun?" I asked. "And how they would prove I had nothing
to do with the murder?"

"You're not still worried about that, are you?"

"Of course I am. Turner and McKinley haven't called
yet."

"So? They're busy. Crime may be down, but it's still
not out. The results probably aren't back from the lab
yet."

"How long can it possibly take to check a gun for
fingerprints?"

"In a *Tod Trueman*," said Johnny, "it takes precisely

as long as the plot demands. For instance, if the gun isn't found until near the end of the show, it takes about fifteen seconds. On the other hand—"

"I don't care about *Tod Trueman*. I want to know how long it takes in real life."

"Call Turner and McKinley. They're the reality experts."

"I don't want to seem too interested. They might get suspicious."

"Stop worrying, Brenda. Turner and McKinley don't have time to call someone who isn't a suspect, to tell her that she isn't a suspect."

"But what if I am a suspect?"

"You're not. What makes you think they'd even consider the possibility?"

"It's not so far-fetched. What if they don't find anybody's fingerprints on the gun? That's a distinct possibility. Think for a minute. If you'd just shot someone, wouldn't you wipe your fingerprints off the gun before stashing it in some innocent bystander's hatbox?"

"No. I'd wear gloves."

That was something I hadn't thought of. It made matters worse. Johnny didn't seem to understand.

"If the cops don't find fingerprints on the gun the only evidence they have points straight at me," I said.

"If that were the case, they'd arrest you. Since they haven't, I'd say you were in the clear."

"Unless they don't have the results yet."

Which brought us pretty much right back to where we'd started.

6

Thoughts of Doreen Sands kept me awake that night. A vague sense of loss had settled over my world. Like a haze, it subtly altered my perception. Against this background sadness, I felt much better about my personal situation. Johnny was right. Nobody had accused me of anything, nor were they likely to do so.

I wanted my hats back. The precinct was no place for fine millinery. The thought of my creative output sitting on a shelf keeping company with far gorier evidence made me shudder.

After a quick breakfast, Jackhammer and I traipsed around the Village, taking in the cool crisp morning air. Overnight, the ginkgo trees on Horatio Street had dropped all their foliage. Bushels of fan-shaped leaves buried the sidewalk under a thick blanket of yellow.

Jackhammer dove in. The shimmering pile rustled.

"Careful," I said. "You never know what you might find just beneath the surface."

A little before noon Turner called.

"Got any lunch plans, Ms. Midnight?"

Lunch plans? This sure wasn't the call I'd anticipated. As a matter of fact, I did have lunch plans. I planned to work through lunch to make up for yesterday's long lunch with Fuzzy. "Is this a social call?" I asked, genuinely perplexed at his question.

"Detective McKinley and I would like to talk to you in a nonofficial capacity."

"Nonofficial means I can say no?"

"Yes."

"No."

"Oh."

I was tempted to ask for my hats back, but sensed it wasn't quite the right moment. After a minute or so of strained conversation we agreed that yes, it most certainly was a glorious fall day, and hung up.

Before I could even ponder how totally weird that conversation had been, the phone rang again.

This time it was McKinley. "Regarding lunch," he said, " 'nonofficial' does not do the situation justice. What my partner actually meant to say was 'extracurricular nonofficial.' "

I had no idea what he meant, however I picked up on the main thrust. "I guess that means I can't say no."

"It means," said McKinley pronouncing the words slowly and carefully, "if you knew the repercussions of a 'no,' you, being a prudent individual and all, would most likely say 'yes.' "

I said yes.

"That's more like it." McKinley told me to meet them at Tepper's down in Soho. "Know where that is?"

"Yes."

"We'll be looking forward to seeing you."

I walked along Bleecker Street to MacDougal, took that into Soho, then wound my way over to Tepper's. I used the time to analyze my churning emotions. No, I wasn't scared. I wasn't happy, or excited, or angry. Slightly irritated and extremely ill at ease probably best summed it up. I detected a cold, sharp edge in the fall air.

I also considered the significance in the detectives' choice of an out-of-precinct restaurant. Did they merely want a change of scene, or did they want not to be seen? They sure hadn't picked Tepper's for the food. At one time, the restaurant had been the Soho equivalent of Angie's—an ancient dark and dingy neighborhood joint, rumored to have started life as a speakeasy. In the early seventies, during Soho's first-wave boom when small factories turned into white-walled art galleries overnight, old man Tepper, who'd been behind the old wood and brass bar for as far back as anyone could remember, sold out to a gigantic midwest conglomerate.

The new corporate owners expanded Tepper's into two adjacent storefronts. A design team tacked up brand-new fake antique tin ceilings that didn't come close to matching the real tin ceilings in the original space. They hung oak-framed sepia-toned photographs that supposedly depicted Soho in the thirties. For that authentic arty touch, management put a glass tumbler of crayon stubs on every butcher-paper covered table.

They billed it as the ultimate Soho dining experience. On matchbook covers, T-shirts, baseball caps, and coffee mugs—all for sale either in person or by catalog—Tepper's promised, ''You'll rub elbows with artists.''

Wake up and smell the turpentine, or rather the lack of it. No actual live artist had dared to set foot in the place since 1973.

There were, however, plenty of Soho shoppers, taking a load off, looking for a sip of wine and bite to eat, their shopping bags shoved under the tables.

I spotted Turner and McKinley near the back at a round table. They were not alone. A blond woman sat to Turner's right—the lady cop with the ponytail who'd been stationed in front of the door at the buying office the morning Doreen Sands was murdered, the one who got stuck with the rotten job of keeping all those uptight designers from leaving the reception area.

When I neared the table, Turner pushed back his chair and halfway stood up. ''So glad you could join us.''

Like I had a choice.

He nodded toward the lady cop. ''Officer Gundermutter, meet Ms. Midnight, the best damned milliner on West Fourth Street.''

I extended my hand. "Please, call me Brenda."

Officer Gundermutter gave my hand an enthusiastic shake. "Nicole," she said, almost like a question.

No wonder; she didn't look like a Nicole. Then again, she didn't look like a Gundermutter either. Dwarfed by the bulk of the detectives, she looked downright pixielike.

Turner and McKinley both ordered steak sandwiches with fries, Officer Gundermutter got a tuna melt on an English muffin, I went for a spinach salad. "Hold the bacon," I told the waitress.

Turner leaned over toward Gundermutter. With a nod in my direction, he said, "Our milliner friend is one of those vegetarian types."

Gundermutter looked for a moment like she might comment, but she apparently thought better of it, and blushed instead.

Anxious to know why I was bidden to this occasion, I could barely participate in the small talk that dominated lunch. Turner and McKinley covered the state of the subway, the mayor, the Giants, the Jets, and platform shoes. Gundermutter didn't say much either. Mostly she kept her head down and chewed tuna, once or twice glancing up to smile at either Turner or McKinley. I was too tense to eat. I picked at my salad, and moved chunks of food around from one side of the bowl to the other.

By the time the waitress returned to ask if we wanted dessert, my stomach had tied itself into knots.

"I highly recommend our homemade apple pie," she said.

In honor of my three companions, I should have asked if Tepper's had any doughnuts.

"Just coffee for me," I said.

Gundermutter, Turner, and McKinley all went for the pie, warmed and à la mode.

Six bites into his slice, McKinley put down his fork, drew in an overly dramatic deep breath, and at long last got to the point. "We've hit a snag in the investigation of the murder of Doreen Sands."

You could have knocked me over with a feather. Not

the part about hitting the snag, that was to be expected. It happened in most investigations. The surprise was that they admitted it. To me. In the presence of an underling. This was significant.

Silence followed.

I began to suspect some sort of trap.

My mind raced. What if, I asked myself, my worst fear about the gun had come true? No fingerprints had been found, and under pressure from higher-ups, Turner and McKinley were forced to make me the fall guy, and they'd arranged this little luncheon charade to arrest me, and they'd brought Gundermutter along because she was a lady cop and maybe they had to search me for some kind of evidence.

I should never have listened to Johnny. I should have realized my desperate situation, and taken it on the lam, got out while the getting was good. Skedaddled. Returned to Belup's Creek. Got a job at the mall. Who said you can't go home again?

I heard a sound, like a pounding.

Turner thumped on the table.

"Hey, Ms. Midnight, you there? Is it something you ate? Some of those leaves maybe?"

"Uh . . . no. I'm fine." I covered my lie with a smile.

"Good," he said. "Because we need your help."

They needed my help.

That cinched it. Obviously I had lost my mind.

As part of the new plateau in our relationship, Johnny and I had agreed it was okay to drop in on each other unannounced.

I lay flat on my back on his couch, staring up at the cracks in his ceiling. Lots of little ones branched off a big long one shaped like a lightning bolt. "What's a panic attack like?"

"Not this," Johnny said. "This is more like Brenda with a very vivid imagination."

"You wouldn't say that if you'd been there," I said.

"Tell me about this Officer Gundermutter."

"Nicole Gundermutter. She's got to be some kind of a spy," I said, "with a blond ponytail."

"Cloak and dagger stuff?"

"The deal is, Turner and McKinley want me to do for Gundermutter what they did for you, except in reverse. I'm supposed to show her how to act less like a cop and more like a department store employee. I'm supposed to teach her fashion and retailing jargon. They claim she's going undercover at Castleberry's."

"You should be flattered. Turner and McKinley have made you an honorary detective." Johnny laughed.

I didn't find it funny and told him as much, in a not-very-nice manner, choosing not-very-nice words.

"You've lost your sense of humor, Brenda. You haven't been yourself lately."

What the hell did he mean by that? "Wrong," I said. "Everybody else is not themselves—Chuck, Elizabeth, and now Turner and McKinley."

"How about me?" asked Johnny.

"You're okay, I guess." So far.

To prove me wrong, he dashed into the kitchen. I mean really dashed, as in fifty-yard dash, from a crouched position. But since no New York apartment actually has fifty interior yards, he dashed in place, edging little by little toward the kitchen. Once there, he slammed cupboards and banged pots and a few minutes later returned with a steaming cup of tea. "Here," he said. "It'll make you feel better."

"I hate tea."

"It's herbal."

"I hate herbal tea."

"Well then think of it as medicine."

"A placebo."

"Drink."

I don't remember dozing off, but I do remember waking up. It was evening already. My first thought was Jackhammer, still at Midnight Millinery, probably hungry, probably having to go, and most definitely mad.

I tore out of Johnny's apartment, and took off running.

As I rounded the corner to West Fourth, I saw Officer Gundermutter, squatted down in front of Midnight Millinery's door, making kissy sounds and tapping on the glass. I braked to a stop.

She looked up at me. "What a cute little doggie."

I caught my breath. "His name is Jackhammer."

Gundermutter stood up and brushed herself off. "I came by to see when we could get together."

I opened the door. Jackhammer rushed up, his tail stub vibrating, and leaped two feet into the air. He landed and leaped up again, but by his second landing he must have remembered how long he'd been alone. He gave me a dirty look and sauntered over to his pile of fabric.

I hadn't yet answered Gundermutter's question. While trying to come up with an excuse not to get together with her, I pretended to study my calendar.

"How about tomorrow morning?" she suggested. "We don't have much time. I have to be ready to start my undercover job first thing Monday."

"Tomorrow's Saturday, right?"

She nodded.

"That's no good," I said. Gundermutter looked so disappointed, I felt the need to elaborate. "Saturday is Doreen Sands's funeral." Too late, I realized I should have kept my mouth shut.

"That's perfect," she said, beaming. "I'd love to go to the funeral with you."

7

A perfect day for a funeral. Gloomy. A relentless rain blew by in sheets of gray. Way off in the distance I could hear an occasional rumble of thunder.

Jackhammer hated the cold wet sidewalks. Yesterday's fun layer of leaves had turned into today's slippery mess. He cut his own morning walk short, quickly got down to business, and trotted past the soggy garbage in front of his favorite Italian restaurant without a sniff.

Once we were back in the apartment I wrapped him up in a big fluffy bath towel. I got myself dried off, then looked through my closet for an appropriate outfit to wear to the funeral. Black was too obvious, I thought. I settled on a dull gray silk dress, a good match for both the day and my mood.

I didn't expect any funeral to be a barrel of laughs, but this one would be especially bad, and now further complicated by the presence of Officer Nicole Gundermutter. How would I ever explain her to Fuzzy and the other milliners?

Despite logic, and Johnny's reassurances, I continued to worry about Turner and McKinley's motive for siccing Gundermutter on me. Did they really want me to show her the retail ropes? Or, could it be they wanted her around to keep tabs on me and make sure I didn't leave New York, in case they failed to find out who killed Doreen Sands and had to hang the murder on me? The thought that my staying out of the slammer hinged on the detectives' crime-solving abilities chilled me to the bone.

The buzzer sounded. It was the doorman on the intercom. "Miss Gundermutter to see you," he said.

"Tell her I'll be right down."

I put on my raincoat, anchored a close-fitting gray velvet cap on my head, grabbed my umbrella, patted Jackhammer on the top of his head, and left.

Gundermutter wasn't in the lobby and no one was at the doorman's desk, so I couldn't ask where Gundermutter had gone. Before I could think much about it, a loud explosion from outside scared the hell out of me. I first thought lightning had struck a nearby object, but when the sound modified down to a continuing growl, I realized it was a muffler-free engine.

I went outside. The doorman stood on the sidewalk in front of the building, watching in awe as some juvenile delinquent in a metal flake blue helmet revved up his gigantic Harley.

Make that her gigantic Harley. Gundermutter.

She lifted off her helmet and shouted over the racket, "Yo Brenda. I brought along an extra poncho to keep you dry. Hike up your dress and hop on the back."

She had to be kidding. No way would I get on that bike. Especially in the downpour. I came to the quick conclusion that I'd rather be under arrest. "I don't think the bike is such a great idea," I shouted.

"How come?"

"We'll draw too much attention. Don't you want to blend in, being undercover and all?"

The doorman took Gundermutter's helmet for safe keeping and promised to keep an eye on the Harley.

"Is he trustworthy?" Gundermutter asked.

"Absolutely," I said.

We crossed the street to the bus stop. Gundermutter alternated between staring longingly at her parked bike and impatiently scanning the approaching traffic for the bus. I applied the Watched-Pot-Never-Boils Theory to the question of bus arrival and turned my back to the street.

I moved under the awning of the pharmacy to keep dry and perused a display of neon-colored toothbrushes in the window.

I was just thinking that the green was kind of nice when I saw a familiar form reflected behind me in the plate glass. The form bobbled up and down. It was Johnny, dripping wet, jogging in place. "Lusting after a new toothbrush?" he asked.

"Waiting for the Number Ten," I said.

"I'm jogging to the Union Square Farmer's Market—a variation of Chapter Seven of my book, 'Jog to the Grocery Store.'"

"In the rain?" I asked.

"Sure. Why not?"

Gundermutter sauntered over. I made the introductions.

"Are you really him?" she asked.

Johnny, who had a lot of experience with that kind of question, smiled graciously.

"Wow," said Gundermutter.

The bus shuddered up to the stop. As Gundermutter and I got on, Johnny asked if I had dinner plans.

"No."

"Good. I've got a ton of experiments for you to try out. Come over at eight?"

"See you then."

Gundermutter flashed her badge at the bus driver. With a nod, he let her pass.

I, a mere civilian, used my Metrocard.

I joined Gundermutter near the back of the bus.

"I can't get over how you know that Tod Trueman guy," she gushed.

"I've known Johnny since before there was a Tod," I said. "In fact, that's how I met Turner and McKinley—through Johnny. They coached Johnny in how to act like a cop."

"Tod Trueman is modeled after Detective Turner? And McKinley? That is so cool."

Actually, that was stretching it a bit, but I didn't correct her.

I used the long ride uptown to teach Gundermutter fashion and retailing terminology. She wrote down my every word in a small black leather notebook. "This is very helpful," she said. "I sure hope I nab this killer. It'll be my first arrest."

She seemed excited at the prospect. I just hoped her first arrest didn't turn out to be me.

At Eighty-first Street we transferred to a crosstown bus. It sailed smoothly through Central Park, and deposited us a short walk away from the funeral.

A mass of black umbrellas clogged the sidewalk in front of the dark gray stone church. Gundermutter and I joined the murmuring crowd, and slowly made our way up the stairs and into the entry area of the church.

I was surprised at the great number of people, most of them complete strangers. Gundermutter scanned the crowd with enthusiasm. "Somebody here has got to be guilty," she said.

I took it as a good sign that she didn't look at me when she said that.

As we jostled along, Gundermutter frequently jabbed her elbow into my ribs, and with a nod of her head indicated someone she thought looked suspicious. "Who's that?" she asked dozens of times.

I could never tell who she meant, nobody looked particularly suspicious to me, so each time she asked, I just shrugged.

I did some looking too, but I didn't see anybody who'd been in Castleberry's waiting room the morning Doreen Sands had been killed.

I felt a tap on my shoulder. Fuzzy.

"Hey, Brenda. What a sweet little gray hat."

That, coming from Fuzzy, was definitely not a compliment.

Perched atop her red curls, was what looked like a tiny conservative pillbox. Upon closer examination it turned out to be a heavily veiled tuna fish can.

"Nice can," I said.

I hadn't figured out a way to explain Gundermutter, so I didn't. I simply introduced her to Fuzzy by name.

"Pleased to meetcha," said Fuzzy.

"Likewise," said Gundermutter. She couldn't take her eyes off the tuna fish can.

"Doreen Sands raved about this hat," said Fuzzy in defense of her fine funeral chapeau. "She told me it reminded her of the sea."

"It's very interesting," said Gundermutter.

"Why thank you, Nicole," said Fuzzy. Then she asked the dreaded question. "Are you a milliner or what?"

I jumped in before Gundermutter had a chance to answer. "Oh my god, will you get a load of that hat over there?" I said excitedly, pointing deep into the church at no one in particular.

"What did I tell you?" said Fuzzy. "I knew the hats here would be fabulous. *Almost* everybody is decked out in their best today."

I was pretty sure that "almost" referred to me. "They certainly are," I said.

"Not even this horrendous downpour could stop them," said Fuzzy. "I'm afraid I had to give up my plan to organize a milliner-only seating area. It would have been nice in the spirit of community and all that, but Doreen Sands had like a zillion friends, and there's too goddamned many people here. Which reminds me, I've got to mingle, make sure everybody knows about the Milliners Milling show. You two stick around after, I'll gather all the hat people and we'll go out for a drink."

Gundermutter and I pressed through the crowd. We found two seats together in a pew near the front of the church. I saw some familiar faces in the chaos, but they were all milliners, no one from Castleberry's waiting room.

Gundermutter twisted this way and that in her seat, straining to see people as they filed in. She flipped open her notebook and every so often, scribbled a couple of lines.

My turn to jab her in the ribs. "They'll think you're a cop," I whispered. "Or a reporter."

With a frown she tucked the notebook away.

I stared straight ahead and focused on the morbid groan of the organ.

The organ music swelled to an unbearable volume, then stopped. In the vacuum, the services began. A prayer, followed by hymns, some standing, some kneeling, then many stirring eulogies delivered by well-spoken friends and family members—none of whom looked like killers, none of whom I'd ever seen before, none of whom had ever been near any hatbox of mine.

The last speaker introduced himself as Doreen Sands's fiancé, Gregory something or other. Gundermutter snapped to attention. She was no doubt operating under the theory that nine times out of ten the spouse turns out to be the killer, and a fiancé is almost a spouse.

Gregory was a pleasant enough looking man, nice suit, slicked-back light brown hair. He seemed dazed, which I thought was appropriate for the circumstances. His voice caught several times as he told of his all-too-brief time with Doreen.

It was a beautiful story. Their eyes had met across a crowded subway—love at first sight. A month later he'd taken her to the Rainbow Room, got down on one knee, and proposed. "Like a fairy tale," he said. They were to be married in the spring. She got killed. And that was that.

The pallbearers bore the casket slowly down the aisle. Gregory followed behind, head bowed.

The ritual was what it was supposed to be—overwhelmingly sad. I got caught up in the mood, a big lump formed in my throat and my eyes welled up with tears. Gundermutter sniffled twice.

Everybody got up and attempted to leave at once.

"I haven't seen Spencer yet," said Gundermutter. "Have you?"

"Spencer?"

Then I remembered. Somewhere in the back of my brain I dredged up the knowledge that Detective Turner's

first name was Spencer. I had never once called him that.
"No, I haven't," I said.

"I thought for sure he'd be here," she said. "Or Detective McKinley," she added.

I hadn't really thought of it before, but she was right.
Turner and McKinley should have been there. Sure, it was
a cliché that cops attend funerals to look for crooks and
killers among the friends and family. That doesn't mean
they don't really do it. That was why Gundermutter
wanted to come.

Back out on the street, the rain pounded down harder than
ever. Umbrellas shrouded the mourners, making it impossible to find Fuzzy. Just as well, I thought.

The hearse and a long line of black cars were parked
in front. I started to head over to the bus stop, but Gundermutter grabbed onto my coat. "Wait," she said, "I
want to meet Ms. Sands's fiancé. You know what they
say: nine times out of ten . . ."

"Yeah, I know."

"Come with me," she said.

I supposed it was the proper thing to do, pay my respects.

We found Gregory by one of the black cars, standing
under a six-foot-wide umbrella. Pulling me along with
her, Gundermutter sidled over to him. "I'm terribly sorry
for your loss," she said.

"Thank you."

"She was a wonderful person," I said.

Suddenly, one of the men who stood nearby collapsed
his umbrella. "Brenda! Brenda Midnight! I hoped you'd
be here."

The man reached for my free hand.

My heart skipped three beats.

"Great to see you, Ray."

8

Ray Marshall and I . . . well, it could have been different, way back when, but things had got all confused . . . and then he adopted this godawful orange and yellow shag rug that used to be Johnny's godawful orange and yellow shag rug, and . . .

"It's been a long time," he said. "Too long."

"Yes, it sure has," I said. Boy, did he look good in black.

"I should stay around a while to see Gregory off. After that why don't you meet me for a drink? Say, in half an hour? I know of a cozy little lounge right around the corner."

Not such a great idea, but tempting.

To cover up my lack of decision, I introduced Ray to Gundermutter, and damned if she didn't take it upon herself to make up my mind for me. She exchanged pleasantries with Ray, then turned to me and said, "You run along with your friend, Brenda. Don't worry about me."

Thus backed into a corner, I didn't see how I could not go. I smiled at Ray. "See you soon."

I walked Gundermutter to the bus stop.

"Why did you have to go and do that?"

She ignored my question. "That Ray Marshall's quite a looker. You and he . . . uh . . . you know?"

"No," I said firmly.

49

"Good. Wouldn't want you to get too caught up staring into that man's dark eyes."

I thought I'd been more subtle.

"Be aware," she said. "That starry-eyed romantic bullshit can really throw a wrench into a police investigation."

"Investigation? What do you mean, investigation? I'm meeting a friend for a drink. That's all."

"No. You are meeting a man who appears to personally know the fiancé of the murder victim. You are meeting him with the express purpose of gathering information."

Wrong. That was not my intent. I actually had no intent in mind. Or if I did, I wasn't willing to admit it. "I don't know," I said.

"Come on, Brenda. Don't let me down. What we've got here is a once in a lifetime chance to get the inside lowdown on the fiancé, stuff I'd never be able to find out. Your job, your mission, your civic duty is to learn whatever you can about Gregory. Later, I'll debrief you."

Like it or not, I'd been deputized. Better than being arrested, I supposed.

"Remember, Brenda. Ask questions. Pay attention to body language. Remember everything. No fact is too obscure."

The bus came and whisked gung-ho Gundermutter away.

A bartender flopped a damp rag over the oak bar.

"I'm supposed to meet someone here," I said.

"Right now, ain't nobody here 'cept you and me. Sit any old where you want. Now, what'll you have?"

"Bloody Mary," I said. "But hold the vodka." For a whole lot of reasons it seemed wise to stay stone cold sober.

I carried my drink over to an alcove and sat down on a dark blue plush velvet couch, thought better of it, and moved to a chair opposite the couch. I was glad Ray hadn't arrived yet. I needed time to think, to figure out what the hell was going on.

First, Turner and McKinley tell me to stay out of police

business as well they should and always do. That made
sense, and was exactly what I expected. Then, in a totally
bizarre turnaround that still had me in shock, the two detectives ask me to help them by teaching Gundermutter
about retailing so she can go undercover to better investigate the case. And now, Gundermutter, a mere uniformed patrol person, assumes way too much
responsibility for the case, and she wants me to help her
investigate, somehow talking me into it. And the only
reason I'm willing to go along with any of this is because
the murderer apparently sneaked the goddamned gun into
my hatbox which made it look like I was somehow at
least somewhat involved.

To summarize my assessment of the situation: I had to
get involved to prove I was not involved.

I felt all right about meeting Ray. There were worse
ways to spend an afternoon than having a drink with Ray
Marshall. I frequently passed through his Chelsea neighborhood on my way to the garment center, always halfway hoping to bump into him. Yet I never had until now.
Like I said, things could have been different between us.
When we first met, he was doing some kind of undercover
work. He never revealed what, or whom he did it for, but
I knew he wasn't a bad guy, even though he did end up
with that bad rug.

And there he was. Smiling. Walking toward me. Looking
good. Carrying a Bloody Mary. I wondered if his had any
vodka in it.

He buzzed my cheek. "Wonderful to see you," he said.
"Even in such awful circumstances."

Oh yes. The funeral. I'd been so deep in thought, I'd
almost forgotten.

He sat on the couch and we toasted to the memory of
Doreen Sands. Ray said, "Terrible business, murder.
Gregory is, as you'd expect, devastated. This will stay
with him forever."

"I can't imagine what it's like to lose—"

"The worst."

"Did you know Doreen Sands well?" I asked.

"No. Not really, mostly through Gregory. How about you?"

"Well, the millinery community is. very close." Another one of those truthful lies.

"Did she buy hats from you?"

"I rarely sell wholesale," I said, leaving the question open. I didn't want him to know I'd been waiting to see Doreen on the very morning she'd been killed. "How do you know Gregory? Do you two, uh, work together?"

Ray laughed at my clumsy attempt to discover what he did for a living. "Gregory is a financier. He's my friend and neighbor. How about Nicole? Is she a milliner?"

Nicole? It took a moment to register that Nicole equaled Gundermutter, and longer to decide how to respond. If I lied and said she was a milliner, Ray might want to know why she hadn't worn a hat. I couldn't say she was my friend because why would a friend take a friend to a funeral, unless they both knew the dead person? On the spur of the moment, I couldn't come up with a plausible explanation of Gundermutter's connection to Doreen Sands.

Except the truth. A refreshing concept. I weighed the pros and cons. Ray had to know the cops were involved. What was the big deal? I gave it a stab. "Actually Nicole is a co . . ." On second thought, because Gundermutter was going undercover, it *was* a big deal. I shut my mouth, stopped myself short, dangerously close to saying too much. To stall, I took a sip of my drink. ". . . or rather I should say Nicole *was* a co-worker of Doreen Sands. She works at Castleberry's, I'm not sure which department. She's like a friend of a friend. I know her through Johnny Verlane. Remember him?"

"Yes. Of course I remember Johnny. How is he? Are you and he—"

"Johnny's writing a book."

"No kidding."

"It's a brand new genre, a workout as you cook book."

"Fascinating. Johnny Verlane is quite the celebrity these days. I don't know about that detective show of his though. To tell you the truth, I think it's over-the-top, especially the part about how at the end of each show Tod Trueman always gets the girl.''

I wondered how much, if anything, to read into that.

"Every week," said Ray, "a different girl. It's not credible. Tod Trueman is not at all like the true-life detectives in charge of Doreen's case. Gregory tells me those two are a couple of real bozos.''

I squelched the urge to defend Turner and McKinley, an urge that surprised the hell out of me. Much as I hate to admit, the detectives aren't really so bad. Sure, they frequently get off on the wrong track, but usually for the right reasons based on their experience and proper procedure.

Ray continued, "Those idiots claim Doreen's murder was a random robbery gone bad. Now that's about the stupidest theory I've ever heard. The cops are trying to take the easy way out. Gregory won't let them get away with it. He lodged an official complaint.''

They say you can never get a cab in the rain in New York. Myth debunked. Ray stuck his arm out; fifteen seconds later a cab splashed up to the curb and we got in.

"Nice day for ducks," said the cab driver. Then he laughed at his joke, uproariously, all the way downtown.

Ray got out at the end of his block in Chelsea and handed me more than enough money to cover his part of the trip. "Next time we meet," he said, "I hope it's under more pleasant circumstances.''

"I'm sure it will be," I said. What could possibly be worse than a funeral?

The cab continued to the Village. The driver didn't stop laughing until he pulled up in front of my building and told me how much I owed. I paid, and as I was getting out of the car, somebody else scooted in.

"Nice day for ducks," said the driver to his new fare.

On my way inside, I noticed that Gundermutter's motorcycle was gone.

*   *   *

I got Midnight Millinery open by early afternoon. I set up for heavy-duty production work, figuring not many customers would venture out into the rain. In fact, there were none, unless Gundermutter counted.

I heard her coming a block away. Jackhammer went wild at the racket and continued to bark furiously when she came in the shop. "What's wrong with the little doggie?" she asked.

"Noise bugs him."

"So sorry, little guy." She pulled out the vanity bench and sat. "Brenda, feel free to go right ahead and keep working while I debrief you."

"Oh, okay." I barely glanced up. Good grief, she was serious.

"What did your friend with the sexy eyes have to say about the fiancé?"

"Ray didn't say much. He and Gregory are neighbors. And friends."

"Is that all you found out?"

"No, I also found out that Gregory thinks the official police theory is a crock."

I'd given that some thought. It seemed to me that if Gregory had killed Doreen Sands, he wouldn't be griping about how the police were such colossal screw-ups. He wouldn't make a complaint. He'd be happy they were not harassing him. Then again, he might do just the opposite to confuse the issue. Or, he might be crazy, and if he were the killer, he might well be. In that case his actions didn't necessarily have to make any sense whatsoever.

"I'll let you in on something," said Gundermutter. "I guess it's all right for me to level with you, since you're helping out with the investigation. Gregory is correct. That particular police theory *is* a crock, intentionally so. You see, Spencer—Detective Turner—leaked a false theory to the press. We want the perp to relax, so he'll slip up and we can nab him. Or her. That's why I'm going undercover."

"I should have guessed," I said. "That Turner is one smart cookie."

"He sure is," said Gundermutter with a sigh.

I glanced up from my work and caught Gundermutter in a full-cheek bright red blush. Something clicked. I put two and two together. The evidence was in. Clearly, Gundermutter was sweet on Turner.

"Now," she said. "Tell me more about fashion and retailing."

9

I dodged a flying tuber. "Since when do you juggle?"

You think you know somebody and then . . .

Johnny tossed three purple heirloom potatoes into the air. He had them all going at once, round and round, round and round. Every so often he altered the rhythm and bounced one off his heel. It was an impressive display of coordination. We were in his kitchen, waiting for his potato casserole to brown.

"I learned to juggle years ago," he said. "To get an edge as an actor, I had to be versatile. Some time you should take a look at the 'Other Skills' section at the bottom of my resumé. You will discover that I can sing on key, tap dance, ride a unicycle, deal and shuffle cards like a pro, and now at long last, legally operate a motor vehicle in the state of New York."

"You got your driver's license! Congratulations." I sure hoped Johnny's driving skills had improved. The last time I saw him behind the wheel, he'd smashed into a concrete wall. That official scrap of paper from the state could quite literally be his license to kill.

"Thank you," he said. "As you know, it's been a long and difficult struggle."

His kitchen timer gonged.

"You keep juggling," I said. "I'll serve the dinner."

* * *

Jackhammer positioned himself three feet away from the table. His big round black eyes stared longingly at the single yellow potato that Johnny had roasted especially for him. When the potato cooled, Johnny rolled it across the floor. Jackhammer dragged the spud over behind the couch and attacked it.

Johnny and I did likewise with the casserole. "You wouldn't believe all the unusual potatoes they had at the Farmer's Market this morning," said Johnny. "I put seven different varieties in this casserole."

"It's delicious. I'm curious, which potatoes juggle best?"

"Depends on the trick. When symmetry is important, I'd have to say new red is the best choice. Otherwise, I'm kinda partial to the purples."

"Will this kind of detail be in your book?"

"Yes. I believe it's important to touch all the bases."

After some more potato discussion, he brought up the funeral.

"I'm surprised Officer Gundermutter went with you."

"I didn't want her to. She sort of insisted."

"What's she like?"

"She rides a Harley, is gung-ho, can't wait to make her very first arrest, and sees the Doreen Sands investigation as her big chance. Oh yeah, she's got a crush on Turner. Blushes and calls him Spencer, if you can imagine."

"That *is* his name, you know."

"He'll always be Turner to me."

"How was the funeral?"

"What you'd expect. Sad. Terrible. Morbid. Doreen Sands had a lot of friends."

"Milliners?"

"Yes, lots of milliners, but lots of normal people too. Fuzzy seemed disappointed. She thought the funeral would be a huge hat event, a preliminary to her own Milliners Milling Around the Millennium show. She wanted all the milliners to sit together, but it was too crowded. Serves her right for being so crass. A funeral is hardly the place for self-promotion."

"Unless it's your own funeral," said Johnny.

"An idea like that proves you've been hanging around Lemmy Crenshaw too much. A funeral is for grieving."

"Closure," said Johnny. "And for cops to attend, where they stick out like sore thumbs, and look for who done it. In one of the *Tod Truemans*—"

"I remember, I saw that one. Gundermutter had to fulfill that cliché all alone. Oddly enough, Turner and McKinley were no-shows, probably to make their random robbery theory look good. Gundermutter admitted it was contrived to fool the guilty party into thinking he's in the clear."

"Or she," said Johnny. "The doer could be a she."

"Right. Meanwhile, Gregory, that's Doreen Sands's fiancé, thinks Turner and McKinley are Class-A jerks. He lodged an official complaint."

"He told you that?"

"Uh, no, not exactly. What happened was I ran into Ray Marshall—remember him?—and it turns out he's friends with Gregory. They live in the same building. Anyway Ray told me about the complaint."

"Ray Marshall, huh. So how is Ray? Did he mention my ex-rug? I kinda miss it."

"I didn't ask about your ex-rug. Ray is fine. Says he watches *Tod Trueman* sometimes."

Later, while we were cleaning up the dishes, I mentioned that Turner and McKinley seemed to be up to something.

"What they're up to," said Johnny, "is using all their resources, including Gundermutter and you, to solve a murder. Tod Trueman does much the same. For instance, in one of the new episodes Tod is closing in on an evil druglord, and in the course of the investigation he needs to learn about tattoos. It turns out an old friend of Tod's from high school is a world famous tattoo artist and—"

"Wait," I said. "The old friend is a she, who grew up to be a gorgeous busty blond, she ends up in jeopardy, and Tod heroically and daringly rescues her from the snatches of the evil druglord by dropping out of a helicopter into a burning building, and in the last minute of airtime the blond throws herself at Tod, and they kiss passionately as the closing credits roll.''

"Wrong," said Johnny. "The tattoo artist happens to be a brunette."

Jackhammer and I walked along Bleecker Street toward home. The rain had finally called it quits and the still-glistening street was packed with people who'd been holed-up all day long.

I felt pretty good. Despite outward appearances, Johnny is much more than a photogenic face. He has a good rational head on his shoulders. Lingering over dessert, a scrumptious experimental dish he called the Hundred Push-up Pudding Cake, we talked once again about my unwilling involvement in the Doreen Sands case. This time I agreed, I'd been out of my mind for thinking that Turner and McKinley could possibly believe I had anything to do with the murder.

Johnny suggested I might have a problem with authority figures. "Put it behind you," he said.

That was sound advice. I'd done my part. I'd fully co-operated with Turner and McKinley. I'd taught Gundermutter enough about fashion and retailing to get by in her undercover role at Castleberry's. I'd put up with her going to the funeral with me. I'd had drinks with Ray Marshall. Sure, I felt bad about Doreen Sands, but the fact was I did not know the woman. It was time to wash my hands of the whole mess.

I pulled my mattress out of the closet and was in the process of sheeting it up when the phone rang.

Not in the mood to talk to anybody, I let the machine take the call.

It was Fuzzy. "Are you there, Brenda, screening perhaps? Well, okay, whatever. I just wanted to let you know that I stuck up for you when everybody was saying that you killed Doreen Sands because she refused to buy your hats."

I dashed across the room and grabbed the phone.

"Who said I killed Doreen Sands?"

"Aha. I knew you were home."

"Who said I did that?"

She hee-hawed. "Nobody. That was an attention-grabber, a clever ruse on my part to get you to answer your phone. However, if someone had said you killed Doreen Sands, you'd never even know because you didn't join our millinery bunch for an after-funeral drink. Where'd you take off to, anyway? I looked high and low for you and that person you were with, but you'd both vanished. Absolutely everybody was there. Except for you."

"Sorry, I remembered something I had to do."

"Who was that hatless person, anyway?"

"Friend of a friend."

"Well, she'd look a hell of a lot better in a hat. You should have loaned her one for the occasion. So anyway, we, the milliners minus you, went out. Naturally, the main topic of discussion was Doreen Sands. Before you know, we're all speculating about who killed her. You'll be happy to know that no one brought up your name. You can thank me for not mentioning you were on the premises that morning."

"Thank you."

"What'd you think of Doreen's fiancé?"

"Sad," I said.

"Ha!" she said. "Good actor, that's what he is. Here's the scuttlebutt on Gregory. A couple of weeks before Doreen was killed, he dumped her."

"The engagement . . ."

"Was off. Could be that Doreen was morbidly depressed and killed herself."

"Who said?"

"Everybody. Nobody. Pure rumor, the kind that floats around and settles and the longer everybody thinks about it, the more real it becomes, until it takes on a life of its own. But you know, it could be true."

If Fuzzy knew what I knew, she'd know that couldn't possibly be true. No way Doreen Sands could have killed herself, because the gun had ended up in my hatbox and Doreen Sands was not the person who put it there. Of course, Fuzzy didn't know what I knew, which actually was a good thing, and I planned to keep it that way.

In the interest of putting the whole episode behind me, I had to tell Turner or McKinley what Fuzzy had told me. I called the precinct.

Saturday night was not the best time to find either detective in. I was surprised when Turner picked up. "Turner here." After hearing my voice, he sighed and said, "What now?" like he really didn't want to hear it, whatever it was.

"Full disclosure," I said. "I've heard, through the millinery grapevine, that Doreen Sands's fiancé Gregory dumped her and she got real depressed and killed herself. I know the part about the suicide can't be right, but I thought you'd like to know about the breakup. I thought it might be relevant to your investigation." Especially since Gregory had complained about Turner and McKinley.

"Thank you, Ms. Midnight. I'll look into it, but as we both know, it couldn't have been suicide. Now, if you don't mind, I have a ton of paperwork."

The connection went dead.

10

Perched atop my rickety stepladder I had a bird's eye view of Midnight Millinery. I gazed down on the roomful of hats, the antique vanity, and a kibble-tossing Jackhammer scrambling across the floor. I allowed myself a self-indulgent moment of pride, then got back to the task at hand—the seasonal wrenching open of the back window.

The window sash was crooked to the left in respect to the window frame, the frame was crooked to the right in respect to the building, the building was crooked in all respects to West Fourth Street, which as part of the West Village was crooked and totally off the grid to New York City and, for that matter, the rest of the known universe. A hundred fifty years of entropy further complicated the situation, making it impossible to determine precisely where the partially deteriorated wood frame ended and the partially solidified dirt and grime from outdoors began.

Earlier that morning when I'd gone through the lobby on my way out of the apartment building, the doorman had said, "Nice football weather we're having."

"Sure is." I had never understood that reference, but whatever it was called, I wanted to get some of that invigorating crisp air into Midnight Millinery. I propped open the front door with a hat block. If I ever got the window open, a nice cross breeze would sweep through the shop. After several tugs, and lots of cursing, I succeeded. With a pane-rattling shudder, the window ground open four inches.

The nice weather would bring out tons of shoppers. To prepare, I straightened up my work mess, steamed and fluffed the displays, and took out several nearly completed hats that needed bits of hand sewing here and there.

Sunday customers, many of them tourists who spilled over from Bleecker Street, were easily intimidated. For one thing, they're in New York, walking in the wild and wacky West Village. Most often, they'd never worn hats, didn't know how to put one on, or even if they should. And if they did want to make a purchase, the prices were hard to fathom for anyone who didn't know what was involved in making a hat.

To help customers get comfortable with the idea of wearing a hat, I did my best to provide exactly the right amount of attention to each so as not to overwhelm them, or to leave them feeling neglected—often a tricky balance, based a little on experience, but mostly on guesswork. I found it helped if I worked on a small project. It kept me from staring at the customers, yet I could easily be distracted whenever someone wanted help.

I glanced up at the first two customers who bounced through the door, a rosy-cheeked couple with a distinctive polyester pastelness about their clothes that shouted "American tourists." I was thinking how this woman would never in a million years wear a hat back where she came from. She plucked a dramatic black hat from a display. I'd have bet money that she did not own a single article of black clothing, not even tights. I was still feeling smug from this admittedly snooty assessment, when she expertly angled the hat on her head, gave it a quick look in the oval mirror, and proclaimed it "to die for." Her husband whipped out his credit card.

Sometimes everything I think I know turns out to be all wrong.

In the early afternoon the drunk-from-brunch bunch reeled in. They presented a unique challenge: how to keep people from making expensive mistakes they'd hate themselves for the next day, while not discouraging sales. Due to a certain white fitted leather jacket that had been hanging in my own closet unworn for several years, I was particularly sensitive to their needs. Before selling a three-hundred-dollar hat to someone three sheets to the wind I always ask questions like, "Do you wear hats often?" or "Does it go with the rest of your wardrobe?" This can save everybody a lot of heartache.

Late in the afternoon Midnight Millinery got so crowded that Jackhammer grew tired of having his head patted and hearing everybody say what a cute little doggie he was and took refuge in the storage room. I wished I could join him. I felt more like a hostess at a party than a shopkeeper. My chances of adequately taking care of any customer plummeted to zero. About the best I could do was to look toward the door whenever the bells jangled.

I couldn't help but notice when a woman wearing a spectacular plaid boater-style hat came in. I watched out of the corner of my eye as she checked out my display hats. She paid as much attention to the inside as the outside. Obviously, she knew her way around millinery. She even helped a customer twist a hat into a face-flattering off-center tilt.

The customer I was working with at the time was having a tough time deciding between two cocktail hats. "I like the red. But then again, the black is so me. Maybe I'm bored with being me."

She put on one hat, then the other, and repeated the process many times. "What do you think?" she asked.

"Well . . ."

The woman in the plaid boater strolled over. "Want to know what I think?"

The indecisive customer looked even more perplexed. "I don't know. I guess so. I mean, maybe, yeah. Why not?"

"Take both the red and the black. You won't be sorry."

The indecisive customer said, "That's a damned good idea." She handed me the hats. "Wrap 'em up."

I smiled at the woman in the boater.

"You do very nice work," she said. "I'll come back during the week when you don't have such a crowd."

I looked forward to seeing her again.

At five o'clock I locked up. It had been a very long day. I was dead tired. Since Jackhammer had spent the last part of the day hiding out, he was hot to trot. As a compromise I walked him over to Sixth Avenue. I put him in his canvas bag and sneaked him into Balducci's where I bought a big grilled portobello mushroom to take home for dinner. While I was inspecting a bunch of arugula for bug holes, Jackhammer stuck his head out of the bag and snatched up a raw *haricot vert*. He swallowed the expensive, skinny, French green bean whole.

When I first moved to New York, fresh from Belup's Creek, certain urban phenomena caused me no end of wonder: the occasional brown water flowing out of the tap, advertising blimps puttering by in the sky, daredevil traffic-dodging jaywalkers, and the fact that some stores opened later and closed earlier than their posted times.

Wasn't there a law or something?

Boy, did I have a lot to learn.

Sometimes life happened. As sole proprietress I had to adapt. I loosened the rules. I changed the sign in Midnight Millinery's window to read "noonish 'til late or by appointment."

A store the size of Castleberry's had no problem keeping regular hours. They stayed open every night 'til nine, seven on Sundays. On the way home I passed by. It was only six, so I popped Jackhammer back in his canvas bag and went into the store.

I was immediately assaulted by a deranged perfume spritzer. Jackhammer sneezed; I hurried over to millinery.

Photos from back in the heyday of hats show glamorous millinery departments prominently featured in stores. These days, hats are often an afterthought, stuck somewhere between umbrellas, socks, barrettes, and hair accessories—pretty much abandoned and left to die.

Castleberry's, under the capable leadership of Doreen Sands, had become a different story. Her millinery department commanded a sumptuous space near the center of the store, with walls of bezeled-edged mirrors and spiffy display furniture.

And the hats? A fantastic collection, lovingly displayed on intricate wire heads, or arranged carefully on shiny countertops. Very special hats like Fuzzy's were locked up in glass cases.

All the hats were the work of local milliners, most of whom I knew. I was trying to match labels to faces I'd seen at the funeral when a saleslady swooped down on me.

"My dear," she said, "has anyone ever told you that you have a hat face?"

"Uh . . . no," I said. As a goof, I wanted to see where she'd go with this.

"Well, you do. It's all in the cheekbones. Please, have a seat. I'll show you." She sat me down in front of a three-way mirror and brought over an armful of hats. One after the other, I tried them on, occasionally backwards. When I put on an exquisite cocktail hat with long feathers sticking up, she gushed, "This is you, positively you."

Coincidentally, the hat that was "me" was the most expensive of the bunch. "Hmmm," I said, scrutinizing my image in the mirror.

"Shall I wrap it, or would you prefer to wear it out?"

"Um . . . I think, I'll have to think about it."

She frowned.

"It *is* a nice hat," I said.

"Well, it's one of a kind and it won't be here forever, you know."

"I'll have to take my chances, I really can't . . ." I started to lift the hat off my head.

Behind me, in the mirror, half hidden by a revolving hat tree, I spotted a milliner I knew vaguely. Laura, I think, was her name. She didn't have her own store, but worked out of her apartment. That's the way most of us start, until we get lucky enough or desperate enough to do something about it.

Laura stifled a laugh. She must have witnessed the whole sales pitch. She walked up and pushed the hat back down on my head. "Lovely. Truly lovely. You have a hat face, you know?"

"Excuse me," said the saleslady to Laura, "do you work here? I don't believe I've ever seen you before."

"No," said Laura, "but I'm thinking about it. I hear you have an opening for a millinery buyer."

Color drained from the saleslady's face. "Yes, I believe we do."

I didn't buy the hat. Laura and I left together. We stopped for a while outside Castleberry's to chat.

"Checking out the competition?" asked Laura.

"No. I was just—"

"Don't be embarrassed. We all do it. Why else would *I* be at Castleberry's? I wanted to know who was doing what, and to see how my latest collection was displayed."

"You sold to Doreen Sands?"

"Many times. She was very supportive, and had a terrific fashion instinct. They'll never replace her."

"I suppose not."

"Except for Doreen, buyers don't know good millinery from a hole in the ground."

"Sorry I never met her."

"I thought you knew her."

"Never had the pleasure."

"Such a waste. They say that after her fiancé broke up with her she killed herself. Can you imagine?"

And so, that rumor was alive and well. It bothered me, but there was not a goddamned thing more I could do. I reported it to Turner the first time I'd heard it. Now, I was out of the loop. Like Johnny had advised, I'd put it all behind me.

Although I couldn't help but wonder who did it.

I had never heard anybody say a single bad word about Doreen Sands. But somewhere somebody must have had a score to settle. Had it been business related—a milliner, another buyer, a co-worker perhaps? Or had it been someone in her personal life—Gregory, the ex-fiancé? Had he really jilted her? In my opinion, that would give Doreen motive for murder, not the other way around.

I felt a degree of guilt. Not that there was anything I could have done to save Doreen Sands, but if I'd been more alert that morning at Castleberry's, I would have caught the killer red-handed, sneaking the smoking gun into my hatbox. Actually, that wasn't true. If I'd been more alert, the killer would never have tried to put the gun into my hatbox.

Later that night I went back to Midnight Millinery to straighten up. Considering the hectic day and all those customers, the shop wasn't in too much disarray. I finished sooner than expected.

So I relaxed. It was the first time in quite a while I didn't have something pressing to attend to. In other words, it was the perfect time to start a fun project—my hat for Fuzzy's show.

I got out my supplies and started goofing around. I allowed whatever wanted to happen to go right ahead and happen. No restrictions. Accidents counted. Inspired by the indecisive customer who couldn't decide between the red hat and the black hat, I even toyed with the idea of a hat for a two-headed human. In the Village you never knew who would walk through that door next, or how many heads they'd have.

11

I dreamed about hats. Hats on heads, hats on two heads, hats under foot, hats over guns, guns under hats. Toward morning the hats sprouted arms and legs and tap danced madly faster and faster until they became a blur of color, feathers, and ribbon and merged into one hat.

I awoke with the desire to make that hat—the ultimate hat, the sum of all hats, the hat which boiled down to the essence of hat. But when I got to Midnight Millinery I couldn't remember what that hat looked like.

So I worked on some regular hats instead. That in itself was exhilarating enough. What could be more fun than sitting around making hats? And getting paid for it. I loved the feel of the materials, the whoosh of steam, the scent of straw. I loved the whole process, not just the finished products. When I thought about it, I was pretty damned lucky.

Time slid by.

Fuzzy called in the afternoon. "I heard you were hanging out at Castleberry's yesterday."

"You must have talked to Laura."

"Yes. She called to R.S.V.P. about my show. She said you two had an interesting adventure in the millinery department."

"It was silly. We goofed on the saleslady. She told me I had a hat face."

"Well you do."

"Oh come on. Everybody has a hat face. Anyway, it was fun, and also kind of enlightening to be on the other side of a millinery sales pitch."

"You know, Brenda, maybe you could pick up a couple of hints from that saleslady. When it comes to sales, you're not very aggressive."

"It's true, I'm not. Yesterday I had this customer who was agonizing over whether to get a red hat or a black hat. I didn't know what to tell her. Then this other customer came along, a woman wearing a stunning plaid boater, and she told the indecisive customer to buy both. And she did, and she was happy about it. Delighted. Paid cash. I couldn't believe it."

"Back up a minute," said Fuzzy. "What did that woman in the boater look like?"

"Attractive. Mid-forties. Well dressed. I paid more attention to her hat than her. Why, do you know somebody who has a plaid boater?"

"Check out my web page, specifically the rotten customer alert area."

"I already saw it."

"Go again, and this time take a more careful look."

I went back to Fuzzy's web page and headed straight for the customer warning area where I found a photo of a woman in a plaid boater. It sure looked like the same woman. According to milliners all over the city, she was a persnickety, demanding, giant pain in the ass. Impossible to satisfy, she measured the distance between hand stitches with a loupe and a tiny pair of calipers. And I'd been looking forward to seeing her again. Damn.

My work was winding down for the day when Gundermutter burst through the door, all pumped up from her first day undercover at Castleberry's. "It was so cool," she said. "Thanks to you teaching me the lingo, nobody in the store had a clue that I was a cop."

She plopped down on the vanity stool, crossed her legs, and smiled at me like we were best pals. Perhaps we had bonded on the bus or at the funeral and I hadn't noticed.

"Where do they have you working?" I asked.

"All over the store. That's the best part. I'm a floater. It's a terrific setup for undercover work. Whenever anybody needs help for an hour or so, they send me to fill in. The only thing they won't let me do is ring up a sale. I guess for insurance reasons. I folded sweaters, hung ties, stacked boxes, dusted displays, and even got to help customers. That was the most fun of all. I also hung out in the employee lunchroom and the loading dock."

"What did you find out?"

"I solved the case. I know what happened to Ms. Sands. But, I've got a problem. It gets complicated. Mind if I shoot some ideas by you?"

Inwardly I rolled my eyes and sighed. Outwardly I said, "Okay."

"How about we grab a bite? This may take a while and I could eat a horse."

We went to Angie's.

The regulars were watching the news on the big TV that hung over the bar. A couple of them gave Gundermutter the eye when we passed through on our way to the back room. I couldn't tell if they thought she was cute or if they smelled cop. She did look pretty good all dressed up in her undercover costume, a flower-print wrap dress and strappy pumps. She held her head up and strutted. Her ponytail flipped back and forth.

By Village Standard Time, it was early for dinner—barely six o'clock. We got a table with no problem.

Gundermutter was appalled that Tommy let Jackhammer in. "I'm sure that bartender saw your bag wiggle," she said.

I shrugged. "Probably."

"He gave you the thumbs-up."

"So he did."

"You can't bring a dog where food is served. It's against the law. I should call that to the bartender's attention, and alert the proper authorities."

"Careful," I said. "You'll blow your cover."

*   *   *

Raphael came around. "The usual?" he asked.

I nodded. Jackhammer climbed out of his bag and put his chin on the table.

Gundermutter ordered a cheeseburger and an orange soda. She must have considered herself still on duty.

When Gundermutter was ready to begin, she cleared her throat and took a deep breath. Then she launched into a moment-by-moment, excruciatingly detailed, phenomenally boring account of her day at Castleberry's. She went on and on, throughout our entire dinner. I had to give her credit, the lady was thorough. It occurred to me that she might actually be a good cop.

Then she told me her conclusion.

"Drugs." She slapped the table with both palms.

Wine sloshed out of my glass. I mopped it up with a napkin.

"Sorry," she said. "I'm so excited. As you and I have already discussed, nine times outta ten, somebody gets offed, it's the spouse or the significant other—".

I interrupted. "I heard a rumor that Gregory dumped Doreen."

"Insignificant," she said. "When it's not the spouse or the significant other, it's almost always drugs." She took a small bite out of her monstrous cheeseburger.

I put up my hand to protest. "Nothing I've ever heard about Doreen Sands hinted she was in any way involved with drugs."

"Hear me out. It's like this: Ms. Sands smoked cigarettes. You can't smoke anywhere anymore—" She wrinkled her nose, sniffed, and looked around Angie's. "—except this place maybe, but I think they're breaking the law, especially here in the back room so far away from the bar. It depends on how many tables they can have, and . . ."

I frowned.

"I know what you're gonna say. I'll blow my cover if I complain. Okay, I'll let it slide. This time."

"Good decision," I said.

"Anyway," she said, "Ms. Sands was not allowed to smoke at Castleberry's, not even in her own office, so she sneaked smokes out on the loading dock, a kind of a no man's land as far as store regulations go. Know what I discovered? Castleberry's gets merchandise from all over the world and all of it comes through that loading dock.''

I had a pretty good idea where she was headed. I hastily downgraded my short-lived good opinion of her abilities.

"And you know what that means . . ." she added.

I nodded again.

"Drugs," she said. Again, she slapped the table.

It didn't mean drugs at all. It meant that Castleberry's was a retail store doing what retail stores do, engaging in the practice of normal day-to-day business. Cartons in, cartons out. You could argue that conspicuous consumption was an opiate . . .

Raphael drifted by. I asked for another red wine. Gundermutter ordered white. I figured that meant she now considered herself officially off-duty.

She continued relating her drug fantasy. "At first, I didn't think Ms. Sands was directly involved with the drug trade. I thought she must have witnessed a deal on the loading dock, and somebody not very nice knew what she saw, and bye-bye buyer." Gundermutter drew her finger across her neck. "But then I remembered those slashed-up hats."

Until that point, I must admit, my mind had been wandering, but the mention of hats, especially slashed-up hats, grabbed my interest. "What hats?"

"At Ms. Sands's apartment. Didn't I tell you about those?"

No, she hadn't. "When were you in Doreen Sands's apartment?"

"I went with Spencer . . . I mean, Detective Turner. He and Detective McKinley took me along when they tossed . . . er, searched the place. I found some hats in Ms. Sands's bedroom and they were slashed apart. At the time, I didn't think much about it. But now, after a full day of evidence-gathering at Castleberry's, I'm in a better position to analyze that evidence. Know what I think?"

I anticipated what was coming next. I picked up both almost-full glasses of wine.

"Drugs," she said.

And yes, she slapped the table.

I put the glasses back down, and asked, "Drugs, huh? In the hats?"

"Hidden under the lining."

I didn't believe it for a minute.

"Now that I've cracked the case," she said, "I've got like a major problem. I thought since you're such good friends with Detectives Turner and McKinley—"

I corrected her. "Not friends, acquaintances."

"I need your help. Remember how I told you how Detective Turner leaked the random robbery story to throw off the perp?"

"I remember."

"After I told you that, Detective Turner confided in me." She stopped talking for a moment, sighed as if remembering the moment, and blushed. "He really does think it was a random robbery. He doesn't believe we'll ever discover who killed Ms. Sands. He put the case on the back burner. But then Ms. Sands's fiancé complained and that's why they sent me in undercover to Castleberry's. It was all for show. Detective Turner wanted it to look like the department was making an effort to solve the case. He didn't think I'd find anything. But I did. I want to excel on this assignment. I want to catch the killer. But I'm worried about Spencer . . ." She looked at me.

"It's all right," I said. "You can call him that."

"Thanks." She blushed again. "Spencer is a good detective. And he's my superior. I can't stand the thought of going against him, but in this case, he's wrong. It's no random robbery, it's—"

I picked our glasses up.

"Drugs."

I set them back down.

"If I go ahead on my own," she said, "I could get a promotion. I want to make detective."

What she really wanted, I thought, was to make a detective. Then I felt guilty for my mind being way down in the gutter swimming in mire and muck. Poor Gundermutter. I tried to imagine what it would be like to be her and to have a crush on, of all people, Detective Spencer Turner.

I took a drink of my wine. She'd given me a lot of information. The drug stuff, of course, was a crock. But I was certainly curious about those slashed-up hats in Doreen Sands's bedroom. And the more I thought, the curiouser I got.

I debated what to do. I truly did not want to stick my nose into police business. I reminded myself I did not know Doreen Sands. I reminded myself how I wanted to concentrate on my own work and make a great hat for Fuzzy's show. I reminded myself that enough time had passed to prove that I was not a suspect. I reminded myself of a bunch of other things. And then I looked Gundermutter straight in the eye and said, "Take me to see those slashed-up hats."

12

"Nope. No can do," said Gundermutter. She held up her empty wine glass and twisted her head around to look for Raphael.

I clamped my hand over her glass. "You're back on duty. Come on, take me to Doreen Sands's apartment. I've got to see those slashed-up hats."

"I can't just go to Ms. Sands's place any old time I want," she said. "Even if I could, I sure couldn't drag a civilian along with me."

"Why not? You're a cop, aren't you? You're assigned to the case. I'm not just any civilian. I'm the consultant, the millinery expert who is trying to help you solve the case and, I might add, get you that promotion you deserve. I say we go."

"A stunt like this would get me demoted, not promoted. Spencer Turner will see to that."

"Don't you worry about Spen . . ." I stopped. Turner's first name got stuck in my mouth, but when I saw Gundermutter's eyelashes flutter, the name rolled out, sounded almost natural, as if I always called him Spencer. I continued. "Solve the case that Spencer, in his great wisdom, assigned you to, and it'll be a feather in his cap. It won't matter if you disprove his theory. Believe me, Detective Spencer Turner is used to being wrong. It's the nature of the job, as I'm sure you know. What's important is that he's good enough to recognize when he's wrong."

I paused to take a drink of my wine. Gundermutter

didn't say anything. I sensed her resolve weakening.

"Spencer will be proud of you," I said, "but you've got to take the initiative. Grab the bull by the horns."

"I suppose I could call Spencer and ask if it's okay." She plucked a tiny yellow cellular phone out of her purse.

"No. Don't. As your superior, Turner will be forced to go by the book. He'll have no choice but to tell you not to go. Then I won't get a chance to see the hats, or to tell you where they're from, or look for hiding places you'd never think to look."

"Yeah? Like what?"

"Like feathers. Did you know that feathers have hollow shafts?"

I rarely use feathers, and had no idea if that was true or not. It didn't matter. Gundermutter put her phone away. I'd made my point.

I quickly paid the bill, hustled Gundermutter out of Angie's, and into a cab that had just rounded the corner.

"What about Jackhammer?" she asked. "You're not bringing him are you?"

"Sure. He'll be fine." I couldn't risk taking the time to drop him off at home. It was crucial to keep up the momentum and not give Gundermutter a chance to chicken out. "If anybody asks, I'll say that he's trained to sniff out drugs."

Gundermutter gave the cab driver an address on the Upper West Side. He flipped on the meter, and a canned celebrity tape recording encouraged us to fasten our safety belts. Gundermutter did; I followed her lead. Given that the cabbie was a maniac with a death wish and a penchant for rapid lane switching for no obvious reason except to cut off other—much larger—vehicles, buckling up was a good idea. I hoped the white-knuckle ride would keep Gundermutter from thinking about the many departmental regulations she was about to break.

Gundermutter stared at the brooding five-story stone mansion and shook her head. Afraid she might bolt down the street, I walked up the steps to the entrance, shoved open the heavy wood door, and held it for her. "We've come this far," I said, beckoning.

"I'm gonna regret this," she said.

A small radiator sputtered and hissed in the corner of the tiny entry area. Takeout menus lay on the cracked tile floor. The intercom system was to the left of a bank of tarnished brass mailboxes.

Gundermutter took out her cellular phone. "I think I'd better . . ."

I took quick action. I pushed the button for the super-intendent.

A loud buzz startled us. Gundermutter and I jumped; Jackhammer barked. I leaned against the inner door.

What a contrast to the grungy preliminary entrance. Everywhere, perfectly maintained dark wood paneling. A carved stone fireplace spread over one wall. Big beams crossed the ceiling. A carpeted staircase curved upwards.

A door creaked open a crack, leaking out the sounds of a local TV newscast. Then the door opened all the way and a stocky gray-haired woman in a gray house dress emerged.

The woman scrutinized us.

"Are you the super?" I asked.

"Yeah? Whaddaya want?"

I waited for Gundermutter to say something. She didn't.

The super reached into the pocket of her dress, extracted a watch, and squinted at it. "Come on, already. It's not like I got all day."

"Police matter, ma'am." I said.

The super frowned at me, then fixed her gaze on Gundermutter. "I remember you. You're one of the ones here the other day snooping around the murdered girl's apartment. I had a feeling you'd be back. I was hoping it'd be one of those good-looking detectives. The white one kind of reminded me of that Urban Detective guy on TV."

The mention of good-looking detectives drew another blush out of Gundermutter. "We need another look-see?" she half asked, like she was just trying out the concept and if the super didn't go for it, she'd be happy to turn tail and split.

"Fine with me," said the super. She cocked her head toward Jackhammer. "What's with the dog?"

"Drug sniffer," I said.

"You won't be finding any drugs around here. I run an up-and-up building." She reached inside her door for a ring of keys, then trudged up the stairs with Gundermutter and me bringing up the rear. On the second landing she turned around, clasped her hand to her heart, and stopped to catch her breath. "A damned shame. She was such a sweet girl, paid her rent on time, didn't play loud music, didn't complain. Couldn't ask for a better tenant."

"Did you ever meet Miss Sands's fiancé?" I asked.

"Seemed like a nice enough fellow." She leveled her gaze at me, and lowered her voice. "Bet you think he's the one who did it." She turned back around and we continued our climb up to the fifth floor.

The building had probably started life a century and a half before as a single family home. It had been carved up to make two apartments on each floor. Doreen Sands's apartment faced the back. The super let us in, showed us how to safety lock the door, and lumbered back down the stairs.

Gundermutter stepped inside the apartment. It was my turn to have second thoughts. I stood in the hallway pondering what I was about to do. I didn't care about the law or departmental regulations or red tape. What gnawed at me was invasion of privacy. If I were Doreen Sands, I wouldn't want some stranger poking around my place. Of course, Doreen Sands was dead and her current place was six feet under. Would she really care? I had no way of knowing.

Gundermutter came back out into the hall. "This was all your idea. Remember? You coming in or not?"

Inwardly I struggled. Dead people have rights. Shouldn't they be allowed their privacy? Then again, this particular dead person had been murdered. She deserved to have her killer caught.

I picked up Jackhammer and entered the apartment.

Doreen Sands had lived well. An eclectic contemporary

mix of furniture contrasted with the high ceilings and elaborate moldings of an earlier time. A beige sectional couch snaked around a corner. She had lots of hat-related objects. Hat blocks served as a bookends, a weather-beaten antique millinery shop sign hung above the fireplace.

I must have looked uncomfortable because Gundermutter asked if I was okay.

"Yeah," I said. "Fine. Show me those slashed-up hats."

She gestured toward a closed door. "In the bedroom."

The bedroom was large by New York standards. Big enough to hold a double bed, a high dresser, a low dresser, a rocking chair, and a long rectangular table.

Laid out on the table were half a dozen high-quality hats. I could see why Gundermutter thought they'd been slashed up. Their guts spilled out. Stiff white buckram was exposed, wires poked through, linings were turned inside out. However, Gundermutter didn't get it quite right. The hats had not been slashed up. Stitch by stitch the hats had been painstakingly deconstructed.

It took me a moment to digest this information.

"Turner and McKinley saw these?" I asked.

"They didn't seem to think they were out of the ordinary," said Gundermutter. "I didn't either until I found out what was going down at Castleberry's on the loading dock. Obviously we've got a drug smuggling situation here."

"Hmmm," I said, not willing to commit myself.

Gundermutter picked up one of the hats. Once it had been a green silk-satin draped cloche. Now it was a pile of fabric and interlining. "All these layers," she said, "a great place to stash contraband."

I frowned.

"Now, I'm not necessarily saying Doreen Sands was the one doing the smuggling," said Gundermutter. "Could be she discovered drugs in the hats and planned to turn in the smuggler. Or, she could have been black-mailing the smuggler. Those who hobnob with low-lives tend not to have a long life themselves. I'm telling you, if Jackhammer really were a drug sniffer, he'd be going nuts right now. My guess is the lab analysis will turn up traces of heroin or cocaine.''

"An interesting theory," I said, "but wrong. You are wrong for the right reason, just as Turner and McKinley are right for the wrong reason."

"You want to run that past me again?"

I pointed to one of the hats that had been completely taken apart. "The lining, and interlinings, stiffeners, and all the pieces have been carefully laid out and flattened. Doreen Sands wasn't looking for, or hiding drugs, she was studying how the hat was constructed."

"What for?"

I took a deep breath and lied. "Quality control."

Doreen Sands had not been checking for quality. Nor were drugs the reason Doreen Sands had cut the hats apart. I'd bet my last number-five needle that Doreen Sands was knocking off hats. Maybe the milliner who was getting knocked off found out and knocked Doreen off. I hated the idea that a fellow milliner was a killer. I couldn't tell Gundermutter. Not yet.

Gundermutter said, "I don't get it. So long as the hat looks okay outside, why bother?"

"A hat is only as good as its inner structure. It's also possible Doreen screwed up. It happens, even to the best buyers. Maybe she ordered too many, or misforecast and picked wrong colors, or woke up to find that trend she hopped on changed overnight and she's stuck with an order that won't sell anywhere at any price. In that case, she might look for any possible reason to return the order. Maybe she ordered silk and got a silk blend, or the sample was cut on the bias and the delivered hats were on-grain. Doreen Sands could have examined those hats to see if the materials—even the insides—were exactly as promised."

"Oh."

A dejected-looking Gundermutter sank down on Doreen Sands's bed and absentmindedly ran her hand over the hat-patterned quilt. "I really wanted to crack this one," she said.

Jackhammer, who's great at sensing when someone needs comforting, jumped up on the bed and climbed into Gundermutter's lap. She scratched the top of his head and sighed.

I examined the pieces. In my mind I put them back together, made them into whole hats. Happily, I didn't recognize the hats as the work of any milliner I knew. I thought about telling Gundermutter my suspicions, but decided against it. I didn't want to be responsible for unleashing her on the millinery community. Once I found out who made those hats, I'd let her know.

Gundermutter put Jackhammer on the floor and stood up. "Let's get out of here," she said.

"I want to look around more," I said. "Just a couple of minutes."

She sat back down on the bed. "Whatever."

I ripped through Doreen Sands's closet. Nice clothes, mostly from the mid-priced lines of big-name designers. Stacked on shelves were lots of hatboxes with the logos of milliners I knew. I was looking for someone I didn't know, the milliner whose hats lay in pieces—the Unknown Milliner.

I checked the waste basket, and the dresser drawers, looking for imprinted tissue paper, labels. Nothing. A quick tour through the kitchen told me Doreen Sands ate cereal for breakfast and probably had the rest of her meals out. From the contents of her bathroom cabinet I deduced she had trouble sleeping. She also used a special tooth-whitening toothpaste.

I wandered into the living room and tried to imagine Doreen Sands sitting on her couch thinking. I could see her smoking, and stubbing out her cigarette in a copper cowboy hat ashtray, all the while conniving and plotting to knock off the designs of the Unknown Milliner.

I found an appointment calendar in the most obvious place, a desk drawer. A must-read, I stuck it in my bag.

I looked into the bedroom to see what Gundermutter

was up to. She'd stretched out on the bed next to Jack-hammer.

"I'm done," I said.

"It's about time," she said.

13

Gundermutter, Jackhammer, and I sat on the stoop outside Doreen Sands's building and observed Upper West Side life—parents pushing kids in strollers and take-out delivery guys zooming by on bicycles.

Poor Gundermutter. She looked awful. I felt bad for her. She'd meant well. Now, her whole drug conspiracy theory had crashed, and with it her dreams for a promotion.

"Look on the bright side," I said. "Now you don't have to worry about contradicting Turner's idea of whodunnit."

"I don't know, Brenda. I still say those slashed-up hats could have been stuffed full of drugs." She stood up. "Guess I better go check in at the precinct."

We shared a cab back to the Village.

Gundermutter didn't seem to want to talk anymore, and that was fine with me. Jackhammer fell asleep in my lap. I pressed my head up against the window and thought about Doreen Sands. Why would she risk her considerable reputation to knock off some hats? I wished it had been drugs. For me, that would have been far less disturbing.

In the silence, the cab driver cranked the radio up, and filled the icky sweet vanilla-scented air with the sounds of desperate people seeking guidance from a call-in psychic shrink. If any of those callers had asked me, I'd have told them to skip the psychic shrink, and go buy a hat.

As the cab neared the Village, Gundermutter took a gold-tone compact out of her purse, snapped it open, and spent the rest of the ride looking into the jiggling mirror, reapplying her mascara and lipstick. Every so often she let go of a big sigh. The only word she uttered was "shit" when the cab swerved to avoid a pedestrian, and she got a streak of lipstick on her chin.

Jackhammer and I got out of the cab in front of my apartment building. Gundermutter continued on to the precinct. "Paperwork," she said. Given her fresh makeup job, I suspected she hoped for something other than paperwork. Like maybe Detective Spencer Turner would be hanging around, looking for someone to have a drink with.

I made a pot of coffee and curled up on the couch to read Doreen Sands's engagement calendar. It was a thick leather book with a gilt-edged page for each day. The entries were made with blue ink in a small, neat handwriting. Doreen was already booked up all the way through the end of the year. A quick thumb-through of her life reminded me how much I cherished my independence and how lucky I was to have Midnight Millinery.

I could never do a job like hers. Her days were a tightly scheduled series of business meetings and business lunches, appointments with sellers and suppliers. On most nights she had at least one business-oriented social event. I admired people like her who could be on all the time. The very thought made my smile muscles hurt. Doreen Sands apparently thrived on that kind of stuff.

A few patterns emerged. She went to the gym twice a week, usually early mornings on Tuesday and Thursday, and always with a trainer. Hairdresser and manicurist on Fridays. Legs waxed once a month. An acting class whenever she could fit it in. Lots of buying trips, overseas and in the United States.

How did she ever find time for Gregory? Maybe she didn't. In which case I could hardly blame him for dumping her—that is, if he really had. It would be nice to know if that particular rumor were true. I could find out with a quick call to Ray Marshall, but at the moment, I was far more concerned with learning the identity of the Unknown Milliner.

I read and reread, backwards and forwards, made some notes, and listed a couple of manufacturers Doreen had visited. If she were scheming to knock off hats, somebody had to make them.

Manufacturing was one area of millinery I knew very little about. I could never hand over a prototype to a factory. That wasn't my kind of millinery. It was also the reason why I'd never sell in the big numbers or be rich and famous.

Around midnight Jackhammer jumped off the couch and dashed into the foyer, barking. Elizabeth was either coming in or going out. I looked through the peephole and saw that she was unlocking her door. Good. I needed somebody to talk to. I opened my door. "Hey."

"Hey back," she said. She looked wonderful, not the least bit tired. I wondered where the hell she'd been.

"Want some company?" I asked.

"Sure, why not? The night is young."

I told her what I'd been up to. "Looks like Doreen Sands was knocking off hats."

Elizabeth shook her head. "Brenda Midnight, if you know what's good for you, you'd keep to your word and stay out of police business."

That's what she said. However, I noticed she had leaned forward in her chair to make sure she didn't miss a word of my story.

I smiled and went on to describe Doreen's hectic schedule.

"I don't understand people like that," said Elizabeth. "Always on the go. And for what, may I ask?"

"Doreen Sands had built up a great millinery department," I said.

"Far better to be a great milliner—Lilly Daché, Mr. John, and maybe someday with a lot of hard work and a little luck, Brenda Midnight—than to run a great millinery department."

"Thanks for the compliment."

"Deserved."

"Here's a question for you," I said. "If there were no great millinery departments, would there still be great milliners?"

"Ah, the age-old question. I pose another: Would there be great artists without galleries, without museums?"

"Sure, I guess. But no one would know of them."

"Right," she said. "Now, getting back to the subject, I hate to say it, but that lady cop friend of yours has a point. Doreen Sands had a damned good setup to move drugs."

"Too obvious," I said.

"Most things are."

"What strikes me as weird," I said, "is that Gundermutter is the only one who thinks drugs were behind the murder. Usually, Turner and McKinley blame any crime in the neighborhood on drugs. But this time, for some reason, they're sticking to their theory that it was a random robbery. According to Gundermutter, Turner really believes that, and wasn't just saying it."

"Perhaps the cops know something you don't."

"Yeah, like maybe they think I did it."

"Will you stop that kind of talk? Your paranoia is beginning to get tedious."

"Sorry. You're right. Even I don't believe it anymore."

"What *do* you believe?"

"I think the Unknown Milliner found out about the planned knockoffs. It's underhanded and sleazy to knock off a design, but unfortunately it's not exactly illegal. With no recourse under the law, the Unknown Milliner got really pissed, confronted Doreen in her office, shot her, and then sneaked the gun into my hatbox."

"Are you saying that Doreen Sands was underhanded and sleazy?"

"That is a big problem. The logic doesn't follow. Everything I've ever heard about Doreen Sands is quite the opposite. She had a reputation for being fair and honest and supportive. Yet I saw the evidence in her bed-room.''

"You ought to tell Turner and McKinley. Let them sort it all out.''

"No way,'' I said. "Don't you understand what would happen? First they'd yell at me for sticking my nose into police business. Then they'd yell at Gundermutter for tak-ing me to Doreen's apartment. She'd be in serious trouble. After they were finished yelling, they'd relentlessly inter-rogate all the milliners. I'd get the blame.''

"Oh, for goodness sakes, Brenda. Why would the mil-liners blame you? How would they even know you'd said anything to anybody? It seems perfectly natural that the detectives, in the normal course of investigating the death of a millinery buyer, might want to talk to some milliners. I don't see why they'd have to bring up your name.''

"Trust me, word would get out. Someone at some time will somehow bring up my name. I'd be an outcast, scorned by the millinery community.''

Elizabeth rolled her eyes. "Now, that'd sure be a trag-edy of epic proportions.''

I was disappointed. Elizabeth was usually so understand-ing. She'd changed. It must have had something to do with those late hours.

I needed to confide in somebody who would under-stand. Fuzzy? I couldn't trust her not to blab it all over. But there was no one else. Okay, then, I'd just point out to Fuzzy how very important it was to keep it under her hat—at least until I found out more. She wasn't stupid. She'd listen to reason.

It wasn't too late to call. Fuzzy rarely slept.

She answered on the first ring. "Have no fear, Fuzzy here.''

"It's me,'' I said.

"Brenda. How nice to hear from you.''

She was shouting. In the background loud music pounded. Ever since she got a cellular phone, I never knew where she was. "Are you out?''

"But of course. Tonight, dressed to kill in my hot-off-the-block, starched-to-hell, I-LOVE-NEW-YORK T-shirt hat, I'm scoping out the East Soho club scene, also known as the East Village Down Under or the Upper Lower East Side.''

"Speaking of neighborhoods," I said, "I'm going to be down in yours tomorrow. Thought I might drop by your loft, say around eleven?"

"See you then."

14

I didn't want to pay for yet another cab. There was no halfway efficient way to get to Fuzzy's neighborhood by bus. So, a little before eleven the next morning, I shoved my way onto a downtown Number Two train.

In most cities the designation downtown pretty much equals the central business district, the part of the city with all the tall buildings, traffic jams, commerce and culture, as opposed to the suburbs where the people who work in the tall buildings and participate in the commerce and culture, go home at night. In New York going downtown means going south. The central business district, otherwise known as midtown, is downtown from uptown, but uptown from farther downtown. Like so many things in life, it all depends on your point of view.

Go far enough downtown and you hit Wall Street, yet another business district complete with skyscrapers. Fuzzy lived way, way, way downtown, on the southern tip of Manhattan, somewhere vaguely below Wall Street, on a short narrow street that's easy to miss. Which I did, first going one way, then the other. Frustrated, I gave up the search, swallowed my pride, and asked a UPS guy. ''Nice hat,'' he said, then kindly pointed me in the correct direction.

Fuzzy had the entire seventh floor of a thirty-story building. In the eighties it was chock-a-block with cocaine-wired brokers who shouted into telephones. "Buy, sell, what the hell?" Some time after the eighties ended, and the brokers either moved on or got sent to jail, the building emptied out and eccentric urban pioneers like Fuzzy moved in at reasonable per-square-foot rents. Then, sometime in the mid-nineties when the *end* of the eighties ended and the beginning of the nineties began, the repurposed building filled up with high-tech new media start-up companies, and the corridors became crowded with bleary-eyed web masters and technowizards, who tried to be, but weren't a tenth as cool, or a hundredth as capable, as Chuck Riley.

The city named the burgeoning area Silicon Alley and invited everybody to come on down and plug in.

And they did. Enough that the fifty-foot-high lobby crackled with activity. T-shirted executives darted this way and that, their sneakers silent on the marble floor.

A burly man pushed a dolly piled high with plasterboard onto the elevator. I followed, and then three pale skinny guys got on. Wired to the hilt, they sucked down espressos and talked a mile a minute about sophisticated new telephone switching equipment, which was surely destined to change modern civilization, and make them all a huge profit.

When I punched the number for Fuzzy's floor, the skinny guys stopped their chatter. They all kind of drew back, and gave me a dirty look.

"Bunch of jerks," said Fuzzy, when I told her how the skinny guys had reacted. "They're insanely jealous. Every last one of them hates my guts because my web page gets more hits than theirs, and the web page is not even what I do. Well, I do it, but you know what I mean."

I knew exactly what she meant. Fuzzy wasn't just a milliner, nor was she just a web page designer. Fuzzy was everything—the original multimedia artist. She was robust and dynamic and bursting at the seams with life and information and stuff. Her web page was only one way she got her many words out. Her web page was good because she was a good, possibly great, artist. That's why her hats win awards, and her sculptures, her video, her one-act plays, her . . .

"Got a hat ready for Milliners Milling?" she asked.

"Working on it," I said.

Slowly, we meandered through a maze of Fuzzy's works-in-progress that filled the entire ranch-sized loft. Along one wall, a row of video monitors pulsated with abstract images of hats. To my left was a sculpture made out of brightly painted antique hat blocks lashed together with paper-covered wire and number-nine belting ribbon. "Are those the blocks from the flea market?" I asked.

"They sure are. I was totally inspired. That was a fabulous find on your part. You were such a doll to let me know. I ought to dedicate the piece to you and the spirit of millinery community."

"I don't know what to say," I said.

Fuzzy's millinery workshop was a large area loosely defined by structural columns and a couple sheets strung up as curtains. When we got near, she speeded up, like she didn't want me to see.

"Working on something new?" I asked.

"All will be revealed at my show."

She'd never been secretive before. Despite her efforts to hurry me along, I managed to sneak a peek into the studio area. I gasped. And then I tried to cover up the gasp with a cough, which came out sounding really weird.

"What's wrong with you?" asked Fuzzy.

"All of a sudden, I don't feel so good," I said.

"Something you ate maybe?"

"Yeah, that must be it." I pushed on my stomach and groaned, then launched into a totally made-up story about eating breakfast at a local greasy spoon.

"Probably undercooked eggs," she said. "You've got to be really careful with eggs these days."

While she prattled on about eggs and chicken handling and inadequately inspected restaurants, I tried to absorb what I'd seen in her millinery studio—a display of very un-Fuzzy-like hats. These hats weren't spray-painted cereal boxes decorated with plastic bananas, or festooned record albums, or kinetic sculptures spinning atop six-part beanies. These hats didn't light up or make sounds or break any new ground. They were quite nice, quite traditional, quite wearable, quite sellable hats.

Hats I had seen before. Recently. In pieces.

Fuzzy was the Unknown Milliner.

Fuzzy. I'd met her a few years ago while making the rounds of Soho boutiques. We were walking toward each other on West Broadway, each burdened down with several black- and white-striped hatboxes.

"Hats?" I'd said.

"Uh-huh. You too?"

I'd nodded.

"Well, then," said Fuzzy in that deep foghorn voice, "let's celebrate millinery."

As luck would have it, we were standing right in front of a wine bar.

"Okay."

That had been the beginning of what I thought was a pretty darned good friendship. Until now.

I did not like this development. If Fuzzy was the Unknown Milliner, that meant she was the milliner whose hats Doreen Sands was knocking off, and that meant she was quite possibly the milliner who had knocked off Doreen Sands. Fuzzy a killer? That couldn't be.

My theory had to be wrong.

All I wanted was to get the hell out of Fuzzy's loft. I needed to think. I needed to be alone.

Fuzzy led me into her kitchen area way in the back of the loft. She insisted on making me a cup of herbal tea. "Whatever you've got," she said, tapping a bright-colored tea tin with a green-painted fingernail, "this'll fix it right up. It'll settle your stomach."

She spooned out a clingy mass of dry brown vegetable matter and dropped it into a raku cup she'd made during her pottery phase.

What was it with everybody wanting to give me tea? First Johnny, now Fuzzy. The scene was replaying itself, only this time menacingly.

She must have realized I'd peeked at her new hats. Did she know what else I knew? Would she try to kill me too? That tea might settle more than my stomach.

"No thanks," I said, "I don't care for tea."

"Don't think of it as tea, think of it as medicine."

Or poison, I thought.

Elizabeth was right. I *was* paranoid.

With uncanny timing Fuzzy asked, "Anything new on the Doreen Sands case?"

"Not a word. Tell you the truth, the shop has been such a madhouse lately, I haven't had time to think."

To keep Fuzzy from seeing the expression on my face, I walked over to a small window that looked down into a narrow vacant lot next to her building. Pretending to be fascinated with the view, which was nothing but a brick wall and a construction trailer, I tried to get my thoughts in order.

The situation might not be so bad after all. Just because Fuzzy had designed some new hats that she might have sold to Doreen Sands who might have been planning to knock them off, didn't mean Fuzzy knew what Doreen Sands had in mind, and even if she did, it didn't mean Fuzzy had killed Doreen Sands, and even if she had, she wouldn't know how much I knew.

Or would she? She was aware that I knew the cops. She might have even found out that Gundermutter was a cop.

The teapot pierced the air with its whistle. Fuzzy called me over. I watched as she poured steaming water into the raku cup, over the pile of twigs. With a flourish she handed it to me. "Bottoms up."

I blew into the putrid-smelling golden brew.

My thoughts came fast and furious and in such jumbled order that I almost overlooked an important fact. It was definitely not Fuzzy who had sneaked the gun into my hatbox. She could never disguise herself. My solace was brief because I immediately realized that she could have hired somebody else to do the actual killing. She knew zillions of people, including some highly unusual characters. I wouldn't have been the least bit surprised to find a professional killer among them.

"Your friend Chuck Riley is a genius," she said. "I am so glad I found him. He's doing up some great lighting effects. It's going to be a killer show."

Again, I blew into the tea. Fragments of herb swirled just beneath the surface.

"So, tell me Brenda," said Fuzzy, "what brings you down to my neck of the woods? A powwow with your broker?" She chortled loudly.

I couldn't tell her I'd come to tell her about the slashed-up hats at Doreen's. I came up with a pretty good lie for spur-of-the-moment. "It's another problem with the state. I had to go to the World Trade Center to get it straightened out. Can you imagine, they claimed I owe over four thousand dollars in sales tax for last quarter."

"Fat chance," said Fuzzy. "You'd have to have grossed like fifty thousand smackers in three months for that to be true. No offense, but I don't think you do that much business."

"Not even close," I said. "So anyway, the state admitted the mistake was theirs, and sent me on my way. I hate this official stuff. I'm stressed out."

"Poor Brenda."

"In fact, now that I think of it, that's probably what made me sick. It wasn't anything I ate. Just nerves. Pure and simple. I won't be needing this tea after all."

"Tea's good for stress," she said.

"Not this kind of stress," I said.

"Have it your way." Fuzzy grabbed the raku cup out of my hand and chugged down the brew.

Okay, so I'd overreacted. Fuzzy was not attempting to poison me.

"I really should be going," I said.

I hoped I was out of my mind.

I decided to walk home, thinking perhaps the long walk would soothe me. Wrong. I'd forgotten about the traffic at the intersection of Canal and Broadway.

It honked, it screeched its brakes, it gridlocked, it

fouled the air, it did everything but stay in its own god-damned lane and yield to pedestrians.

Later, safely back at Midnight Millinery, I felt foolish for believing—if only for a moment—that my friend Fuzzy . . . well, it was so ridiculous I couldn't even give form to the thought. I mean, really, I needed to get a grip on myself.

It occurred to me that if I could put two and two together and come up with Fuzzy as the killer, Turner and McKinley or even Gundermutter might eventually put those same facts together and reach the same conclusion. Being cops, and not Fuzzy's friends, instead of rejecting the idea, they'd latch right on to it. They'd go after Fuzzy.

I couldn't let that happen. I had to prove that Fuzzy was innocent before the police got the crazy idea that she wasn't. Okay, so I knew what I had to prove, the question was how to do it. The answer to that came quick. I couldn't prove a single thing, not with what I knew.

I needed more information. Hard as it was to believe Doreen Sands was knocking off Fuzzy's hats, I'd seen the evidence. Perhaps Fuzzy wasn't the only milliner she was knocking off. I could hardly ask Fuzzy, or any of the other milliners, but I could go to the manufacturers Doreen Sands had met with. But on what pretense? How could I possibly wheedle my way into the confidence of a man-ufacturer's rep who was nothing more than a broker?

I got stuck on that idea. Brokers. I'd thought about brokers when I first got to Fuzzy's building. What was it? Buy, sell, what the hell. Buy, sell.

That was it. Buyers. Them I could cozy up to by pre-tending to sell.

I did some quick phone work and set up two appointments with prominent millinery buyers, one for the very next day. That meant I had to hustle to get some samples to-gether to take with me.

I called Turner hoping he'd spring my hats. That would make things a lot easier.

As soon as he heard my voice, he growled, "Now what?"

"Are you finished with my hats yet?"

"Afraid not. Be patient, Ms. Midnight."

As long as I had him on the phone I took the opportunity to very casually inquire about the investigation. I wanted to know if he was on to Fuzzy. "Any leads in the Doreen Sands case?"

"A word to the wise, Ms. Midnight. You best not be stirring up trouble."

On that sour note, he hung up.

15

I called Johnny. "Dinner? Angie's? My treat." I couldn't tell Johnny my suspicions about Fuzzy—he'd tell me to go to the cops—but that didn't mean I didn't want a dinner companion. I desperately needed to talk to somebody about anything. It didn't matter what.

"Can't," he said. "I'm making dinner tonight to test out one of my new workout recipes on Lemmy. He's already here. Come on over. I'll get another dumbbell out of the cupboard and set another place at the table."

Not the ideal situation, but hey, what was?

"Be there in a few," I said.

"Bring Jackhammer," he said.

Lemmy threw open Johnny's door. He had on a greenish-hued rumpled sharkskin suit. "Brenda. Jackhammer. Long time, no see." He buzzed both my cheeks Hollywood style. The man positively reeked of citrusy after shave, like he'd splashed it from the tip of his toes to the top of his shiny pink, fresh-shaved chrome dome.

"Where's Johnny?" I asked.

Lemmy jerked his thumb toward Johnny's kitchen. "In there. Our boy's doing jumping jacks while cooking up a storm."

Jackhammer sniffed the savory air and ran full-steam into the kitchen. Through the doorway I saw Johnny jumping around, a strange kitchen utensil in each hand. He lifted one in greeting. I waved back.

"Take a load off," said Lemmy.

My small frame hardly qualified as a load. Lemmy joined me on the couch, and moved in a little too close. A lascivious grin spread across his face, and he winked. "Go to hell," I said, not the least bit offended. Lemmy was just being Lemmy—in other words, a jerk.

"So, Brenda," he said, "how's it going?"

"Not bad," I said. "And you?"

"Can't complain."

"I hear you got Johnny a good deal on this book thing."

"Please," said Lemmy, "don't refer to the deal of my career as 'this book thing.' It is far more than a book, far more than a thing. Trust me, it's gonna be The Thing. I'm talking like big-time runaway best seller. The talk shows will be bidding against each other to get Tod Trueman, Urban Detective as a guest. And that's only the beginning. We've gotta hit while we're hot. I'm thinking we could license kitchenware tie-ins and workout gear. Hell, who knows, maybe a movie. I'll get our Johnny on the big screen yet."

A movie out of a cookbook? I shouldn't have been surprised. Lemon B. Crenshaw saw movies everywhere. The only project he'd ever convinced Hollywood to take on was so incredibly stupid, Johnny turned it down. That made for some high tension in the client-agent relationship, but they'd eventually worked it out. Lemmy dug up another of his clients for the role, Hollywood changed the name of the protagonist from Tod Trueman to something else, and the movie got made. It was due to be released soon.

"Did you find a ghost writer for the book?"

"Not yet. I've been working night and day to narrow down the field. I've got some definite possibles. As a matter of fact, I brought along some material to show Johnny. After that movie fiasco a while back, I'm careful to make sure he feels involved in every inch of the decision-making process. Know what I mean?" He winked again.

"As long as you're here, I might as well get your opinion too. You're an artist. You've got not half bad taste."

"Gee, thanks Lemmy."

"You're most welcome."

He opened up a snazzy brown leather monogrammed briefcase, and pulled out a manila folder. Inside were several eight-by-ten glossies. He laid them side by side on Johnny's coffee table. Some were headshots, some full-body poses. He jabbed at the photos with a short stubby forefinger. "Now this here redhead dances, check out those long luscious gams; and the blond sings, as you can well imagine given that enormous set of bazooms."

What did I expect from Lemmy, the man who had an extensive brassiere collection mounted on his living room wall? However, I had never seen an author photo that revealed quite so much cleavage. "Excuse me, Lemmy. Are you positive these women are writers?"

Lemmy rolled his eyes. "Brenda, Brenda, Brenda. Of course they're writers. Anybody can write. It's a *recipe* book for chrissakes. A cuppa this, a cuppa that, heat it up, slap it on a plate. This isn't literature, you know. What these ladies are is yummy cover decor, and I must say—"

Just then, Johnny skipped out of the kitchen.

Lemmy clammed up.

Johnny circled the dining room table many times while pressing a covered casserole dish over his head. Finally, with great ceremony, he set the plate down. He cocked his head at the photos on the coffee table. "Who're they?"

"Writers," said Lemmy, grinning from ear to ear. "For your book. The cream of the crop for our Tod Trueman, Urban Detective recipe and workout package. Come over here and feast your eyes."

Frowning, Johnny scrutinized the glossies. "These don't look like writers to me. These ladies look more like actresses or models or—"

"You are *so* right, Johnny," said Lemmy. "Perceptive. That's what I like about you. For an actor you have real depth. What we're gonna do is give one of these ladies the opportunity of a lifetime."

"What do you mean by that?"

"Well," said Lemmy, "whichever one you pick—and Johnny the choice is completely up to you—that babe not only gets to help you write the book, we're also gonna stick her on the cover."

"But I already have an idea for the cover," said Johnny. "I thought it would be me pictured with—"

"Of course you're gonna be on the cover. It would hardly be a Tod Trueman book without Johnny Verlane on the cover, now would it? It's just that you're gonna have company on the cover, and I might add, rather nice company."

Johnny shook his head. "I don't think so, Lemmy. I want the cover to show me peeking out from behind one of my fluffy soufflés, urban-detective-like."

Lemmy shook his head. "You don't get it, Johnny. You don't know a goddamned thing about marketing. I tell you, we need one of these juicy broads on the cover."

"No," said Johnny, with surprising force.

Lemmy said, "Don't you mean, you don't think so, until your hard-working self-sacrificing agent or a professional from your publisher's marketing department knocks some sense into your thick skull?"

"No," Johnny said, "that's not what I mean. What I mean is no, no way, never, I won't do it. No."

"He won't do it," mocked Lemmy. He looked at me. "Guess our boy is getting too big for his britches, refuses to help a struggling actress, like it's any skin off his nose." He glared at Johnny.

Johnny glared back.

It was time for me to jump in. "Lemmy," I said, "you wouldn't happen to be dating any of these, uh, writers, would you?"

Lemmy looked as if I'd slapped him across the face. "Shame on you, Brenda Midnight to even think such a thing. You know me better than that. This is business, pure and simple. I'm a businessman. I know not to mix business with pleasure. My only concern is Johnny and what's best for his career."

"Yeah, right," said Johnny. "If you were really only thinking of me and not casting about for your next *ex-*

girlfriend, then you'd find me a writer who's really a writer. And you'd make goddamn sure my fluffy soufflé got on the cover.''

Lemmy slapped his forehead with the heel of his hand. ''I give up. I freaking give up.'' He stuffed the glossies back in his briefcase and snapped it shut.

They got over it. Neither Lemmy nor Johnny was much prone to reflective thought, yet they each realized three fundamental truths: Without Lemmy as his agent, Johnny wouldn't be *Tod Trueman, Urban Detective*. Without Johnny as his client, Lemmy wouldn't be Lemon B. Crenshaw, super agent. And without each of them keeping the other firmly in line when necessary, they'd both be bicycle messengers.

''Okay,'' said Johnny. ''One and two and three and four.''

My fingertips grazed the floor. I held onto my ankles and pulled. ''This is nuts,'' I said.

''Ugh,'' said Lemmy.

''I'm merely testing the concept,'' said Johnny. ''A perfectly natural progression of the workout-as-you-cook book idea is to workout before you sit down at the table. It gets the blood to your head and involves the whole family.''

''Bad for digestion,'' I said.

''All I need,'' grumbled Lemmy, ''is more freaking blood in my head.''

''And now,'' continued Johnny, ''we will march in place. Hup, two, three, four.''

Jackhammer danced around our marching feet, no doubt wondering why, with a table full of great-smelling food, we didn't just sit down and eat it.

Eventually we did.

The food was good. I wasn't sure what it was, and Johnny refused to say. ''You'll have to read the book,'' he said, ''but I assure you, there's absolutely no meat involved. I wouldn't want to upset the vegetarian among us.''

"Don't you go overboard on that meatless chapter," warned Lemmy. "We wouldn't want to alienate the normal people with a way-out wacko book that only has fringe appeal." He smirked.

I didn't let Lemmy get to me. Rather than get into an argument about meat, I changed the subject. Unfortunately, the subject I chose was millinery and before I knew it, Lemmy said, "Heard you had a little trouble with a hatbox."

"Hatbox? Trouble? Not me. I don't know what you're talking about." I shot Johnny a look that would have killed had he seen, but he was busy looking under the table, tossing a chunk of crusty, hand-kneaded bread to Jackhammer.

Lemmy plowed right ahead, paying no attention to my denial. "What I heard was that those idiot detectives Turner and McKinley found a gun in your hatbox—of all places—and then, damned if it didn't turn out to be a murder weapon."

"Oh that," I said. "It was nothing. A mistake. Really."

"Doesn't sound like nothing to me. You musta freaked. Makes you look like the bad guy. Victim's a millinery buyer, right? Never bought any of your hats. Sounds like motive to me. You were there, that's opportunity. And the smoking gun in your possession? Even those clowns Turner and McKinley could figure that one out."

"Nobody ever thought I killed her," I said, about ninety-seven percent sure that was the truth.

"I don't know," said Lemmy. "I mean, what if you're one of those split-personality types? One of the other yous coulda killed the buyer lady, then regular you blacked it out. You know, I like that. In fact, I'm liking it a lot. It's got huge potential. Tell you what, I'm gonna pass it along to the *Tod Trueman* writers."

I tried not to react because that would make Lemmy all the more likely to follow through. However, I felt my face blanch.

"Don't worry, Brenda," said Lemmy. "I'll make sure you get credit—inspired by Brenda Midnight. How's that sound?"

*   *   *

I was glad that Lemmy took off immediately after dinner.

While we were carrying the dishes into the kitchen, Johnny complained, "Lemmy could have at least offered to help clean up."

"He's got a pretty short fuse," I said.

"I should be used to him by now. I am right, aren't I, about the book cover?"

"Of course," I said. "At least, you're more right than Lemmy."

We did the dishes. Johnny washed, I dried, and Jackhammer sniffed around on the floor in case some scraps of food fell his way. After some thought, I came up with a way to tell Johnny some of what I'd been up to without getting him worried I was sticking my nose into police business. I merely changed the emphasis.

"You'll never guess what gung-ho Gundermutter did yesterday," I said.

"What?"

"She took me to Doreen Sands's apartment."

"On whose authority? Do Turner or McKinley know?"

"I don't think so. They sure didn't hear it from me."

"Sounds risky. Why'd she want you along?"

"She wants to solve the case on her own to impress Turner. She had this crazy idea that Doreen Sands was smuggling drugs inside of hats. Either that or somebody else was, and Doreen found out. She showed me the so-called evidence."

"Which was?"

"A bunch of hats that had been cut apart. I'm afraid Gundermutter was mighty disappointed when I told her that, in my expert opinion, the hats had not been used to stash drugs. Although I didn't tell Gundermutter, I'm pretty sure Doreen Sands was knocking off someone's designs." I didn't tell him that I believed that someone to be Fuzzy.

"Why would anybody want to knock off hats?" he asked.

"I don't know. Money I suppose. Although it's hard to imagine that there'd be enough profit in such an endeavor for Doreen Sands to jeopardize her considerable reputation. It appears she did though.''

''Don't write off Officer Gundermutter's drug theory so quickly. It's more credible than your theory. I hate to tell you this, Brenda, but you've got hats on the brain. You see millinery as the end-all, the center of the universe. Since when was millinery, even knocked-off millinery, a motive for murder?''

''There you go again,'' I said, ''siding with the cops.''

As Jackhammer and I walked along Bleecker Street toward home, I calmed myself down. Maybe Johnny had a point. Maybe I did have millinery on the brain. It clouded my perception and made me think my friend Fuzzy was a killer.

I still didn't go for the drug explanation. The fight between Johnny and Lemmy emphasized the fact that, cliché or not, most murders are committed by someone known to the victim, a lover, a spouse, a lover's spouse, a spouse's lover. Maybe my millinery-addled brain had made this whole thing too convoluted.

It wouldn't hurt to look into the rumor that Gregory had dumped Doreen. All I had to do was call Ray Marshall and ask. That's exactly what I intended to do as soon as I got home.

I picked up the phone, punched in Ray's number. Midway through the first ring I hung up. I was afraid Ray might get the wrong idea as to my intentions. Or that Johnny would find out I'd called Ray and then he would get the wrong idea.

I decided to sleep on it.

16

Early the next morning I went to the shop and gathered up a bunch of hats to take uptown for my sales appointment. Every time I dropped a tissue-wrapped creation into a cardboard Midnight Millinery hatbox, I cursed Turner. I suspected his refusal to release my travel hatboxes and sample hats from the precinct had more to do with him being a big bully than with rules, regulations, or police procedure.

I had designed those hats especially for department store sales. With them in the lockup I was forced to put together a collection from the shop, none of them appropriate for the department store market or to turn out in big numbers. I'd probably make a fool of myself.

I closed up the hatboxes. Right before leaving the shop, after wavering half the night and most of the morning, I picked up the phone and dialed Ray Marshall's number. I did it fast, almost like it was an accident that I couldn't blame on myself if it got screwed up.

"Brenda," he said. "I was hoping to hear from you."

"You were?"

"Yes."

"Oh." To get the conversation moving in a safer and more constructive direction, I blurted out, "I've heard some talk on the millinery grapevine about Doreen Sands and Gregory, that they'd broken up and called off the wedding. I thought maybe Gregory would want to know. If it's not true he might want to set the record straight. It makes him look bad, especially after the eulogy he gave at the funeral.''

''Poor Gregory,'' said Ray. ''The guy's been through an awful lot. How I hate to be the bearer of bad news.''

''But you'll tell him?''

''Yes. Somebody's got to. Thanks, Brenda. I'll let you know what he says.''

We disconnected.

I felt like a first-class heel. I'd used Ray to get to Gregory, hoping to get a rise out of him. At least I hadn't lied. The part about the rumor was true.

It had been easier than I expected to get appointments with two millinery buyers, one uptown at a large store where I was now headed, and one later in the week downtown in Soho at an exclusive boutique. In both instances, I'd been immediately put through to the millinery buyer, and told when to show up. The thought that my name and reputation were getting around greatly inflated my ego. I spent much of the bus ride uptown trying to get it back down to size.

I needn't have bothered. The long wait to see the buyer took care of that nicely. Minute by minute, my ego shriveled.

There I was, at another department store, in another waiting room jammed with hopeful designers all waiting to see buyers, and another receptionist who put me on another list, and another buyer who kept me waiting a long time. Was this one dead too? I sure as hell hoped not.

I propped up my feet on my hatboxes, leaned back and daydreamed my way back to the Castleberry's waiting room on the morning of the murder. Once again I dredged up every memory, and, once again I reached the same conclusion: there was simply no way anybody could have put that gun in my hatbox without my knowledge.

Yet there had been a gun in my hatbox.

''Ms. Midnight?'' The receptionist said.

I snapped back to the present. ''Yes,'' I said.

"Go through those doors, turn right, third door on your left. Good luck with your collection."

I knocked. When no one answered I cracked open the door. "Is this, uh . . ." I faltered, suddenly realizing the buyer hadn't told me her name when we'd talked on the phone. ". . . millinery?"

"Yes, yes, yes. Come in. You're in the right place. Put your hats on that table." The buyer flung an arm toward a white plastic-topped table. A multitude of silver bracelets jangled.

I approached her large messy desk and extended my hand. "Brenda Midnight," I said, with a smile that I hoped could pass for real.

The buyer grunted, gave my hand a quick, weak shake, then picked up her phone, punched in a number, and lambasted someone on the other end. It sounded like a personal call, and didn't seem to have much to do with millinery, or for that matter, murder.

Okay, so she wasn't going to introduce herself. I was embarrassed. I should have done my homework. Too late now. I had little choice but to think of her as the Uptown Buyer.

Uptown Buyer was dressed in a stylish suit with big lapels and quirky plastic buttons shaped like hats. She was reasonably attractive in a bland blond sort of way. She seemed in a mighty big hurry to get viewing my hats out of the way so she could get on with the important part of her day. Inwardly I laughed at my formerly inflated ego. Whatever had I been thinking?

I reminded myself that my ego was not the issue, my mission was not to sell hats or to make myself feel good, it was to fact-find. I wanted to learn if Uptown Buyer knew about Fuzzy's new line and maybe, if I got really lucky, what she thought about Doreen Sands. Still, no matter what my ultimate long-term goal, running through the act of selling felt exactly like selling.

The office was filled with swatches of fabric and veiling, samples of feathers, and pictures of hats. I maneuvered around a maze of stacked-up cardboard cartons, and made it over to the table. The surface was in terrible condition, chipped, stained, and scratched. In art school, they'd hammered into me the importance of a good presentation. I'd come prepared for a lousy display surface with a piece of red satin. I unfolded it, spread it over the table, swooshed it around into casual gathers, and laid out my hats in a pleasing array. Checking to make sure my smile was still in place, I turned around.

The buyer's telephone conversation had ended with a curse and a slammed receiver. Now she had her nose buried in an inch-thick foreign fashion magazine.

I cleared my throat.

She looked up. "Are we ready now?"

"Yes."

She marked her spot in the magazine with an envelope, then pushed herself out of her chair, and walked briskly over to the table. With her hands behind her back, she half bent over my arrangement of hats, grimaced, and said, "Hmmm."

That's all. One hmmm. For the longest time after, she said nothing. My smile started to feel very out of place, the muscles holding it began to quiver.

I steeled myself for rejection.

But then a little voice inside my head spoke up: Don't take it so goddamned personally, it told me.

Rejection means the hats are wrong for the direction of the store, or that the buyer has already ordered similar styles from someone else, or that she got up on the wrong side of the bed, or that she's already blown her budget for the season.

Rejection does not mean the hats are lousy. It does not mean they are bad art.

Don't take it personally. Don't take it personally. Like a mantra, I kept that refrain going in my head. It was not a big deal, I told myself. Especially considering selling was not my goal.

Uptown Buyer tapped her forefinger on a black cotton velvet hat. "Here," she said. "Put this little cocktail number on. I want to see it in action."

The hat was from several seasons ago. Kind of cute, I

thought, though I'd only sold six. I put it on and checked in the mirror to be sure I had it positioned properly.

"Hmmm," said the buyer again. She cupped my chin in her hand and twisted my head this way and that. "Miss Midnight, is it?"

"That's right," I said. "Brenda Midnight, Midnight Millinery."

"Well, Miss Midnight, I'm tempted, but quite honestly, I believe the cocktail craze has already peaked, taking with it of course, the cocktail hat craze." With a world-weary shrug, she strode back over to her desk, sat down, and picked up her magazine. Clearly, she was done with me and was sorry she'd wasted her time.

Don't take it personally.

I quickly stuffed my hats back into the hatboxes and started for the door. I was far too sensitive.

Don't take it personally.

Yeah, right. I felt awful.

In a last-ditch effort to get me toward my stated goal, I took a deep breath and ventured forth with, "Interesting that you're attracted to that cocktail hat. You must have known Doreen Sands, over at Castleberry's? She ordered six dozen of this very style not long before she was murdered."

That was one hell of an effective big fat fib. It got the buyer's nose out of her magazine pronto. "Of course I knew Doreen Sands," she said. "Terrible, terrible thing, her being murdered like that. I understand it was a robbery. Poor Doreen, not even safe in her own office. Of course, we have far better security in this store. That doesn't mean I'm not concerned. You say Doreen Sands ordered how many of your little hats?"

"Six dozen," I said. "Doreen said that in her opinion, while the cocktail craze may have appeared to have peaked some time ago, that particular peak was premature. She forecast a rapid resurgence in cocktail-related fashion, swizzle sticks, olives, and bar accessories."

"What is the status of that order now?"

"Up in the air," I said.

"Well then, perhaps you and I can work something out."

What we worked out was that she'd buy the six dozen hats I had falsely claimed Doreen Sands had ordered. This meant I'd be plenty busy making cocktail hats. It also revealed quite a bit about Doreen Sands's reputation among her peers.

The Uptown Buyer typed the order into a computer, then swiveled the screen around so I could see and approve before she printed it out.

"That's fine," I said.

With a few keystrokes she sent the order to a laser printer next to her desk.

"Who else are you buying from this season?" I asked, nonchalantly.

"The usual suspects," she said. Her phrasing almost caused me to choke. "Why do you ask?"

"Oh," I said casually, "I always like to know whose hats are going to be displayed with mine."

"I see." She named several milliners I knew.

"Any hats from Fuzzy?"

"Goodness no. You're uptown now. The uptown customer does not purchase bad jokes or funky hats."

"I understand, but I heard, you know through the grapevine, that Fuzzy is coming out with a new collection. It's supposed to be more firmly rooted in wearability."

"Not that I've heard of."

I didn't know if that was good or bad, or even if it was true.

The printer spit out my order. The buyer scrawled illegible initials on the bottom, folded it over twice, and slid it into an envelope. "Nice doing business with you, Miss Midnight," she said.

"My pleasure."

So, I got a big order from a prestigious uptown store, and I got it by lying. What did that say about the state of millinery? I couldn't think about the subject without getting angry, mad as a goddamned hatter.

I was disappointed with myself. As a fact-gatherer, I'd failed miserably. I hadn't picked up a shred of information I didn't already know about Fuzzy or Doreen Sands.

And I had six dozen cocktail hats to make.

Time now equaled money, so I splurged on a cab back to the Village. I spent the ride downtown tossing around a new idea.

Could Doreen Sands have been killed by a rival buyer? This morning's buyer, whatever her name, had demonstrated the power of Doreen Sands. If Doreen wanted it, Uptown Buyer wanted it too. Doreen was the one who got the exclusives, the attention, the coverage in the fashion press. She was the one who had the big bucks. She was the one who made all the other buyers look inferior. It could be simple jealousy. Or maybe another buyer was after her job. How nice it would be to slide into a big success story with none of the hard work or talent.

In truth, I didn't think so. I tried not to be misled by my hat-centric view of the universe. However, I made a mental note to ask Gundermutter if Castleberry's was actively looking to replace Doreen Sands.

I got back to Midnight Millinery and checked my answering machine. The first message was from a snippy-sounding woman who asked why wasn't the shop open during regular hours, didn't I want to sell hats? The next message was from Ray Marshall. "Please call," he said, so I did.

"I told Gregory," he said.

"How'd he take it?"

"Pissed off. Hurt."

"I can imagine."

"He'd like to talk to you, to see if he can do some damage control before this thing gets out of hand. Would you come over to my apartment this evening?"

"All right."

We agreed on seven o'clock.

17

That was stupid.

Despite Turner and McKinley's bullshit random robbery theory, despite Gundermutter's bullshit drug smuggling theory, and despite what even I thought I knew about Fuzzy, anybody halfway reasonable, anybody who knew how these things usually turned out, would realize that Gregory looked real good as the killer, especially if he and Doreen had broken up.

And I had just agreed to meet with Gregory at the apartment of a man I barely knew. Good going, Brenda.

I liked Ray Marshall and felt confident he liked me. That still didn't make it okay. The most concrete thing I knew about Ray was that due to the secretive nature of his line of work, I never would know much about Ray. And the most concrete thing I knew about Gregory was that nine times out of ten . . .

I would not go, not to Ray's apartment. However, I thought of a possible way to save the meeting. All I had to do was call Ray and switch to a public venue, some place like Angie's, where I knew everybody and would be perfectly safe. The problem was I couldn't come up with a good, believable reason why we had to meet in a public place.

However, I did come up with dozens of plausible reasons to move the meeting to Midnight Millinery, a semi-public place, where I would be semi-perfectly safe. I could increase the safety factor greatly if the semi-public place had an armed cop hiding in the storage room.

Since I didn't have Gundermutter's cell phone number, I had to wind my way through Castleberry's voice mail. I finally branched off to a far-flung location where a recording told me to hang on and a human would come on the line. After five minutes, one finally did. I told her I needed to talk to a new employee, Nicole Gundermutter. I spelled her name.

"I have no listing. Do you know the department, ma'am?"

"No. She's a floater, could be anywhere in the store. I guess you'll have to page her."

"I'm sorry, we don't do that, ma'am."

"It's a life or death emergency."

"That's what they all say, ma'am."

"This time it's true."

"They all say that, too, ma'am."

"All right then, let me talk to your supervisor."

"I am my supervisor, ma'am."

"Great, then make an executive supervisory decision. Otherwise, the blood will be on your hands."

"You sound serious, ma'am."

"I am serious."

"What's that name again, ma'am?"

"Gundermutter. Nicole Gundermutter. Tell her to call Brenda Midnight immediately."

The call came less than two minutes later. "What's up?" said Gundermutter.

"First, give me your cell phone number."

She did so.

"Thanks," I said. "I've got a situation here, but I don't want to go into it on the phone."

"It had better be good to pull me away from folding lightweight twinset sweaters."

"Trust me, it is. Six-thirty. Midnight Millinery. Don't forget to bring your weapon. We're talking potential pinch of possible suspect." That was a bit of a stretch, but I wanted to be sure Gundermutter was armed.

Next I called Ray Marshall. "About our meeting this evening. Could you and Gregory possibly come to Midnight Millinery instead? I'm stuck here waiting for a messenger. The dispatcher says it'll probably be after seven before they can send someone."

"No problem. I'm sure Gregory won't mind. We'll see you then."

Gundermutter showed up on time. I filled her in.

"I simply cannot believe you expect me to waste my personal time off the job on a wild-goose chase. Yeah, yeah, I know the doer could be the fiancé, nine times outta ten blah, blah, blah, and all that rot, but the more I hang out at Castleberry's, the more positive I am that Doreen Sands was killed because of drugs."

"I told you those slashed-up hats were not used to transport drugs," I said.

"So what?" said Gundermutter. "Granted, at first that little factoid of yours had me depressed, but then I had this realization. You see, drugs don't have to be hidden inside of hats to get somebody killed. I've spent a great deal of time observing the action on Castleberry's loading dock, and you would not believe the shit that goes on."

The woman was obsessed. "Okay," I said. "How about this scenario? Maybe Gregory is the one moving the drugs. Maybe he's the kingpin. He uses Doreen's position to run the whole operation out of the store."

"Not bad, Brenda. I'll think on that."

"Good," I said. "You can think while you're hiding."

"Hiding?"

"Yes, hiding. In there." I pointed to the door of the storage room.

"You've got to be kidding."

"I can't think of a better place."

She opened the door and stuck her head inside. "No can do. It's pitch black in here."

"Directly in front of you is a cord. Pull it."

The light came on and Gundermutter stepped in. "This had goddamned better be worth it," she said, slamming the door.

It was a sentiment I shared.

Jackhammer bounced over to greet Ray and Gregory. "This," said Ray to Gregory, "is Jackhammer."

"Hey little guy," said Gregory. He bent over to scratch Jackhammer between the ears. Jackhammer's tail stub vibrated.

Although I'd spoken to Gregory at Doreen's funeral, I hadn't formally met him. Ray took care of that.

Gregory had a firm handshake, sad eyes, an Armani suit, and a Rolex watch.

"Please," I said, "sit down."

I'd arranged the two farm chairs so that they faced away from the storage room. I didn't want either Gregory or Ray to notice the crack of light around the door. As they got situated, I moved my work chair into position facing them.

After an uncomfortable silence, Gregory started the ball rolling. "It's a very bad time for me," he said. "Did you know my Doreen well?"

"Mostly by reputation," I said, hedging for the umpteenth time. "Doreen Sands had earned the respect of all milliners."

"Yes, I know. Long hard work got her to a position of great success. She loved what she did, and was brilliant at it."

I nodded, encouraging him to go on, hoping he'd eventually talk his way into a trap.

"I'm very much troubled by these rumors you mentioned to Ray," he said.

"Then they're not true?"

"You see—" He looked down at his hands, then at me. "—they are true, up to a point. That's the tragedy. I fear I made a terrible mistake."

He talked weird, I thought, a little removed, as if he were floating above it all. I couldn't put my finger on it. Maybe it had to do with grief. Or guilt.

He continued. "Doreen and I had frequent arguments about her long hours. Her job consumed her. It left her little time for me. Then, a few months ago, out of the blue, she decided to take an acting class, which took up even more of her time. I believe it was a last-minute freak-out before our wedding, a declaration of independence, so to speak."

"That's common," I said.

"I suppose," he said. "Doreen never did anything halfway. She threw herself into the class wholeheartedly. She went several times a week. I was very angry. Doreen often promised to come to see me after her acting class. Later, she'd tell me she was too tired. It was one of those nights that a former girlfriend of mine called. She pleaded to see me again. I was weak and agreed to see her one time. The one time turned into two, and three, and . . . I thought I was discreet, but now you tell of a rumor that Doreen and I had broken up. That is not true, but I'm afraid that Doreen somehow learned about my affair. To save face, she must have told people we'd broken up."

Gregory babbled on for a while, giving a bunch of lame excuses for cheating on Doreen. I guess he expected me to feel sorry for him.

Ray got up and wandered around the shop. He was no doubt embarrassed that his friend was such a cad. I tensed up when he neared the storage room. I was afraid he'd notice the light, or think it was the bathroom, open the door, and discover Gundermutter. I held my breath. Ray walked on by.

I relaxed and turned my attention back to Gregory, who was finally winding down. "Don't you see," he said, "I must determine if Doreen knew about my affair when she died, if she thought we were through. Please find out for me."

"I'll see what I can do," I said, intending to do no such thing. As far as I was concerned Gregory was pond scum. He didn't deserve one more second of my time.

"Thank you, thank you so much," he said.

"One question," I said. "Do you know if Doreen was working on any particular projects?"

"Hats. What else?"

"Any special hats, perhaps a line manufactured exclusively for Castleberry's?"

"I wouldn't know. Like I said, near the end, I didn't see much of her."

"What an asshole," said Gundermutter. "Did you ever, in all your life, hear such a load of crap? I should have burst out of my hiding place and arrested him on principle. Or even better, I should have smashed him over his cheating head with one of those hatblocks you've got lined up in there."

"Poor Doreen," I said. "I've heard rumors that she killed herself."

"Over that jerk? Give me a break. I tell you, it was drugs. Anyway, Brenda, nice try, even it was a total waste of time. Now, if you don't mind, I'm outta here."

Gundermutter and her one-track mind. She'd been right about one thing though. The meeting with Gregory had been a total waste of time. Much as I didn't like him, I didn't think he'd killed Doreen. Given his philandering, it made more sense that she'd want to kill him.

I still had no information to prove Fuzzy hadn't killed Doreen. Or even that she had killed Doreen, which would at least get this over with once and for all.

The time had finally come to talk to Chuck Riley. It was also time for dinner. I figured I could kill two birds with one stone.

18

"You want my advice?" asked Chuck.
"That's why I'm here," I said.
When I'd called Chuck to invite myself over, he told me he didn't want company, and gave me some bull that his place was a mess. When wasn't his boarded-up storefront a mess? From its thick plank floor to its sagging ceiling, it was totally jammed with computers and cables and communication devices and lasers and synthesizers and antique oscillators, all in various stages of repair, all doing technical things I didn't even want to know about.

To get him to agree to see me, I promised to bring a pizza. Only then did he give the go-ahead.

While we ate I filled him in on the Doreen Sands case.

"Next time," said Chuck, when I'd finished talking, "bring a real pizza, one piled high with disks of greasy pepperoni, not a cesspool of goat cheese and basil."

That gourmet pizza had been my attempt to expand his horizons. Obviously I'd failed. I started to defend my choice of pizza, but he held up his hand.

"As to the murder," he said. "You've got it ass-backwards. You're trying to prove a negative—that some milliner didn't do it. Why don't you try to prove who *did* do it?"

"Because I don't care who did it, as long as it's not a milliner."

"Got any ideas who this Unknown Milliner is?"

"No." I had stopped my story short of telling him that Fuzzy was the Unknown Milliner, and therefore my main suspect. I couldn't risk telling him until I found out how he felt about her.

"Look Brenda, unless you've got some kind of supernatural powers, your finding out won't change what is. It's like this: If a milliner whacked her, a milliner whacked her, know what I mean? And if you think you know which milliner whacked her, you ought to tell your cop pals Turner and McKinley."

This, from Chuck?

Not so awfully long ago I could count on Chuck to fully support, without question, any behavior of dubious legality, and to do so with great verve. Lately, he'd been growing more cautious. Last year when I'd gotten myself into a little difficulty, he'd refused to hack into a computer to get the information I needed. Chuck had always been weird. Now he was weird in a weird new way. All the spunk and sizzle was out of him.

From my vantage point in one of his red beanbag chairs, I looked around his apartment. It still sizzled. It still had spunk. LEDs emitted, beepers beeped, lasers lased, modems modulated and demodulated, computers computed, cooling fans whirred. But Chuck, he sat in the middle of it all, in the other red beanbag, looking glum and cranky.

"So," he said, "you gonna do it?"

"What?" I asked. I'd lost track of the conversation that didn't seem to be going anywhere.

"Rat to the cops," he said.

"No, I'm not ready to tell Turner and McKinley yet."

"What are you waiting for?"

"I have a few leads to check out first."

"You're not gonna help that Gregory guy, are you?"

"No, of course not."

"Good. I hate the rat bastard."

"Do you know Gregory?"

"Not personally. I hate his type of low-life cheating sons of bitches."

"So," I said, to change the subject, "how've you been? What have you been up to?"

"The answer to how I've been is crappy, lousy. What I've been up to is not a goddamned thing."

"How's that lighting job for Fuzzy going?"

"Okay. It's a piece of cake."

I'd hoped he'd be more expansive.

"How about Fuzzy? Do you like her?"

"Look Brenda, I thought you came over here to tell me stuff. What's with all the questions about me?"

"Sorry. I was just curious. It's obvious that something is bugging you. I thought maybe I could help."

"Nothing's bugging me."

"Okay."

"And even if there were, you couldn't help anyway."

"You can tell me," I said.

We went back and forth like that for a while, me asking, him denying. Finally he spewed out a long, complex, invigorating string of expletives, jumped up off his beanbag, stood in the center of the room, waved his arms around, and yelled at the top of his lungs. "You wanta know what's wrong with me? You really want to know? Okay, then, I'll tell you what's wrong with me. I, Chuck Riley, I am the love child of Elizabeth Franklin Perry."

I was stunned. Chuck stared at me like he was waiting for me to speak, but I couldn't.

"Did you hear me?" he said. "Elizabeth is my mother. Elizabeth is not merely old enough to be my mother, Elizabeth *is* my mother." He waited a couple of beats so that could sink in, then added, "Maybe."

"You're joking." I exploded in laughter, but stifled it when I saw the hurt look in Chuck's eyes. He might be dead wrong, but he sure as hell wasn't joking.

"Tell me, Chuck."

He jerked his head up and down and around as if surprised to find himself standing. Then he shrugged and collapsed back down in his beanbag. "It happened during that fight I had with Dude Bob."

Dude Bob was Elizabeth's boyfriend some of the time. He lived in Montana. At least, that's what he claimed.

With him, you could never be too sure. Elizabeth met him online. They typed back and forth to each other in a cyber chat room. Their romance eventually progressed to face-to-face meetings. After a couple of misunderstandings about politics and who exactly Dude Bob was, they'd been all ready to tie the knot. But then Dude Bob and Chuck got into a fist fight over an unrelated matter and Elizabeth had taken Chuck's side.

"Dude Bob? Don't tell me you believe that scoundrel. He'd say anything to keep you away from Elizabeth."

"Give me some credit. I know Dude Bob is a lying sack of shit. He told me I was born of a test tube and raised by wolves. I paid no attention to him. Then, after he crawled back under his rock in Montana, he barraged me with e-mail. He said stuff like: 'You know, Chuck old buddy, you bear an amazing resemblance to my former fiancée, Ms. Elizabeth Franklin Perry. Why don't you find out what she was doing on the day you hatched?' "

"What did you do?"

"I e-mailed back, and essentially told him to go straight to hell, but not in those words. My language was a tad stronger." He managed half a crooked smile.

"I can imagine," I said.

"But then after Dude Bob stopped harassing me, I started to think, it wasn't totally impossible. I know it's weird, but I could have been adopted. Nobody ever said I wasn't. I scanned photos of both Elizabeth and me into the computer, measured and compared our features, pixel by pixel, morphed her into me and me into her. As I suspected, Dude Bob was full of shit. Elizabeth and I do not look alike."

"That must have been a relief," I said.

"It was, but it soon passed. I rapidly came to realize that lack of familial resemblance didn't prove that Elizabeth is not my mother. It's like she *could* be, you know. And as long as there's the teeniest pico-speck of possibility, I can't bear to be around her. When I'm not around her I feel like shit, and when I feel like shit, I can't do a goddamned thing, including find out if she's my mother."

I'd never met Chuck's family, but I'd seen pictures.

Freckled redheads. Every last one of them. "What about your family? Have you asked them if you were adopted?"

"After all these years? If I am and if they were gonna tell me, they woulda already. And if I'm not it would be like an insult to ask."

Chuck made me promise not to breathe a word of his craziness to Elizabeth. He didn't call it craziness though. He called it "an existential quagmire."

"What does that mean?"

"Either I don't know who I am, or I don't know if I want to be who I am, or I am who I'm not."

"I see," I said. Whoever he was, that person teetered way too close to the edge.

Now I knew what was bugging Chuck, and there was nothing I could do about it. It was a touchy situation. It would be hard not to blab about this to Elizabeth the next time I saw her.

Before I got all the way home, my secret-keeping ability was put to the test. I ran into Elizabeth in the hall outside our apartments.

"Been out?" she asked.

It was a perfectly normal, friendly-neighborly question. One that didn't require a real answer. A nod of my head would do fine. But because it was so soon after hearing Chuck rave, I was thrown for a loop.

"Uh . . ." I felt my face flush. I couldn't tell her I'd been at Chuck's. "Nowhere," I said. "Just around. Thought I'd get some fresh air."

"Why didn't you take Jackhammer with you?"

Another neighborly inquiry.

"Jackhammer? Oh. He was asleep when I left. Pooped out from barking at the radiator all night." That was true, but it sure felt like a lie.

Elizabeth gave me a strange look. "Would you like to come in? I'll put a pot of coffee on."

"Sorry, can't. Gotta take care of some stuff."

"Right. Okay. See you."

*   *   *

What a mess.

Fuzzy might be a murderer. And I was in the middle. Chuck was nuttier than a fruitcake. Elizabeth knew something was up. And again I was in the middle.

About the only thing I wasn't in the middle of was my fall line.

I needed to prioritize.

I took a very long, very hot bubble bath.

First, I told myself, first things first, then I decided which first was the most first, and that first was saving my own butt.

Should I tell Turner and McKinley what I knew about Fuzzy? Yes and no. Absolutely yes some time, but maybe not right away. How long could I go on knowing Fuzzy had a motive and not tell the fuzz? If Turner and McKinley knew what I knew, they'd put aside their random robbery theory. This situation was truly terrible. There was a distinct possibility the cops would interpret my nonaction as withholding evidence.

I backtracked. Could a few slashed-up hats be considered evidence? No. Could a friend's secret line of hats be considered evidence? No. However, when put together with everything else I knew . . .

Fuzzy had been a good friend for a long time. I wanted to prove she hadn't killed Doreen Sands. That wasn't the right way to look at the problem. Chuck might be out of his mind on some subjects, but had a good point about the Doreen Sands case. I had been looking at her murder ass-backwards. I should start with the refreshing premise that no one I knew had killed Doreen Sands, and go from there. I was still tossing that idea around when the phone rang.

I climbed out of the bathtub, threw on my terrycloth robe, and made it to the phone on the fourth ring.

"Hi Brenda. Ray Marshall here. I'm sorry about today. I could tell you didn't think much of Gregory."

"Did it show?" I'd tried to listen and not judge.

"All over your face. Take my advice and don't ever play poker. You're not planning to help Gregory, are you?"

"You read me right."

"I don't blame you. Gregory's values leave much to be desired. However, deep down he's really not such a bad sort. He truly loved Doreen. He's devastated thinking she found out about his affair."

"He goddamned well ought to be." I was losing my patience with Ray's defense of Gregory.

"Please, Brenda, see if you can find out how much she knew. Please."

A well-placed please weakened my resolve. I hated this. Somebody was always asking me to do something I didn't want to do.

I'd used Ray to get to Gregory. Now Gregory was using Ray to get to me. And he was succeeding.

While Ray went on and on about what a great guy Gregory was, I wondered what I could do to find out— just in case he talked me into helping. I couldn't ask Fuzzy, and I didn't want to ask any other milliners behind Fuzzy's back because she'd find out and ask me why I hadn't asked her, and then I'd have to tell her it was because I thought she might possibly have killed Doreen Sands, and boy would that piss her off, and then we wouldn't be friends.

Okay, so the millinery route was out.

I tried to put myself in Doreen Sands's place. If I were engaged and found out my fiancé had cheated, who would I confide in? Nobody. Not me. It would be far too humiliating.

Maybe Doreen Sands didn't feel the same. She might want to confide in a friend or an acquaintance. But who? Certainly not someone in her work life. That would be unprofessional, which was too bad because those were the people I had easy access to. I considered her other activities. How about the trainer, the leg waxer, or the hair dresser? No. I would not get my hair cut to help out sleazeball Gregory. However, there was one thing I could do without risking my tresses. I could go to Doreen's acting class. That is, if Ray ever managed to talk me into helping.

I brought myself back to the conversation with Ray,

who was saying, "Shall I take your silence to mean you'll help?"

"Maybe."

I called Johnny and asked him if he knew of an acting class on Fourteenth Street.

"Yeah. I hear it's pretty good. Why? Are you thinking about a career change?"

"Doreen Sands went to that class."

"And?"

Here's the part where I had to lie. For one thing Johnny had made it clear that he didn't approve of me poking my nose where it didn't belong. In that respect, he was as bad as Turner and McKinley. Another thing was that I didn't want him to know I'd seen and talked to and was cooperating with Ray Marshall. So, I steadied my voice and said, "Gundermutter asked me to go check it out. I thought you might like to come along."

There. I'd done it. I'd flat-out blatantly lied to the man who was the best friend I'd ever had. And for what?

"Sounds like fun," said Johnny.

I felt awful, consumed by guilt.

19

I'd lied to Johnny. Tormented, I tossed and turned most of the night. The one time I managed to doze off, I fell straight into a nightmare. I don't remember the details, but the plot and three subplots all revolved around lying to Johnny.

Around 6 a.m. I gave up trying to sleep, got up and downed half a pot of coffee, and waited for the caffeine to do its stuff. I also made a decision. I would tell Johnny the truth. I would tell him I'd lied.

But later. I didn't want to wake him up with the bad news that I was a rotten friend.

The sun was barely up when Jackhammer and I arrived at Midnight Millinery. I needed an early start. Somehow I had to adjust my work schedule to fit in those six dozen cocktail hats for the Uptown Buyer's upscale uptown department store.

As a first step, I did an inventory. I rooted through boxes of fabric and supplies, and made a list of all the stuff I needed to complete the order. Then, to clear the way, I worked on hats I'd already started. By the end of the day I had them all done. Well, almost all. I didn't have the heart to work on the hat for Fuzzy's show. The show was still a few days away. If nothing panned out at the acting class that night, I'd have to tell Turner and McKinley what I knew about Fuzzy. Once I did, there was a very good possibility that she would be forced to cancel Milliners Milling Around the Millennium.

That evening, right on time, Johnny popped by Midnight Millinery. "Ready for your debut acting class?"

"First we have to talk."

"What's wrong? Why so somber?"

"I don't know of a good way to tell you this, Johnny, so I'll get it over fast." I gripped my blocking table to steady myself, took a deep breath, and let it all out. "I lied to you."

Johnny laughed. "You mean that bit when you told me Officer Gundermutter asked you to go to Doreen Sands's acting class? You don't really think I fell for that, do you?"

"You didn't believe me?"

"Face it, Brenda, you can't lie worth a damn, not even over the phone. Your voice gets all funny, strained and kinda shaky. From the minute you started in, I knew exactly what you were up to."

"Why didn't you tell me you knew? I mean, weren't you mad?"

"For chrissakes Brenda. You and I have been friends—more or less—long enough that I trust you. A transparent lie doesn't count."

If you tell a lie and nobody believes it, is it still a lie?

"Besides," he said, "I know you'll do the right thing."

For the moment, I no longer trusted my ability to judge right from wrong. "What is the right thing?"

Johnny placed his hands on my shoulders and looked hard into my eyes. "You will go to Turner and McKinley once you satisfy your curiosity."

"Oh. Okay."

"And you will satisfy your curiosity in the very near future."

"Yeah."

I really didn't mind. I was ready to go to the cops. This had gone on long enough.

Walking up to Fourteenth Street, I leveled with Johnny. I even told him that Fuzzy was the Unknown Milliner.

"This is damned serious, Brenda."
"I know."

The entire storefront was covered with a weather-beaten banner that had been up for years. It read, LIQUIDATION! EVERYTHING MUST GO!

A surly bald man, dressed head to toe in camouflage, was perched atop a high metal stool on the sidewalk in front. His fingers drummed idly on a baseball bat that rested across his thighs. His job description could be summed up in one word: intimidate. He was good at it. He watched over shoppers as they sifted through bins of sneakers and T-shirts and underwear.

Below him, on the sidewalk, scores of plastic battery-operated toys quacked and whistled and spun and whirred. A realistic-looking hairy rat writhed.

Under the man's vigilant eye, Johnny and I stepped around the tumultuous toys, and made our way to a doorway wedged into the building behind a small lean-to structure which housed a collection of supernaturally bright colored wigs.

Johnny looped his finger around the tendril of a hot pink banana-curl, pulled it out, let it go. It snapped back. "Amazing recoil," he said.

The man with the bat shifted his weight and glared.

The heavy metal door clanged shut, leaving us in a drab entry area. A flyer advertising the acting class was taped to a wall. An arrow pointed us up a steep narrow stairway.

"Isn't Fourteenth Street an unusual location for an acting school?" I asked.

"Not at all," said Johnny. "It's perfect." He jerked his thumb behind him in a northerly direction. "Remember a decade or so ago when they chased the drug dealers out of Union Square? Dozens of trendy new restaurants opened up and attracted waiters and waitresses to the neighborhood."

"Oh, I get it." Waiters and waitresses waiting for their first big break in show biz. It hadn't been so long ago that

Johnny had been waiting for his first big break. It had come, amazingly, in the form of Lemon B. Crenshaw.

Our plan, hastily concocted while we walked up the stairs, was that Johnny would go in first. A couple of minutes later, I'd slip in and get lost in the excitement surrounding his arrival. Johnny knew that the school had big classes with lots of turnover among the students. Probably no one would notice me at all.

"Break a leg," I said as he went in.

"Break yours," he said. "You're the one acting."

Alone in the hall, I wondered if pretending to be an actor would give me stage fright.

When the moment felt right, I eased open the door.

It was immediately obvious that our plan had worked. Johnny stood at the center of an adoring crowd.

A woman plowed into me. " 'Scuse, 'scuse," she said. "Coming through."

"What's all the excitement?" I asked. "Who is that guy?" I nodded in Johnny's direction.

"Don't tell me you don't recognize Johnny Verlane. He stars in the *Tod Trueman, Urban Detective* TV show. Dreamboat, don't you think?"

I shrugged.

She gave me a look like I was nuts, and resumed pushing and shoving her way toward Johnny.

A group of men with strong jawlines, sharp haircuts, and tight T-shirts hung back from the crowd. I joined them on the periphery of the room and asked them the same question. "Who is that guy?"

"Nobody," said one.

"Wrong," said another. "Today, he's somebody, but yesterday he was nobody, and tomorrow he'll be nobody again."

"I see," I said.

I hung around and made small talk, waiting for the right moment to bring up the subject of Doreen Sands. All of a sudden, the noise level dropped.

A stooped-over man banged his cane against a chair. "Your attention, please." He waited for everyone to stop talking, then continued. "As most of you have already noticed, we're honored to have an unannounced special guest with us this evening, Johnny Verlane. This event is a welcome change after recent tragic events."

That gave me the opening I needed. I turned back to the group of men. Keeping my voice down, I asked, "What tragic events? Did I miss something?"

"Where've you been?" said the guy who had admitted Johnny was somebody, if only for a day.

"It's the busy season at my day job. Lots of overtime," I explained. "I haven't been to class for the last couple of weeks."

"You missed a real-life murder," he said. "Doreen Sands got blown away."

"Doreen Sands. I remember her. She was real nice. Do you know what happened?"

"Robbery, I think. At the store where she worked. She was some kind of buyer. Must have kept a lot of money around."

"It only goes to show," said one of the other guys. "Day jobs are murder."

"You. You over there in the hat." The instructor's voice boomed.

I scanned the room for hats, but didn't see any. What I did see was everybody in the room looking in my direction.

"Me?" I asked, timidly.

"Yes, you. Mr. Verlane has kindly agreed to read a scene. He's picked you to be his scene partner."

"Oh no. I couldn't possibly do that, but thanks anyway."

"Don't be shy."

"I really can't."

"What are you here for if not to learn?"

Somebody shoved a script at me.

Johnny came over to where I was standing. The class formed a circle around us. I whispered to Johnny, "What am I supposed to do?"

"Read," he said. "You be Tina. I'm Tom."

I read.

In the script Tina and Tom, engaged to be married, were battling over china patterns. It rang a little too true for comfort. Johnny and I had a history of breaking up over interior design.

TINA (*holding up plate*): "This is the ugliest color I've ever seen."

TOM: "I like it."

TINA (*emphatically*): "Well, I don't."

TOM: "That's too damn bad. You picked that atrocious flatware. Now it's *my* turn."

Johnny's eyes flashed with anger.

I shot Johnny an equally angry look.

TINA: "Oh it is, is it? You've got lousy taste . . ."

ME (*not realizing I was ad-libbing*): ". . . like for instance that hideous orange and yellow shag rug . . ."

TINA: ". . . in every damn thing."

TOM (*hands on hips and yelling*): "That's right. I chose you."

That set Tina off, and rightfully so. Who could blame her? I'd be pissed too. In fact, I was pissed.

Tina lashed out at Tom.

Tom came right back at Tina.

The insults escalated. The scene ended with Tina screaming an ultimatum, "You choose. The china or me." With that she stormed out of the room.

Except it wasn't really Tina, it was me, and it wasn't really a room, it was a circle of acting students. I slammed into some guy.

The guy turned me around, and headed me back into the center of the circle, back toward Johnny.

I heard applause.

Johnny took my hand, bowed to the audience, and coaxed me to do the same. I forced myself to look at him. He was smiling. He seemed completely normal, as if what had happened was nothing at all. I was confused. Hadn't we just had a big fight?

The answer, of course, was no. It was all an act. It sure felt real to me. Ever since Johnny and I had agreed to agree, we hadn't fought, not once, not even when he threatened to buy a new hideous shag rug.

The applause died out.

Johnny got rushed by the crowd. He blushed. Johnny may have bad taste in home furnishings, but he handled his fame well. He was truly humble. Like that guy had said, tomorrow he'll be nobody again. Nobody knew that better than Johnny.

Other students did scenes. I milled around, too upset to talk to anybody. This had been a crazy idea anyway. I'd tell Ray to tell Gregory that I'd given it a shot. Then I'd take what I knew about Fuzzy to Turner and McKinley. Let them do their job.

When the class officially ended, some of the students approached me. One of them slapped me on the back. "Good work," he said. "You're a natural."

I forced a smile and said thank you.

A woman said, "I was impressed that you weren't intimidated by *the* Johnny Verlane. Me, I'd have swooned looking into those smoky gray eyes of his. And those cheekbones . . . to die for."

"Yeah," said someone. "You ought to audition to be one of Tod Trueman's damsels in distress. Week after week, our man Tod has got to rescue someone from the clutches of an evil drug kingpin. That someone might as well be you."

I laughed. That made me feel a little better.

"You're new around here, aren't you?"

I nodded.

"Who've you studied with?"

I mumbled a made-up name.

"I hear he's very good."

The small group of acting students nodded in agreement.

People were leaving. I edged toward the door.

"You want to come along with us?" asked the guy who thought I was a natural. "We usually get together after class. We hang out, throw back a few drinks, have a couple of laughs."

"I don't know."

It would be a great opportunity to ask questions about Doreen Sands, but I was still shaken up, hardly in the mood to socialize.

"Oh, come on. It'll be fun."

Through the crowd, I spotted Johnny. One look at him settled it. I might not be in the mood to hang out in a bar with a bunch of actors, trying to help a cad find out if his dead fiancée knew he was a cad, but the alternative, walking back home with Johnny, was worse. To me, it still felt like we were fighting.

"All right," I said. "I'll go."

It turned out to be a very good decision.

I was halfway through a glass of red wine when one of the women got out a packet of snapshots, divided it in half, and passed each stack around the table going in different directions.

One of the guys shuffled through the photographs. "What a difference time makes," he said with a sigh.

When some pictures came my way, the man sitting next to me said, "See that girl. She's the one who got murdered."

"Sad, very sad," I said. "Did you know her well?"

"Not in the biblical way. She was engaged—"

A woman leaned over. "Not any more she wasn't. She told me, the night before she was murdered, that her fiancé's old flame was back in the picture with a vengeance."

Bingo.

"Did she catch them in the act?" asked the man.

"No. From what I heard, the old flame must have been a real bitch. She telephoned Doreen and told her to keep her hands off the man, or else—"

Or else? I'd have to remember to tell that to Turner and McKinley.

"Yes, according to Doreen, that's what she said. Of course, Doreen had a real flair for the dramatic."

I downed the rest of my wine. I'd heard enough. I had the information I'd come after. It was not what Gregory wanted to hear, but it was what he deserved to hear. There was justice in that.

As I got up to go, someone handed me two more snapshots. Doreen Sands was pictured in both. I started to pass them on, but something caught my eye.

I sat back down. I hung on to one of the photos and passed the other on. During a toast, when I was pretty sure no one was looking, I covered that snapshot with my napkin. A little later, during another toast, I got out a pen and pretended to write something on the napkin. Then I folded the napkin carefully over the snapshot and tucked it into my purse. After the next toast, I bolted.

At home I examined the snapshot in good light. Standing behind Doreen Sands, on what had to be one of the last nights of her life, was none other than my good buddy, Detective Spencer Turner.

20

Yes, the man in the picture really was Turner. Detective Spencer Turner. There. And no, he wasn't part of the background. He hadn't merely been passing by the table on his way to the other end of the bar. Turner was rock solid there, very much part of the picture. He looked straight at the camera and smiled. I could almost hear him say "cheese." In front of him stood Doreen Sands, also smiling. Turner's hands rested on her shoulders.

Holy flipping cow.

So, Turner knew Doreen Sands. As the idea surged through my brain, some switches flipped, while other switches flopped. The rules had changed. Topsy-turvy, the universe was now a totally different place.

Turner and Sands. Sands and Turner. Doreen and Spencer. The cop and the millinery buyer. Friends? More than friends? One of them dead. Wispy ideas touched down for the tiniest increment of time, then fluttered away before I could pin them down.

Not in my wildest dreams would such a possibility occur to me. At first I was angry that Turner hadn't told me he knew Doreen Sands. But then again, why would he? Since he was the cop, he was the one who got to ask the questions. More than once, he'd made that point abundantly clear.

That made us sort of even. A time or two, I'd held back some little tidbit of information from Turner. Like recently, for instance, about Fuzzy. There was one big difference though: I had never found a murder weapon in Turner's hatbox.

Oh yeah, that. A complicating factor. I still hadn't figured that part out.

I sat down in the chair by the window. Jackhammer jumped up in my lap, curled into a doughnut shape, and went to sleep. For hours I stared out at the glow that passes for dark in New York City. I went over everything again, this time plugging the Spencer Turner variable into the rapidly expanding complex equation. By the time the sky lightened I had a glimmer of an idea as to what had probably happened.

What to do about it was a whole other question. I knew one thing: If my hunch was true, I had every right to be angry.

Johnny Verlane was the absolute last person I wanted to talk to, now or ever again. I still reeled from the fight we'd had the night before in the guise of Tina and Tom.

However, I was reeling much more from what I had found out about Turner. I had to call Johnny. He was the only person I could trust with this information.

I waited until nine in the morning.

"Where'd you run off to last night?" he asked. "I saw you leave with a bunch of people from the class. I tried to catch up with you, but by the time I got down to the street you'd disappeared."

"They went to a nearby bar and invited me along."

"You should have told me," he said. "I would have gone with you."

"Tell you the truth, Johnny, I didn't want to see you."

"Why not?"

I didn't answer.

"Oh, I understand," he said. "It was that stupid scene we did, wasn't it? Lousy play. I think the instructor wrote it. But you were great. You really threw yourself into it whole hog. I should have realized you'd get mad for real. Next time we'll do a romantic scene. Kinda like at the end of a *Tod Trueman*, we could kiss and—"

"There won't be a next time," I said. "My acting career is over and done. That's not why I called. None of that matters anymore. Everything's all different now."

"Different? You mean between us? I thought we were moving along in a good direction."

"It's the murder, Johnny. Detective Turner is involved. I think he killed Doreen Sands."

"Very funny, Brenda."

"I mean it. Not only that, he tried to frame me, must have had second thoughts, and now he's trying to frame Fuzzy, and not doing such a bad job."

"What the hell are you talking about?"

"I don't know. I can't put my finger on it. Nothing makes sense, but something stinks."

"Really, Brenda, you've got me in stitches, doubled over, with tears streaming out of my eyes. You have a very fertile imagination."

This is what I got for lying to Johnny. I no longer had credibility. "It's not a joke," I said, "and it's not funny."

Johnny kept right on laughing.

Talking on the phone was getting me nowhere fast. The only way he'd believe me was if he saw the picture. "I'm coming over."

"Great," he said. "Do me a favor and stop by the fruit stand on your way. See if they have any fresh chives."

I would have forgotten the chives—cooking was the last thing on my mind—but when Jackhammer trotted by the green grocer on Bleecker Street, the little vittle spotter zeroed in on a green grape rolling across the grungy gray linoleum floor. Before I knew it, he'd darted into the store, and pulled me in with him. He made a dive for the grape, got it. Seconds later he spit it out. Jackhammer forgot that he hates grapes. I, however, remembered the chives.

I handed Johnny the bag.

He pecked me on the cheek. "Thanks."

"You're very welcome," I said, a little stiffly.

"What's this about a murderous detective?" he said.

"Please don't make light of the situation."

"What exactly is the situation?"

I showed him the photo.

He shrugged. "So, Turner has a life. I always suspected he did. It's allowed, you know."

"Do you know who that is standing in front of him?"

"Can't say that I do."

"It's Doreen Sands."

"I'll be damned. Why didn't you say so in the first place?"

"I thought I did. You must have been laughing too hard to assimilate the information."

"What do you think it means?"

"It's a long story."

I thought out loud, laid out all the evidence. We started out in Johnny's kitchen. I sat on the high stool and talked. He chopped up the chives and threw them into a bowl with a bunch of other ingredients. Every so often he tossed Jackhammer a morsel. For once, he wasn't working out as he cooked. I hoped that meant he was paying close attention. After a while, he poured the contents of the bowl into a casserole dish, and stuck it in the oven. We relocated to the living room.

When I'd finally said everything I had to say, Johnny scratched his head. "That's pretty strange, all right."

"Pretty strange? That's all you've got to say?"

"Well, it *is* pretty strange. Pretty goddamned strange."

"It's more than pretty goddamned strange. It's criminal."

"Since when is getting your picture taken standing behind Doreen Sands a criminal act?"

"It isn't. But standing with her, and then her ending up dead, and then the gun . . ." I drifted off, trying to remember exactly how I'd connected up all the dots. It had happened sometime in the middle of the night. Now, in the light of day, it all seemed a bit hazy. I couldn't grasp it.

"I'm sure Turner will have a very good explanation," said Johnny. "Anyway, no law says he has to tell you everything. In fact, he doesn't have to tell you anything, and none of what he chooses to tell you has to be the truth. Cops sometimes lie. It's part of the job. Remember that *Tod Trueman* where I—''

''I don't give a damn about *Tod Trueman*.''

''I thought you respected my work as an actor.''

''This is not about your work. It's not about you, or me, or you and me. It's about murder. I don't understand why you don't understand.''

''And I don't understand what you're so hot and bothered about. You can trust Turner. Whatever he's done must be for a reason. He's a good cop.''

I felt betrayed. By Turner, who had used me and kept me in the dark. Worse, I felt betrayed by Johnny. And that made me flat-out, full-tilt pissed off. I did what came naturally. I blew up. ''How can you sit here and defend Turner?'' I shouted.

Johnny opened his mouth to answer. I stuck my fingers in my ears. I didn't want to hear. I already knew the answer. Johnny had fallen into his *Tod Trueman, Urban Detective* role so hard he really believed that all cops were all good all the time, and even when they were bad, they must be defended.

''To hell with the brotherhood of blue,'' I said.

I went on to say a lot of things I probably shouldn't have, using a lot of words I probably shouldn't have to say them. Johnny said some things too, but I was too angry to decipher his words as actual content-communicating speech. When Johnny excused himself to stomp into the kitchen to get whatever it was he'd put into the oven out of the oven, I grabbed Jackhammer and, just like the Tina character from last night's scene study, stormed out of the room.

Only this time it really was a room, not a circle of acting students. More significantly, I was not acting. I definitely was mad. With Jackhammer at my heels, I ran down the stairs and out onto Bleecker Street.

I stood on the sidewalk, not thinking straight, for what seemed like a very long time, until Jackhammer pawed at my leg. I looked down at him.

He looked up at me. His tail stub vibrated. I snatched

him up and hugged him. That made me feel better.

Okay, I thought, I could either stew in my own juice, or walk it off. I opted to walk. Jackhammer got to decide where.

He dragged me along Bleecker Street, past cheese and pasta and sausage and vegetable stores, over to Sixth Avenue by Castleberry's, then back west along Christopher and onto Hudson Street, to Greenwich and West Street and back again. I completely lost track. We did Sheridan Square, Abingdon Square, and Washington Square. We went uptown, downtown, east and west, until we were both pooped and sat down on a stoop to rest.

I leaned back and tilted my face toward the late morning sun. The wind off the river whipped Jackhammer's reddish topknot into punk-like peaked spikes. I closed my eyes and breathed deep. Then, when my anger emptied out, and fresh oxygen energized my brain, and I was once again capable of rational thought, I opened my eyes and realized where we'd ended up.

Straight across the street from the Sixth Precinct.

21

From my vantage point on the stoop, I stared across at the yellowish tan brick building. Compared to some of the older grand precincts around town, this one resembled a suburban grade school, except a little less foreboding. It was a bad fit—too low for this vertical city, too featureless and new for the historic charming West Village neighborhood. A couple of blocks away was the former precinct, a building that had tons of style and dignity. It had been gutted and turned into a stately apartment building.

On the sidewalk in front of the precinct two cops talked. About what, I wondered. Doughnuts? Long Island real estate? Or perhaps how to lie to, mislead, and set up helpful citizens who happened to be at crime scenes.

Turner and McKinley got a lot of mileage complaining that I'm always around whenever there's trouble in the neighborhood—a ridiculous exaggeration. I was at Castleberry's the morning Doreen Sands was murdered. Big deal. Crime may be down, but it still exists, and wherever it exists, there is, by definition, a crime scene. It stands to reason that somebody's got to be at the crime scene. And this time that somebody was me. It's a crapshoot.

I was tempted to go inside, confront Turner, and settle this once and for all.

I thought better of it.

I considered the consequences. I knew not to act in

haste, fueled by my still-smoldering rage. I knew to count to ten. And I did.

At best this was a delicate situation. At worst, dangerous. Although I'd raved to Johnny that Turner killed Doreen Sands, I was probably overreacting. Still, something was up and Detective Spencer Turner was in the middle. The gun in my hatbox was the key. I had no idea what it might open.

I finished counting to ten, then did it again. I debated the pros and cons until I got fed up with hearing myself think. The only way to find out for sure was to go. Throw caution to the wind. Get it over with.

"Come on," I said to Jackhammer, "let's go visit the nice policeman. The one who is our friend." I hoped. Really, really, really hoped.

I scooped Jackhammer up, tucked him under my arm, walked across the street, nodded at the two cops who were still talking, opened the door of the precinct, and walked in.

I was a familiar face around the cop shop; the uniforms on the first floor didn't twitch a mustache when I passed through their territory. No one even made a comment about Jackhammer.

I headed up the staircase that led to Turner—and truth. When I got upstairs, I paused a moment to take a deep breath, and to check my purse for the photo of Turner and Doreen Sands. I almost chickened out when it occurred to me that I should have the photo copied and give the original to Johnny in case Turner was the killer and something happened to me. But that was a crazy thought. I refused to let my paranoia run rampant.

I plunged ahead, and marched into the grim cubicle Turner shared with McKinley. I didn't bother knocking on the door frame. I was not there to demonstrate good manners. I had come to confront the detective.

He was leaning way back in his chair, feet up on his desk, a phone receiver stuck between his jaw and shoulder. When he saw me he made a face, covered the mouthpiece with his hand, and mumbled. It sounded like "not you again." Then he jerked his chin in the direction of a broken-down typing chair.

An invitation to sit.

I chose not to.

Instead, I stood Jackhammer on the chair so he could be eye level to the action. I slammed the photograph down on Turner's desk, and watched as the expression on his face shifted from irritation to something much more complex. He said a few more words into the phone, and cut the connection. Then he swung his legs off his desk and looked down at the photo. He said nothing.

Neither did I.

McKinley came in carrying two cups of coffee. "What's she doing here?"

Turner gestured at the photo.

McKinley looked. "Shit."

The two detectives stared at the photo, as if that would make it go away. Isolated muscles in their faces quivered in spasm. They both cleared their throats several times. I got the impression they were attempting some kind of nonverbal communication. It must have failed, because after several exceedingly uncomfortable minutes, Turner came out with, "Excuse us a moment, Ms. Midnight. If you'll please step outside."

"No," I said. It came out strong and loud and clear, full of resolve.

Jackhammer spun his head around and gave me a puzzled look. I scratched the spot between his ears to let him know that the "no" hadn't been meant for him.

Turner looked at McKinley and shrugged.

McKinley shrugged back.

"I can explain," said Turner.

I made no comment. I crossed my arms and tapped my foot, ready to hear his explanation, thinking this better be good.

Turner said, "But not here."

"Too goddamn many ears," said McKinley.

Jackhammer and I followed Turner as he rolled the typing chair through a long, depressing, fluorescent-lit corridor.

The chair's splayed wheels kept getting caught on broken tiles, which slowed our progress.

"Where are we going?" I asked more than once.

In reply, Turner grunted.

We turned one way, then another, and finally stopped in front of a gray steel door stenciled with the words "broom closet." Turner fumbled with a huge ring of keys, until he found the one that unlocked the door. He pushed the chair in and told me to sit down. This time I honored his request. Jackhammer zoomed back and forth, and gave the room a quick once-over.

McKinley clomped in and handed me a cup of coffee. "Wait here," he said. Before I had a chance to protest, he and Turner left. The door swung shut behind them, making a solid thud and a tiny click.

Locked?

I put my ear up to the door, waited until the sound of the detectives' footsteps faded, then very slowly tested the doorknob. It turned.

Not locked.

Okay, I thought, here I am, not exactly locked in, but pretty much confined, in a broom closet, in my local precinct, having just tipped my hand to Turner, the cop I claimed not to suspect of murder even though deep down I still wondered, and McKinley, who must have been in on it, whatever it was. Around me was a building chock full of cops, with guns, all between me and the outside world.

I looked around my confines. A slop sink in the corner, floor-to-ceiling shelves loaded down with industrial sized containers of cleaning chemicals, econo-packs of toilet paper, and paper towels. Brooms and mops leaned against the wall.

Not such a great place to be. My heart pounded. I reached for Jackhammer, and hugged him close.

I should have counted to ten more than twice. I should have counted to ten a hundred times. I should have waited. I should have come up with a safer course of action. Now I was stuck in a smelly broom closet in enemy territory, with a five-pound Yorkie, thinking of all the things I should have done. I was very sorry I'd dragged Jackhammer, an innocent, into possible danger.

Jackhammer's ears perked up. I, too, heard approaching footsteps. Okay, what if my worst imaginings came true? Just in case, I picked up a broom. Thus armed, and feeling very foolish, I waited.

The door opened. Turner and McKinley quickly stepped in, and shut the door.

I brandished the broom at them. "Lay one finger on me and . . ."

Jackhammer bared his tiny teeth and growled.

In unison, Turner and McKinley rolled their eyes.

"Get real," said McKinley.

Boy, did his attitude make me angry. That felt a whole lot better than being scared. I put down the broom and told Jackhammer it was all right. The policemen really were our friends, sort of.

Turner sat down on an inverted bucket. "I guess I owe you an explanation."

"Yes, you do." And a big apology.

"Blame it on Johnny Verlane," he said. When he saw the look on my face he rephrased. "I don't mean blame *it* on Johnny. What I mean is, when I saw his success with *Tod Trueman, Urban Detective*, I thought 'Why not me?' I signed up for an acting class, where I met Doreen Sands. That's why I'm in the photograph, and that's all there is to it. You know what Ms. Midnight, the funny thing is, I'm a pretty damned good actor."

A big, warm let-bygones-be-bygones smile spread across McKinley's face. "It's really nothing to be concerned about. My partner here"—he jokingly elbowed Turner in the ribs—"would never live it down if some of the men around the precinct found out he was taking that class."

"I was preparing for the future," said Turner. "Can't blame a guy for that. Someday I'll retire. What am I gonna do? I don't want to be a rent-a-cop sitting all night long in some unheated warehouse listening to water dripping and rats scurrying. I don't want to be a private dick hunkering down in a dark car staking out a cheating spouse and wondering when I'm finally gonna get the chance to take a pee.'' Turner flexed his fingers, then continued. ''I guess you may as well know the whole sorry tale. My lady friend and I recently called it quits. I thought maybe, the acting class would perk me up. I was hoping, you know . . . that I would meet somebody.''

''It's really no big deal,'' said McKinley.

I grew tired of hearing them express in different ways how not a big deal it was. ''Not true,'' I said. ''It *is* a big deal. Doreen Sands is dead—murdered. If that's not a big deal, I don't know what is. And the gun, that's a big deal too.''

''You figured out about the gun?'' said McKinley.

He and Turner looked at each other, again attempting nonverbal communication.

This time I thought I detected fear in their faces. The wispy idea that had flitted through my brain the night before and had tried to come into focus when I was talking to Johnny came in for a hard landing. At last I knew exactly how that gun got in my hatbox.

My turn to lie. ''Sure. I knew about that gun from the get-go.''

''Shit,'' said McKinley. He looked scared. Turner too. That pretty much confirmed it.

No matter how many times I'd gone over the events that occurred at Castleberry's the day Doreen Sands was murdered, it always came down to the fact that there was no way anybody could have put that gun in my hatbox without my noticing. And they hadn't. Not in the waiting room. It happened at Midnight Millinery. McKinley did it.

For a long time, none of us spoke. During the silence, I detected a change in the atmosphere, a shift of power. I resituated myself in the chair, sat up taller. Jackhammer stood at attention.

Turner put his head in his hands and groaned.

McKinley stood in front of the door. He looked ill.

Turner finally broke the silence. ''Okay, Ms. Midnight. You win. Here's the deal. One night after acting class, some of us went to a bar. It was there that Doreen Sands liberated my gun.''

"She what!''

"She swiped his gun,'' said McKinley, as if I hadn't understood.

I'd understood the words, but it was hard to believe them. Cops do not get their guns lifted off their persons.

Turner said, "I thought Ms. Sands was putting the move on me. She must have been reaching for the gun. I rebuffed what I thought were her advances—not that she wasn't attractive, but it was too soon after my breakup. A little while later, Ms. Sands left the bar.''

"With your gun?''

"Yes.''

"Didn't you notice it was gone?''

Turner sighed. "Not right away, no. I was seated when it happened, and I'd had a few. Well, more than a few. Okay, I had a shitload of alcohol in me. I'm not much of a drinker. Never have been. But ever since the breakup, well, I guess you could say I fell apart. Do you understand how this makes me, a big city detective, look?''

I nodded.

"You don't ever want to lose your service revolver,'' said McKinley. "The only thing worse is getting killed in the line of duty.''

"I wouldn't be so sure,'' said Turner. "With that, there's honor.''

We all thought on that for a minute.

Turner went on. "After I left the bar, I realized I didn't have my gun. Hoping I'd left it in my locker, I went back to the precinct to look. No gun. By the next morning I'd sobered up enough to suspect Doreen Sands had taken it, maybe to get back at me for spurning her. Before I could check it out, the call came in and we found her dead. I can never know for sure what was in her mind, but the bottom line is she killed herself with my gun.''

"Killed herself? Suicide? You're kidding?'' I'd never really believed those rumors.

"Do I look like I'm kidding, Ms. Midnight?''

"No, you don't. Was there a suicide note? Is that how you knew?"

"No note. That's frequently the case. Suicide notes are for TV. It was clearly suicide from the way the gun was situated and the angle of the wound."

"Not murder? Couldn't a knowledgeable killer make it look—"

"Please, Ms. Midnight. Trust me on this. When I found the gun with Ms. Sands's body, I took it. She was already dead. I could do nothing more for her. I had to save my own ass. I was positive the employee who discovered the body hadn't seen the gun. Nor had Castleberry's security, or EMS, or the first uniforms on the crime scene. From that point on, I covered up. To keep my gun out of it, I couldn't let it go down as a suicide. Actually, I did Doreen Sands and her family a big favor by calling it a murder. You know how society looks down on those who kill themselves."

"So you faked a murder investigation, and that whole bit with Gundermutter was . . ."

"Subterfuge," said McKinley.

"Then you weren't trying to set me up?"

"Come on, Ms. Midnight," said Turner. "You didn't think that."

"I didn't know what to think. I'm still not too clear as to why you needed your gun in my hatbox."

"First off," said Turner, "that was not my gun that McKinley put in your hatbox. It was a throw-down, untraceable. In order to add credence to our claim that Doreen Sands's suicide was murder, we needed to come up with a murder weapon. It seemed possible that the killer, if there had actually been one, could have used your hatbox to transport the weapon off the premises."

I looked at McKinley. "You slipped a throw-down in my hatbox when you were at Midnight Millinery."

"That's about the size of it."

"I still don't understand how that would do you any good," I said. "Ballistics, forensics, whatever—can't they determine that the throw-down was not the murder weapon?"

"Yes, they can," said Turner. "But only if the alleged murder weapon hadn't got lost in the system. I saw to it that it did."

"I suppose my hats and hatboxes are also 'lost' in the system?"

"Sorry, Ms. Midnight."

I put Jackhammer on the floor, snapped on his leash, and stood up. "I'm out of here."

Turner got up off the bucket. "Please keep this under your hat, Ms. Midnight."

I didn't answer or even look at him. McKinley moved away from the door. I left.

22

Keep it under my hat? That Turner had a lot of nerve.

I was bursting to tell Johnny and everybody I knew the extremely illegal stunt Turner and McKinley, those fine upholders of the law, had pulled.

In particular, I wanted to tell Lemmy Crenshaw. He'd be thrilled to hear what his two least favorite detectives were up to. Though mightily tempted, I could not tell Lemmy. If I did, it'd be all over—in more ways than one. First it would be all over the media, then it would be all over for Turner. His police career would screech to a totally humiliating dishonorable and sleazy end. He wouldn't even be able to get that night watchman job he dreaded. McKinley would be in bigger trouble. He's the one who'd tampered with evidence and sneaked the throw-down weapon into my hatbox.

I hoped I never saw either of them again.

For once I held all the cards. That might have been nice had I wanted to be in the game. This time I didn't want to come out and play.

I took my time walking back from the precinct. Jackhammer saw it as an opportunity to sniff at every parking meter and fire hydrant along Hudson Street. I was sad and mad, but mostly plain old relieved that the whole mess was over.

It was good to hear Turner and McKinley actually state

that they never thought I had killed Doreen Sands. It was also good to know they didn't think Fuzzy or any other milliner had killed Doreen Sands.

It was odd how those rumors of suicide turned out to be true. Turner, with his incredibly large male ego still intact, hinted that Doreen Sands had committed suicide because he himself had spurned her. Wrong again, Detective. Doreen Sands had killed herself because of that two-timing fiancé of hers, Gregory.

That was close to good news. Yes, Doreen Sands was still dead, that fact had not changed, and her death was still a great loss to her family, the millinery community, and anybody else who knew her. It seemed callous, but if she wanted to die bad enough to steal Turner's gun and use it to blow herself away, so be it. It was none of my business.

I opened up Midnight Millinery. Jackhammer puttered around and rearranged scraps of fabric. Not in the mood to work, I did much the same until I happened to glance at my calendar. The appointment with the store in Soho, which I'd completely forgotten about, was for two o'clock that day. At first I thought I'd already missed it. It was hard to believe, after all that had happened, that it was not yet noon.

I could easily make the appointment, but there was no longer much reason to go. What did I care if some millinery buyer was jealous of Doreen Sands or knew about Fuzzy's new line?

I picked up the phone to cancel, but changed my mind. It didn't matter that I no longer needed to go. Canceling was simply not professional. To protect my reputation, I had to go through with the appointment.

I hadn't sold hats in Soho since my friend Margo closed her boutique, Einstein's Revenge, and ran off to Europe with her trashy boyfriend. In the short time it took her to realize the boyfriend was a creep and to get herself back to New York, commercial rents in Soho had quadrupled, so Margo never reopened the store. Instead, she became a stylist.

Soholo et Noca was on West Broadway pretty far down in Soho, almost all the way to Canal Street. A man who looked as if his last gig had been linebacker for the New York Giants hulked on the sidewalk out in front of the pink-painted glass-fronted emporium. The upscale boutique bouncer, last year's edgy trend, had become a fully ensconced institution.

Through ultradark sunglasses, the scowling bruiser watched my approach. When I veered toward the store, he pushed open a tall glass door. "Welcome to Soholo et Noca." His voice was smooth and deep.

"I have an appointment to see the millinery buyer."

"You are expected." Even though he appeared to have no neck, the bouncer somehow managed to nod his head toward an elegant man in a two-thousand-dollar suit who was standing in the back of the huge, almost empty space, talking into a cellular phone.

I felt really stupid, but I didn't know the name of this buyer either.

"Brenda Midnight," I said.

The man I came to refer to as the Downtown Buyer shook my hand. When he smiled his face barely moved. "Coffee? Chardonnay perhaps?"

"Coffee would be nice," I said. "Black."

We sat facing each other in white leather Barcelona chairs, right smack in the middle of the store. All around us stylish customers glided silently from display to display. An employee of indeterminate sex, wrapped up in indeterminate layers of gray garments, served steaming dark coffee in white porcelain cups, then swiftly disappeared into the back.

"I've heard of your work," said the Downtown Buyer. His diction was flawless, voice even.

I didn't know if that was a compliment, figured I'd better smile anyway, did so, then felt foolish.

We sipped coffee in silence, checking each other out. Finally he said, "Show me your hats."

"Here?" Again I felt foolish. Of course it was here or he wouldn't have said that. It was just that I didn't want it to be here. Not with customers around. I find the act of selling almost unseemly. I wanted to do it in a back office, out of sight, perhaps with a plain brown bag over my head.

"Yes," he said. "Here will do nicely."

First I took out some little hatlettes I'd brought along. I thought they would look good with the elegant gowns for which Soholo et Noca was best known.

The Downtown Buyer thought otherwise. He made a sour face. "No, no, no," he said. "I purchase real millinery. I do not purchase hair baubles and doodads."

"Oh." I hastily got the hatlettes put away and showed him the rest of the collection, what he called the real millinery.

His examination was very thorough. He peeked under every headsize band, checked for handwork, questioned the materials. I wouldn't have been surprised if he sniffed for the aroma of glue. Finally he proclaimed, "Delightful collection. Your reputation is well-deserved."

"Thank you," I said.

"Do you have a presence in Soho?"

"No. Not since Einstein's Revenge closed."

"I'm sure you understand that I require an exclusive below Houston Street. Up there"—he brushed his hand toward uptown—"you can sell whatever you want to whomever you want."

I agreed to this restriction.

We discussed price. I almost tumbled off the Barcelona when he said my prices were too low and suggested a higher amount. I agreed and doubled. Next, we went over delivery dates and quantities. He swept a silver fountain pen over a purchase order, rapidly filling it out. "I'll expect the same high-quality work as in your samples," he said. "The Soholo et Noca customer expects perfection. And they pay for it. It's my job and my passion to see that they get it."

With that, he rose, shook my hand, and walked briskly

over to a customer. They did a two-sided air kiss. Our meeting was over.

I couldn't shake the feeling that I'd forgotten something. About halfway home, it finally dawned on me what. The entire time I'd been at Soholo et Noca I'd not once mentioned or thought about either Doreen Sands or Fuzzy.

Another order. I had more work to do and even more supplies to buy. I did another inventory, and was in the middle of updating my shopping list when the customer from last Sunday strode into the store, the one with the plaid boater, the one featured in the bad customer section of Fuzzy's web page. Today, she didn't have on a spectacular hat. She was hatless. And smileless.

"Well," she huffed. "Nice to see you're actually open. It's about time." Not exactly friendly.

She must have been the one who'd left the message the other day to gripe that I was closed. I started to tell her how sorry I was, but changed my mind. To apologize for being closed would put me at a distinct disadvantage. If Fuzzy was right about this woman, if she turned out to be a pain in the butt, I sure didn't want to start out on the defense. I stuck out my hand. "I'm so glad to see you."

She shook my hand. "Harriet," she said. And almost cracked a smile.

I took that as a good sign. I wanted to like anybody who knew good millinery. I hoped Fuzzy's web page was wrong about Harriet.

"Thanks for helping me with that indecisive customer the other day."

"Oh, you remember me, do you? From the day you *were* open. I simply could not deal with the crowd. When I came back later in the week—"

"Please," I said, "take a look around. If you have any questions, feel free to ask."

"Of course." She snatched up one of my sample hats, tsk-tsked, and moved on to the next.

I wondered if Harriet really measured the space between stitches with calipers like it said on Fuzzy's web page. While that seemed a bit obsessive, I agreed that

handstitching should be well done. If not, why bother?
Why not use a machine?

Harriet seemed content to peruse my collection. I left
her alone and went back to my shopping list.

Not long after she came over to me. "I want that exact
hat." She pointed across the room to my all-time favorite
cocktail hat, a little cap with a point.

Fantastic, I thought. Harriet wasn't difficult at all. I
could do up one of those hats in no time flat, especially
now that I was gearing up into a high-production frame
of mind.

"Except," she added, "I would like you to make a
couple of minor changes. I want a big floppy brim and
scads of veiling. That should be simple enough."

What the hell was she talking about? To add a brim
where there was no brim required that I draft an entire
new pattern, and totally rethink the design. It wasn't re-
alistic. It was stupid. And this woman was most definitely
not stupid. Fuzzy was right after all. Harriet was being a
pain in the neck for no good reason, as an end in itself.
Clearly, she had challenged me, probably as punishment
for the shop not being open when she wanted it to be.

I gathered up several hats that already had brims to
show her.

No, no, no, and no. "I know precisely what I want,"
she insisted.

I couldn't argue with that. However, I could refuse to
make the hat. I started to do so, but then I remembered a
lesson I'd learned the hard way long ago: The easy way
out wasn't always so easy.

And so, standing tall and proud of myself and my work,
I rose to Harriet's challenge. Fresh and exhilarated from
my experience at the precinct, I felt no customer was too
tough for Brenda Midnight. I could almost hear trium-
phant music swelling in the background as I thought to
myself how I'd prove all those other milliners wrong. I'd
work with Harriet. I'd make her the happiest hat owner
in millinery history.

I turned to Harriet, smiled sweetly, and said, "I'd be
delighted to make the hat of your dreams."

I sat her down at the vanity and offered her a cup of coffee. Naturally she wanted tea. "Make that with lemon and honey."

I called in the order to the deli.

"One tea?" said the deli owner. "You want us to deliver one lousy tea?"

I turned away from Harriet, lowered my voice, and spoke directly into the phone. "Please, as a favor. I'm in a bind here with an important customer."

He grumbled, but agreed.

"Don't forget the lemon and honey," I said.

"One tea, lemon and honey. Got it." No matter how unreasonable the request, he knew that the customer was always right.

The tea arrived a few minutes later. I gave the delivery man a generous tip.

Harriet wrinkled her nose when she saw the logo dangling from the tea bag. She plunged it into the steaming water anyway, held it down with a plastic spoon, and strangled it with the string to extract the juices. Then she squeezed the lemon slice over the cup, poured in the honey, and sniffed the resulting concoction. "Hmpf," she said. She put down the cup without taking a sip.

I brought out my fabric samples. She pawed through all the swatches. True to Fuzzy's warning, Harriet zeroed in on my most expensive fabric, a shimmery elusive silk. She jabbed at it with her forefinger. "I want this."

Inwardly I groaned. Working with that stuff was like working with mercury. It was here, then it was there, then everywhere all at once. It was very beautiful though. That's why I'd kept it around. Harriet had good taste. I had to respect that.

As Harriet described in painstaking detail the hat she wanted, I made a sketch. "Is this what you mean?" I asked.

"Well, no, not quite. A little wider perhaps."

I erased and made changes.

"Taller."

We went through bigger, smaller, softer, and harder. Eventually she settled on a version of a hat that bore no resemblance to the original cocktail hat. I named an ex-orbitant price, stapled the sketch to her order, along with the swatch of fabric, and had her sign.

"So there's no misunderstanding," I explained.

"There won't be," she said. Her face relaxed and she actually parted with a full smile. "Do you require a deposit?"

"That won't be necessary," I said.

23

What a day. Not long after Harriet thanked me for the tea she'd not taken a single sip of and finally went away, I closed up Midnight Millinery. I was too pooped to pop, and almost hungry enough to eat meat. I went home, scarfed down a bowl of broccoli. Then I relaxed.

Too much had happened way too fast.

I hadn't even had the chance to call Johnny and gloat over what I'd learned about his detective pals. In fact, I hadn't talked to Johnny since I'd stormed out of his apartment yelling about the goddamned brotherhood of blue.

I fought the urge to call. Let Johnny make the first move. Then, once he apologized for blindly taking the side of the authorities, I'd tell him the dirt and see if he still thought the detectives were such stand-up guys.

For the time being, I'd have to keep all the juicy information to myself. Too bad. I couldn't even trust Elizabeth not to blab. Not any more, not the new Elizabeth, the one who no longer concocted weird cookies, and who secretly went places at all hours of the day and night. What in the world was going on with her?

No sooner had I posed the question, then the answer came. All the signs were there. I should have figured it out much sooner. Obviously, Elizabeth was in love. But why the secrecy? That still didn't make sense. It was not Elizabeth's way. She was rather notorious for letting it all hang out. Maybe the guy was married. But that didn't sound like Elizabeth either.

Whatever the details, if I was right, it looked bad for poor Chuck. He would be devastated. He was already extremely far off the wall, obsessed with the idea Elizabeth might possibly be his mother.

As soon as I got my hat orders under way, I'd make it my business to find out for sure what Elizabeth was up to. Then I'd know how to keep it from Chuck or, if necessary, break it to him gently.

Later that night, when the phone rang, I assumed it was Johnny with that apology he owed me. I picked up the phone before the answering machine got it.

Not Johnny. It was Fuzzy.

It was good to hear from her, especially now that I could talk without worrying that she might be a murderer. That had definitely put a crimp in our friendship.

"Just checking up," she said. "Have you finished your hat for Milliners Milling?"

"Almost."

"Get cracking, girl. Think beyond millinery, think art, pure unadulterated sculpture. I want to see you in the biggest, wildest, most fabulous fantastical, most gravity-defying Brenda Midnight creation ever to sit on a head. I'm counting on you."

"Don't worry, I'll get it done in time. The last few days I've been very busy."

"Oh yeah. Doing what? Snooping around the Doreen Sands case?"

"No."

"Come on, you can tell me the truth. You're friends with those cops who are working on it. Haven't they clued you in?"

"Hard to keep a secret from you, Fuzzy. Okay, here's the inside lowdown. The cops are convinced it was a random robbery gone bad."

"Oh come on. Don't give me that crap. That's the same as the bullshit printed in the newspapers."

"The facts do seem to support the theory, or so they

tell me.'' I hated going along with the official line, but I couldn't tell Fuzzy that Doreen Sands had committed suicide.

"Does that mean they're done with the investigation?"

"Yes, I believe they are."

To get off that subject I bragged about my big orders. I started with the first, the uptown order.

"Six dozen cocktail hats," said Fuzzy. "That's amazing. How'd you pull that off?"

"The millinery buyer believes cocktail hats will be big this season. I'm probably the only milliner who showed her any."

"Why would she think that? The cocktail craze is like way over and out."

"I can't imagine," I said.

"I suppose she knows what she's doing, even though the woman despises my hats, claims my stuff is too funky for her hoity-toity uptown market."

"I also got an order from Soholo et Noca."

"You cracked that nut? Wow. I *am* impressed. What did you sell to them?"

"Traditional, what the buyer referred to as real millinery. He didn't think much of my little hatlettes."

"No, he wouldn't. I've talked to him before. Can't stand him. He's got a stick up his ass. Doreen Sands would have bought your hatlettes. She could make anything work in her department, just so long as it sits on a head—my hats, normal hats, teeny little fluffs of veiling, hats that aren't really hats. Doreen Sands could have sold purple babushkas as couture."

"At least those that weren't burned," I said, laughing.

"What do you mean burned?"

"Don't you know about the babushka burnings?"

"No. Sounds intriguing. Do tell."

"Well," I said, "back in the fifties, teenage girls took to wearing head scarves. You've probably seen pictures. You know, the whole glamorous, convertible, blond pageboy, high-heeled slip-in mules, polka-dot capri-pant thing. However, the millinery industry absolutely did not see the glamour. What they saw was a nation of scarf-wearing women-to-be who were not spending their baby-sitting money on hats. The industry freaked out big time. They labeled the scarves babushkas and claimed they made the girls look like a bunch of potato diggers. And yes, there really was a babushka burning somewhere in the Midwest.''

"You're making this up, right?"

"I swear it's true. Big bonfire. The media covered it. You could probably look it up."

"Don't think I won't. This is fabulous stuff. It deserves a whole section on my web page. Speaking of the media, I have, of course, invited every fashion writer and photographer within the tristate area to my show. It would be super cool if I could get Johnny Verlane to be my master of ceremonies. Do you think he'd do it?"

"He's pretty busy with his book, but I'll ask him."

"I'd be forever grateful," said Fuzzy.

"Don't get your hopes up. I can't promise."

"He'll do it. I've seen the two of you together. Johnny Verlane cannot say no to you."

"Not true. He can and he has, frequently."

"Sure Brenda, whatever you say."

"So anyway," I said, saving the best for last, "I never told you about my last order."

"I'm all ears."

"Harriet."

"No."

"She came in today and ordered a custom hat."

"Don't say I didn't warn you, Brenda. You should have tossed her out of your shop."

"Harriet's not so bad. She's demanding because she knows exactly what she wants. I admire that."

I promised Fuzzy that I'd call Johnny right away, which screwed up my plans not to call him until he'd called me and apologized.

In honor of my anger, I made it short and to the point. "Fuzzy wants you to emcee her Milliners Milling show. I promised I'd ask."

"You mentioned that show before. What is it exactly?"

"Half performance art, half fashion show. She'll rant. Chuck's doing the lighting, including laser effects. She invited the media, of course."

"You're going to be there, right?"

"Yes. Fuzzy talked me into parading around in a catsuit with my most bizarre hat on top of my head."

"I wouldn't want to miss that."

"Is that a yes?"

"I guess."

"Good. Call Fuzzy for details."

"All right, I'll do that."

I waited a couple of beats to give him a chance to apologize. When he didn't, I said, "Goodbye." I held the receiver at arm's length, trying to decide whether to bang it down or simply hang up, when I heard his voice.

"Uh, Brenda, I'm sorry about this morning."

That was more like it. Exactly what I wanted to hear. I put the receiver back to my ear. "It's okay."

"You were right. I was wrong."

I couldn't wait to tell him just how wrong he was. It was such a delicious moment, I felt guilty. But I didn't let that stop me. "After leaving your place this morning," I said, "I dropped by the precinct and had a little chat with Turner and McKinley."

"I knew you'd do the right thing."

"More than I can say for Turner and McKinley. You've been quite an inspiration for Turner." I told him the whole story, from Turner signing up for the acting class to McKinley sneaking the throw-down gun in my hatbox. "And, if you don't believe me, ask Turner and McKinley. Or actually—don't. Turner told me to keep this under my hat."

At long last I called it a day. Or so I thought. I was dragging the mattress out of the closet when the doorman buzzed me. "That lady with the Harley is here to see you. I went ahead and sent her up."

I shoved the mattress back into the closet and threw on a pair of jeans and a T-shirt.

Gundermutter looked like hell. Her ponytail was disheveled, eyes rimmed with red, and drunk as a skunk, as drunk as Turner must have been when Doreen Sands lifted his gun.

She flopped down on my banana-shaped couch. "I messed up bad," she said.

"What's wrong?" I asked.

"Spencer took me off the case because I'm a crappy cop."

"You are not a crappy cop," I said. "I'm sure it was nothing you did personally." It was a safe bet that Turner hadn't told Gundermutter the whole story, or even part of it.

"That's right. I'm off the case because of what I did not do. Personally, I did not solve the case. I haven't turned up anything definite about the drug connection. I'll probably never get a better opportunity and I blew it. All I want to do is arrest somebody. Why is that so damned hard?"

She toppled over on the couch. At first I thought she had passed out, but then I heard her whimper.

Now, if possible, I was even more angry at Turner. He'd let Gundermutter believe she was a failure. If she knew she was taken off the case because there was no case, that it was a ruse, a scam, a coverup, she wouldn't feel so bad.

To distract her, I babbled on about my new orders.

It seemed to cheer her a little. She made it back into a sitting position. By the time I'd finished she'd started to redo her ponytail. "Soholo et Noca," she said. "That is one cool store. Can't afford it on a cop's salary, and now I'll never make detective."

I had news for her. Damned few detectives could afford Soholo et Noca.

She fastened her ponytail with a large, S-shaped, beaded barrette. The Downtown Buyer would have scorned it as a hair bauble. "Nice barrette," I said.

Gundermutter smiled. "I was assigned to the hair accessories department for an afternoon and I got to meet the buyer. She was so nice to me. I fell in love with the barrette, and she let me have it at cost, better even than my employee discount, which I guess I won't get any-more. I'm not even a fake employee. I'm not undercover, I'm not overcover. I'm nothing going nowhere fast, a cop who's never made an arrest. My mother was right. She always said I shoulda gone to auto repair school.'' She fell over onto the couch again.

I roused her. ''Where's your gun?''

She patted her jacket.

''Do me a favor and put it in a safe place.''

She pushed herself off the couch and staggered into the kitchen. ''How about on top of the fridge?''

''Fine,'' I said. ''I don't want you rolling on it. It could go off or something.''

''It won't, but you are right to be cautious,'' she said.

She made it back to the couch and flopped down. Except for sticking a pillow under her head, I let her be. She was in no shape to ride her motorcycle back to Queens. I didn't want a cop crash on my conscious.

I resigned myself to another night in the chair by the window with Jackhammer curled up in my lap.

24

The chair might have been great to sit in, but it made a lousy bed. I didn't sleep. Mostly I shifted positions and daydreamed about hats—big hats, little hats, hats that weren't really hats, barrettes, puffs of veiling, and burning babushkas. Milliners danced, millinery buyers sang, the babushka bonfire got out of control. Flames were everywhere, Doreen Sands was running, dogs were barking . . .

Wrong.

Only one dog was barking, and I knew him well. Jackhammer was raising a ruckus out in the entry foyer.

Friend or foe?

I crept to the door, slid the peephole shutter open, and looked through.

Friend. Specifically, Elizabeth. She double-locked her door. Then she moved out of range. On her way out, I presumed.

It was close to midnight. Where in the world could she be off to at that hour? To see her secret lover? When would I ever get a better chance to find out? I was fully dressed and couldn't sleep anyway.

I told Jackhammer to keep an eye on Gundermutter, put on my leather jacket, then held my ear to the door and listened for the sound of the elevator door banging shut. When it did, I raced out and ran down the stairway to the lobby.

"Did you see Elizabeth?" I asked the doorman.

He nodded and pointed downtown. "She went that-away."

I caught sight of her as she headed down Hudson. She had a large canvas bag slung over her shoulder. She moved fast, with a lively spring to her step. Wherever she was going she sure seemed happy about it.

It was Friday night, and the weather was wonderful, so the streets were filled with people, even at midnight. It made following her a snap. If she happened to turn around she'd never pick me out of the mob.

She continued downtown. South of Christopher Street, the crowd thinned out. I moved into the shadows, and occasionally ducked into a doorway. Still, I managed to keep no more than a block behind her.

The farther downtown, the fewer people. Gone was the feeling of safety in numbers. I wished I'd brought Gundermutter along—better yet, Gundermutter's gun. Not that I'd know what to do with it.

To my relief, before it got any more desolate, Elizabeth hung a right on Spring Street, a fairly active east-west running street. I rounded the corner in time to see her go into a ramshackle building.

I now knew where Elizabeth was going. All I had to do was find out why.

It was an ideal neighborhood for a tryst, centrally located, yet off the beaten path. It was precisely right smack dab in the middle of nowhere—too far south to be the Village, too far west to be Soho, and too far north to be Tribeca. Some day, it'd get a name, and be somewhere.

I wanted to get off the street before Elizabeth looked out a window and spotted me. I had my pick of two bars directly across from the building she'd disappeared into. I chose the one with the largest window, since it would give me the best view.

The place was packed, smoke-filled, and noisy. Over the din, the squeal of a pedal steel guitar sliced the air. It sounded live. As I pushed through the crowd, homing in on a spot by the window, I caught sight of the band. It was actually one guy, in a red T-shirt, string tie, and a New York Yankees cap turned backwards. Pretty good if you like pedal steel.

The people hanging out between me and the window were working artist types, the kind who really make art, and don't just work hard at being arty.

When a seat at the bar next to the window opened up, I grabbed it. The bartender ambled over. He was a heavy-set bearded guy in baggy overalls. I told him I wanted a red wine.

"I woulda bet you'd be a red wine," he said.

What did that mean?

Once situated, I stared out at the building that had swallowed up Elizabeth. I could see lights on in most of the windows, but if I expected any tell-tale backlit silhouettes of kissing couples, I was plumb out of luck.

Who could Elizabeth be meeting? What for? If it was a lover, it had to be the guy who required all the secrecy.

The building itself offered no clues. Four stories, yellow brick, rundown, no storefront, nothing remarkable. It was a plain old apartment building, like thousands of others in the city.

The bartender again made his way down to my end of the bar. He raised his bushy eyebrows at my empty glass. "Want another?"

I thought for a moment before saying yes. I didn't want to end up like Gundermutter. Or Turner.

The bartender reached under the bar for the bottle. It was the same house brand they used at Angie's. As he poured, I ventured a question. "Do you know of any apartments for rent around here? I heard there might be something available in that building across the street."

The bartender frowned. "Save yourself the trouble. That place is bad news. Leaky pipes. Hardly any heat in the winter."

A craggy-faced man on the barstool next to me spoke up. "You looking? I know of a loft coming up soon, raw, down on DesBrosses Street. It's a real honey. Two thousand wide-open square feet. A bargain in this incredibly tight real estate market."

"Thanks." I scribbled down the particulars on a napkin. Never knew when I might need more space. Someday maybe Johnny and I . . .

The man took a big swig of beer and slammed the mug down on the bar. "But don't you go telling the landlord you heard about the joint from me. I got a date to have it out with that bastard in court."

I laughed, hoping that would be the end of it, but he went on to detail his landlord problems. Every single human in New York City has their own personal harrowing landlord story. His didn't interest me. I listened long enough to be polite. The guy seemed nice enough, and the landlord probably really was a bastard. He wound down one episode, and was about to launch into another, when I excused myself, paid for my wine, and elbowed my way out of the bar.

On the street I ran into yet another milliner I knew vaguely. I wasn't sure of her name, but she knew mine.

"Brenda, Brenda Midnight. Shame on you. You're a disgrace to our fine profession. You've got no hat on your head."

"I couldn't decide which to wear."

"I know how that is. Hey, I heard you were working with the police on the Doreen Sands case, doing the cloak-and-dagger bit."

"Where'd you hear that?"

"I don't know. Fuzzy maybe. Yeah, I think it was Fuzzy."

Damn Fuzzy and her big mouth. "I'm afraid it's not true," I said. "Fuzzy, or whomever, must have been misled by the fact that I am slightly acquainted with a couple of the detectives assigned to the case. They're friends of a friend. I don't know them very well at all."

"Friends, friends of friends, whatever, it's close to the same thing."

"Not really." Most especially not in this case.

"So, what do the cops think happened? My money's on a rival buyer or maybe a hatter with hurt feelings."

"Nothing like that. It was a random robbery gone bad."

"I hear she was in her office."

"So they say."

"That's the downside to safe New York City streets. Crime got up and moved indoors."

We both chuckled.

"I suppose you'll be at Fuzzy's Milliners Milling show next week."

"Uh-huh."

"I'll catch up with you there. But now, I want to get inside. I hear they've got some guy on pedal steel tonight. I'm a country girl at heart. I could sure use a good dose of that twangy stuff."

During that entire conversation I'd kept my eyes on the building, fearful that Elizabeth might come out at any moment, see me, and wonder what the hell I was doing hanging out on Spring Street at one o'clock in the morning. The fact that she hadn't emboldened me. I decided to investigate the vestibule.

I moseyed across the street and kind of nonchalantly slipped into the building.

I looked at the names mounted alongside the individual mailboxes and got a big surprise. Elizabeth herself was listed as E. F. Perry. If the apartment was in her name, did that mean she footed the bill and not her lover? I didn't think she was *that* much of a feminist. The apartment number was 2N. I surmised it was a back apartment, facing north, away from the street.

The bartender was right on the money about the building's condition. It was a gloomy hellhole, grimy, and devoid of any vestige of security. There was no buzzer system. The outer door was not locked; the inner door didn't even have a lock. Anybody could walk all the way inside any old time.

I took that as an engraved invitation. No RSVP required.

Once inside the innermost door, I found the ambiance oddly comforting, familiar. I tried to figure out why. Could it be the wooden floor, spongy under my step? The fluorescent light that buzzed in the ceiling and cast an unearthly glow over everything? The cockroach crawling up the cracked stucco wall? Or the blues riff playing somewhere in the distance?

I sighed deeply.

My next intake of breath held the answer.

I knew that smell. Sniffing, I followed my nose upstairs to the second floor, stopped in front of apartment 2N, and breathed in the familiar odors. Linseed oil. Turpentine. Paint.

Elizabeth Franklin Perry, formerly famous artist, was back at the easel again.

Good for her.

Now that I knew what Elizabeth had been up to, I was ashamed I'd ever thought she'd been having a secret affair. I knew her far better than that. I should have trusted her to be her. I didn't understand why she was so secretive about her return to painting and was a little insulted that she hadn't confided in me. I supposed it was her way of working through her decades-long artistic crisis.

I vowed to keep Elizabeth's secret. I wouldn't even let her know I knew. When she was good and ready, she'd tell me herself.

Gundermutter was up and looking much better, her ponytail was securely fastened on top of her head, gun back in her holster. "I made a pot of coffee," she said.

I went into the kitchen and poured myself a cup, then joined her in the room.

"Where'd you go?" she asked. "I was worried sick."

"There was this pedal steel player down on Spring Street." I was appalled at how easily the deceitful, oblique half-truths rolled off my tongue.

"At that honky-tonk art bar?"

"How'd you know about that joint?"

"Hey, I'm a cop, remember? I may not have arrested any crooks yet. That doesn't mean I don't know things. It's my duty. So, was the guy any good?"

"Not bad."

"Maybe I'll catch his act some time. I'm really sorry about earlier. I guess I was messed up."

"You were upset. I understand. How long have you been conscious?"

"Half hour or so. I've been entertaining Jackhammer with exciting stories of police dog rescues. Right, little guy?"

Jackhammer wagged his stub.

Gundermutter drained the last bit of coffee out of her mug. "I'm outta here," she said.

"Do you think you're in any condition to drive yet? Or ride?" I didn't quite know what to call what you did on a Harley.

"I most certainly am not. I'll walk down to the precinct. We've got a fold-out cot down there for just this circumstance. I think my Harley'll be okay parked outside your building for a few more hours."

25

Instant replay. Hadn't I already dragged my mattress out once that night? That seemed like hours ago. A quick look at the clock on the wall confirmed that it actually had been hours ago. No wonder I was so tired. As soon as the mattress hit the floor, I fell onto it, headlong into a deep sleep.

Better than any alarm clock, Jackhammer is a foolproof wake-up system. One of his more effective methods is to apply one cold nose on my neck for approximately two seconds, stand back, and wait for me to jump up and say, "What the hell time is it anyway?"

His answers vary. Today's was a little woof.

The clock said nine. I was reasonably refreshed, considering.

After a quick walk around the block with Jackhammer, I set out for the garment center with my shopping list of supplies.

Gundermutter's Harley was still parked out in front of the building. I hoped she'd be back to pick up the bike soon. It had already attracted a circle of unsavory-looking admirers. I went back inside and asked the doorman on duty to keep a watchful eye. "That bike belongs to a friend of mine," I said, "a lady with a blond ponytail."

"No problem," he said.

On the way to the bus stop I went into the corner deli for a blueberry muffin and a cup of coffee.

"Thanks for yesterday," I said to the counterman.

"You mean the single tea delivery? With lemon and honey?"

"Yeah."

"So, who was it for?"

"A very special customer."

He rolled his eyes. "Tell me about it."

The strip of West Thirty-eighth Street between Fifth and Sixth Avenues used to be the center of the millinery universe. By the time I got into the field, little remained from the glory days. Each year more suppliers went belly up, got taken over, or were squeezed out of ground-level storefronts by wholesalers of lavishly decorated sparkly polyester dresses and costume jewelry.

I took a minute to stand at the corner and look along Thirty-eighth toward Fifth Avenue. With a little imagination I easily conjured up the past. I imagined the street abuzz with the hustle bustle of the millinery trade and hat gossip. It was a time when the daring forward tilt of a hat made big news, fashionable women demanded pink, and milliners fretted about those nutty babushka-wearing teenagers.

From my modern-day vantage point it seemed like a big flap over nothing. If they thought they had troubles in the fifties, wait until the sixties when milliners went head-to-head with bouffant hairdos and wild psychedelic wigs, and hatters were confronted with John Kennedy, who went bareheaded to his one and only inauguration. And the seventies? Forget it.

I snapped back to the present, happy for what remained of the district. I worried about the rapidly approaching day when I'd be forced to order all my supplies over the Internet. Sound effects and cute dancing graphics would never replace the feel and smell of the materials.

It was a damned good thing for me that Bucky's was still in business, although reduced to half the size it used to be. I'd been doing business with them since I started. Bucky's was strictly wholesale, a long, terrifying, claustrophobic, jolting ride up from the street level in what had to be the world's smallest and darkest elevator. I peered through a tiny round chicken-wire impregnated window at the concrete wall sliding by at about an inch a minute. Eventually it ground to a stop on the sixth floor, the door creaked open, and I entered millinery supply heaven.

Floor to ceiling, narrow aisle after narrow aisle, I basked in the abundance of material and supplies. If Bucky's didn't have it, they'd order it, if they couldn't get it, it didn't exist. I spent a half hour just browsing and getting inspired before I finally got down to work and picked up the items on my list, including the most recent addition, the veiling for Harriet's hat. When I'd gathered everything I needed, I took it all up front to Bucky the Third. He was slouched behind the counter sucking an unlit cigar and reading yesterday's *Daily News*.

Bucky's had been in Bucky the Third's family for many generations, passed on from one Bucky to the next. I always figured the Bucky name came from buckram.

Bucky the Third closed up his newspaper and asked, "How's business?" He was thinner and balder and paler and more stooped over than I'd remembered. Tacked up on the wall behind him were photos of various Buckys shaking hands with glamorous hat-wearing celebrities and politicians.

"Can't complain," I answered. "I'm gearing up for big wholesale orders from two new clients. That's why I'm here."

"That's the kind of news I like to hear. But Brenda, I must warn you: be sure to insist on C.O.D. with any new accounts."

"That's not always easy."

"Well worth the effort if you can pull it off. Some of the girls come in here with stories you would simply not believe. It's a sin how these stores and even some individual customers take advantage."

Bucky, a man who saw disaster in every direction, was exaggerating, but not by much. Only once had I been out-and-out ripped off. That was when a client wrote a rubber check and refused to make good on it because the hat got stolen right off her head the first day she wore it. She blamed me, claiming I should have known such a good hat would attract a bad element.

Many stores habitually paid late. I'd learned to work around the problem, but sometimes things could get pretty hairy cash-flow wise. It was one of the reasons I preferred not to wholesale. The landlord for Midnight Millinery maintained he didn't give a rat's ass how much money some boutique owed me. He was only interested in how much money I owed him and for how long I'd owed it. Can't say that I blamed him.

Bucky the Third ambled over to an ancient wooden cash register, rang up the sale, and returned with my change. Then he wrapped my purchases in heavy brown paper.

"Sad about Doreen Sands," I said.

"Yes it is. Did you ever sell hats to her?"

"No, but I wanted to. She ran a great millinery department at Castleberry's."

He frowned. "You're entitled to your own opinion, I guess. But if you asked me, Doreen Sands sold too many frou-frous, too many nonhats. Don't take me wrong, her death is a tragedy, especially to be murdered like that. Makes you wonder though, doesn't it? But I still say the kind of millinery department that takes on everything but the kitchen sink and lumps it all together as millinery confuses the customer. In the long run, that's bad for the business, bad for all of us."

I took a cab downtown. It let me off in front of the building, in the exact spot Gundermutter's Harley had been parked. I hoped Gundermutter was the one who'd taken it.

"Did my friend come back for her bike?" I asked the doorman.

"Yeah. Not long after you left. She said to give you this." He handed me an envelope.

I waited until I got on the elevator to read the note. Gundermutter's handwriting was a big childlike scrawl. "You know those hatboxes you wanted? The ones that got lost in the system. I think I found them. A bunch of hats inside. Looks like your stuff. I left both boxes on Spencer's desk." On the bottom of the page, she had drawn a big round smiley face.

Lost in the system? Yeah, right.

Jackhammer skidded into the foyer to greet me. I leaned the packages from Bucky's against the wall, picked him up, and gave him a squeeze. When I put him down, he ran over to his favorite spot by the radiator and sat down on a piece of paper—a note from Elizabeth. Strange. Nobody ever left me notes, now I had two in one day. "Come over," it read. "Any time, but knock hard. I might be asleep."

And I knew why. She'd been up all night painting.

I debated whether to go. I wanted to see Elizabeth, but I also needed to open the shop and get to work on all my orders, as well as the hat for Fuzzy's show, which was now way behind schedule. I decided to compromise. I'd go to Elizabeth's, but stay no more than fifteen minutes.

Before I left, I checked my answering machine. One call. Ray Marshall. Where had my mind been? I was so shaken up when I'd seen Turner in the picture with Doreen Sands, and all that had led to, I'd completely forgotten to call Ray to tell him I had bad news for Gregory, that Doreen had known he was having an affair.

I'd call Ray later, after I got to Midnight Millinery.

Elizabeth was dressed in her robe and flip-flops.

"You got my note, I see."

"Actually Jackhammer got to it before I did."

"That little devil. Coffee?" she asked.

"Yes, I could use another cup of wake-up juice. I've got a very full day ahead of me."

She went to the kitchen to make a pot of coffee. Her flip-flops slapped hard against the wood floor. Jackhammer, wary of the noise, followed a respectable three feet behind.

While Elizabeth was gone I poked around her apartment, looking for new paintings. My search turned up nothing, not even preliminary sketches.

From the kitchen, she called out. "No cookies today, I'm afraid. I've been too tuckered out to bake. How about some toast or an English muffin?"

"No thanks. Just coffee will be fine."

The cookie mystery was solved. Back in the sixties when Elizabeth had given up painting, she'd taken up cookie concocting as a creative outlet. Now that she was back to painting, there'd be no more banana dill jalapeño surprises. I was happy for her, but I'd sure miss the exotic cookies.

She brought out a pot of coffee and two mud-colored ceramic mugs. After some blather about the wonderful weather we'd been having, she said, "How's Johnny doing?"

"Johnny's fine, just fine. Really, really fine."

"What's he been up to?"

"Exercise and recipe development. Battling Lemmy."

Elizabeth shook her head. "What this time?"

"Cover concepts. Johnny wants a picture of his fluffy soufflé on his book cover. Lemmy's pushing for another kind of dish all together."

"A dishy dame, right?"

"How'd you ever guess?"

We both got a good laugh at the expense of Lemon B. Crenshaw.

"I believe the cover decision is up to the publisher anyway," said Elizabeth.

"I hope so," I said. "That'd save everybody a lot of angst."

I sneaked a peek at my watch. I didn't think Elizabeth had gone to the trouble to stick a note under my door specifically inviting me to come by just to make small talk about the weather and Johnny. "So," I said, "I haven't seen much of you."

"Oh, I've been busy with this and that."

"Really?" I said, hoping she was on the verge of telling me about her secret painting studio, but that wasn't what she had in mind.

"It's Chuck," she said. "He's why I wanted to see you. I'm terribly concerned about him."

"So am I."

"Then you've noticed the change in him, too? He's not like himself. I call him, he doesn't want to talk. I send him e-mail, he doesn't answer. Have you seen him or spoken to him recently?"

It was inevitable that I tell her. As sure as gravity exerted downward force I was going to break my promise to Chuck. He'd never forgive me. And I wouldn't blame him. I'd never forgive me either.

For Elizabeth's benefit, I did my best to ease into the conversation. "Did you ever think you were adopted, you know like when you were little?"

Elizabeth smiled. "Not adopted, kidnapped. By a sexy swashbuckling pirate with a black eye patch holding a long curved knife between his pearly white teeth. I believed he sold me to the people I knew as my parents. Why do you ask?"

"Chuck's got this crazy notion that he might have been adopted."

"First I've ever heard of it."

"It's a brand-new concept for him. I'm afraid he's become rather obsessed with the idea."

"What makes him think he's adopted?"

"Somebody said something that he misinterpreted."

"Somebody in his family?"

"Not exactly."

"Who then?"

"Dude Bob."

"Dude Bob? *My* Dude Bob? Why in the world—"

This was very difficult for me. "According to Chuck, Dude Bob told him you were old enough to be his mother."

"Well, I am."

"You *are* his mother?"

"Don't be ridiculous. But I *am* old enough."

"Chuck kind of took that idea and ran with it. He thinks—"

"Wait a minute. Did I hear you right? Chuck Riley

believes Dude Bob? Chuck thinks I'm his . . . that he's my son?''

I nodded. ''Your love child. That's how he puts it.''

''I don't know if I should be insulted or flattered.''

''He made me swear not to tell you, but I had to. I'm afraid he's going off the deep end, or at least treading in dangerous waters. Maybe if you talked to him you could knock some sense into his head. In one of his more lucid moments I got him to admit that he's more bugged by the possibility that you *could be* his mother than the belief that you actually *are*.''

I felt better having got that off my chest. At the same time, I felt bad for dumping it on Elizabeth, and really rotten for betraying Chuck—even if it was for his own damned good, which it certainly was.

Wasn't it? On the way to Midnight Millinery I tried hard to convince myself of that.

26

I stood in the center of my storage room wishing the word tiny didn't apply. In this context tiny didn't mean cute or adorable, nor did it mean fitting into amazing bargains at designer sample sales, it meant there was no room to put the stuff I'd just bought. In this context, tiny was a big fat pain. It was also a fact of life in New York. Deal with it, I told myself. Take pleasure in the fact that you can touch all four walls without budging an inch.

I shifted stuff around to make room for the new supplies. When I finally got everything all wedged in, I stood back as far as possible and studied the space. It definitely needed some serious rethinking. More shelves might help. Or, I could move the collection of antique hatblocks into the studio. As they were now, brooding on a high shelf, they weren't doing much good. Once I got all my orders done, I'd take some time out to attack the storage problem.

I decided to tackle Harriet's hat first to get her and it out of the way before fully throwing myself into high production mode.

I got out my design head block and pattern paper. Despite what Harriet believed, I had no plans to redraft the existing pattern. A change to one part would require a change to another part, one that she didn't want changed, which meant *that* part would have to be changed to make it seem unchanged. Forget that. I started from scratch. I used the drawing I'd made under her supervision for reference. What Harriet didn't know wouldn't hurt her.

Once I had the pattern well under way, I took a break and returned Ray Marshall's call. I was delighted when his machine answered. That would make it a little easier to drop the bad news. I'd just started to leave a message, when Ray picked up the line. "I'm here," he said. "You caught me on my way out."

"That's okay, I can call back later." I hoped he'd go for that.

He didn't. "Sounds like the news isn't good," he said.

"I suppose it depends on your point of view," I said.

"Hit me with it."

"Doreen definitely knew about Gregory's affair."

"Damn. Gregory will be—"

"—reaping what he sowed," I said, completing Ray's sentence.

"He'll be devastated," said Ray.

"He's getting what he deserves."

"I understand how you feel, but Gregory's really not such a bad sort."

He sounded like Johnny defending Turner. "You keep saying that," I said. "You'll never convince me though. Gregory is a bad sort. So is his paramour. According to my informant, a woman in the acting class, that's how Doreen found out about the affair. It came straight from the horse's mouth, so to speak."

"Do you mean Gregory's ex?"

"Yep. When Gregory got involved with his ex again, the ex called Doreen and told her to keep her hands off Gregory. Nice, huh?"

"What a witch," said Ray.

I didn't tell Ray everything. I left out the part about the ex telling Doreen to keep her hands off Gregory "or else." It was probably exaggeration anyway, but the real reason I kept it from Ray was because it made the ex look like a suspect, an unnecessary complication. The ex may not be much of a lady as far as playing by the rules was concerned, but she couldn't have been a murderer because there'd been no murder. Doreen Sands had killed herself, a fact I couldn't share with Ray.

"Are you going to tell Gregory?" I asked.

"Yeah, sooner or later I'll have to tell him. Lucky me."

"I know exactly how you feel."

I finished up the pattern and had started cutting out pieces for Harriet's hat when the bells on the door jangled. I looked up. What a surprise. Turner was coming in. Bigger surprise. He was toting my two hard case travel hatboxes.

"Good afternoon, Detective. I see you 'found' my 'lost' hatboxes." I made no attempt to tone down the sarcasm.

"Yes," he said. "Damnedest thing. They turned up after all." He put them down on the counter.

He could have at least mentioned Gundermutter's role in finding the hatboxes. I was beginning to think Turner was just as much of a jerk as I always said I thought he was.

"I don't suppose the gun also 'turned up'?"

"The gun did not turn up. Please, Ms. Midnight, don't make a big deal out of this. Be happy I got the hatboxes back for you."

I was. And even more so when I opened the hatboxes and saw all my sample hats, resting peacefully on their bed of tissue paper, in perfect condition.

"Thank you," I said.

I had to bite my tongue to hold back all the other thanks I had in mind. Like: thank you very much for using me and my hatboxes in your plot to cover your own ass, thank you very very much for allowing me to think, for however short a time, that I might possibly be a suspect, and then all the other milliners, and Fuzzy . . .

"You're welcome," he said. He looked ill at ease.

"Does this mean the Doreen Sands case is officially closed?"

"No. Not closed, but not a high priority either. It's like this, Ms. Midnight. Enough time has passed that we no longer feel it necessary to keep up pretenses. To that end, we pulled Gundermutter off."

"I know, she told me. She's quite upset, you know. She thought she'd turned up some promising leads at Castleberry's."

"Since when have you been talking to Gundermutter?"

"Wasn't it you who introduced me to Gundermutter and wanted me to talk to her? Since then, we bonded. But don't worry, I didn't tell her anything that would embarrass you. I assume she doesn't know about how you and McKinley—"

"No one knows, Ms. Midnight. Only you, and me, and Detective McKinley, and whoever else you've blabbed to."

"No one," I said. "Not even Johnny." After all the damaging lies Turner had told me, I felt I'd earned the right to one, maybe even two.

"I appreciate that," he said.

"I'm glad it worked out for you, Detective."

"Believe me, Ms. Midnight, it's better this way for everybody involved, including Ms. Sands's family and friends. It's a well-known fact that the murder of a loved one is somewhat easier to deal with than suicide."

"Even an unsolved murder?"

He glowered at me, a definitive nonverbal answer.

"Tell me, Detective, why do you think Doreen Sands killed herself?"

"I already told you. From the position of the gun as it related to the position of the body, a million technicalities. You wouldn't understand."

"That's not what I meant. Why do you think *she* did it. From what I hear Doreen Sands had a lot to live for." It saddened me to think she'd killed herself over a two-timing cad like Gregory. She should have shot him, not herself.

"One never knows, does one?" said Turner, shaking his head.

After that, Turner and I small talked. I told him about my sale to Soholo et Noca and how I hoped to satisfy a notoriously difficult customer.

"Good for you, Ms. Midnight. I always said you had lotsa pluck."

"Why thank you, Detective Turner."

"By the way, how's Johnny's book progressing?"

"He's working very hard, day and night."

"What's so difficult about a bunch of recipes and exercises? If he's having trouble on the aerobics angle, my sister—"

"I'll be sure to mention it to Johnny."

"Thank you, Ms. Midnight."

"And thank you, Detective Turner, for getting my hatboxes and hats back."

"Glad I could be of service."

Speaking of Johnny, I decided I wanted to. He picked up on the first ring.

"How about Angie's for dinner?" I said. "Sevenish, be there or—"

"That's a wonderful idea, Brenda. By this evening I'll be far too exhausted to cook. I've been testing and retesting my Hundred Sit-up crispy apple pudding. The recipe is almost perfected, but my abs have had just about all they can take."

On a Saturday night, Johnny and I were lucky to get into Angie's at all. The fact that we didn't get "our" booth didn't much matter. Jackhammer was positively thrilled; the table we got was right next to the kitchen, and Raphael kept the special little burger balls coming fast.

Halfway through my grilled cheese I switched from red wine to black coffee.

Johnny cocked his head in question.

"Long night ahead of me," I explained.

"I thought you were caught up with your work."

"I was. Then I got two big wholesale orders, and then a complicated custom order from Harriet."

"Who's she?"

"She's a very exacting customer. She knows millinery, but she's also a pain in the neck. Lesser milliners quake in her presence. I, Brenda Midnight, will rise to the challenge. The hat I am making will pass her grueling caliper test with flying colors."

"You've got spunk, Brenda."

"Turner called it pluck."

"Same difference. When did you talk to Turner?"

"He came by this afternoon to drop off the hatboxes he not-so-accidentally lost and then apparently lost for real. Gundermutter found them. And wouldn't you know, Turner took all the credit—not for the losing, but for the finding."

"Turner *is* Officer Gundermutter's superior. Anything an underling does . . ."

"Please," I said, "don't defend Turner. It pisses me off that he got clean away with his little coverup. I think that's really low down. And get this: he rationalizes that it's better for Doreen Sands's family to go right on believing she was murdered."

"It probably is," said Johnny. "With a suicide, there are many complicated issues. Everybody—friends, family, whomever—either blame themselves or each other for something they did or didn't do. I'm afraid I have to agree with Turner on that."

That came as no surprise. "I say Turner's little deception wreaks havoc with New York City crime statistics. I bet the mayor would have a few choice words if he knew. The truth is always best."

"I wouldn't be so sure," said Johnny. "Are you speaking from experience? Did you ever know anybody who committed suicide?"

"No."

"Well then, it's a safe bet that Turner knows more than you do on that subject. He's almost certainly had friends who blew themselves away. Cops do it all the time. Especially bad cops."

"Oh, so you finally admit there is such an entity as a bad cop?"

"I never said there were no bad cops. As a matter of fact, in Episode Six of *Tod Trueman* a bad cop kills himself after Tod catches him taking payoffs from a drug dealing pizza shop owner. And we've got another episode in the works. At the end—well, not the final, final end where I smooch the rescued girl, but the end before that end—the bad cop, realizing he's about to be exposed, sticks his gun in his mouth and kablooey, all over the kitchen table.''

27

Kablooey.

I couldn't shake the horrifying image of the cop's brains spilled out all over his kitchen table.

It made it damned near impossible to concentrate on Harriet's hat.

The splattered brain, that part was bad enough, but the image of the kitchen table haunted me more. To me kitchen tables have always seemed sunny and cheerful. Kitchen tables are about greeting a new day with a zest for life and an invigorating glass of fresh-squeezed orange juice. They're not about tragic endings. Kitchen tables are not about kablooey.

A vendor at the flea market specializes in nifty nineteen-fifties-type kitchen tables. Their improbable color combos, tacky materials, and general goofiness always make me smile. They're a hoot. I've got my eye on a pink and gray model with scalloped edges and four matching chairs in case I ever end up with what the local real estate industry refers to as an eat-in kitchen. Most New York kitchens, including mine, are of the stand-in variety, and only then if you're alone, not claustrophobic, and not overweight.

Thanks to Johnny's kablooey comment, I'd never again think of a kitchen table without seeing a cop face down on the pink Formica, the pool of red blood growing larger, moving toward a corny set of salt and pepper shakers shaped like straw hats.

I might have been looking at Harriet's hat, carefully placing my hand stitches at regular intervals, but what I saw were visions of cop heads face down on kitchen tables. The tables changed shapes and colors. So did the salt and pepper shakers, the blood, and even the cop's head. Sometimes the cop was a man, sometimes a woman.

The longer I worked, the faster the scenes changed, one ghastly vision shifted into another. The cop heads changed faster than the tables, and then all of a sudden it wasn't a cop anymore. I pictured Doreen Sands. She was in her office, face down on her desk in a pool of blood. There was not a salt or pepper shaker in sight.

Freeze frame. That image of Doreen Sands stuck. Doreen. Desk. Gun. Blood. Doreen. Desk. Something didn't fit. I thought and thought and finally realized it was the desk. It was not a kitchen table. And Doreen was in her office, not in her kitchen, and that was strange.

I tried to think like Doreen. If I, for whatever reason, had arrived at the end of my rope and had made the momentous decision to kill myself, why would I go to the office? Why not kill myself in the comfort of home, metaphorically the kitchen table?

The gun was all wrong, too.

Doreen Sands kept sleeping pills in her bathroom cabinet. Easy enough to wash down a handful with a glass of booze and never ever have trouble getting to sleep again. Wasn't that the female method of choice? Not guns. Guns were for men. Guns were for cops. Why would Doreen Sands go to all the trouble and considerable risk of stealing a gun from a cop, and then go to her office the next morning and shoot herself? Why would she take the hard way out?

I stood up and stretched. I splashed cold water on my face. I bent over to get blood to my head. No matter what I did, I couldn't get rid of the feeling that it wasn't all over yet. More than once I'd washed my hands of the Doreen Sands mess. It kept oozing back to the surface. And here it was again.

Turner's theory that Doreen Sands had killed herself was wrong. It was based on what he knew, his experience as a cop, an experience that, according to Johnny, included a lot of distraught cops blowing their brains out.

Turner was understandably shaken when he found Doreen's body along with his gun. He must have felt terribly guilty. Whether or not his rejection of Doreen's advances had caused her to kill herself, his gun had provided the means. Or so he thought. His guilt and subsequent freakout caused him and McKinley to wrongly conclude that her death was a suicide.

What was funny—well not funny, Doreen Sands was dead and that would never be funny, but ironic perhaps—was that the detectives' coverup story, that Doreen Sands had been murdered, was almost true.

But even though the detectives' lie was truer than their truth, it still missed the mark.

Yes, Doreen Sands had been murdered. However, it was not the work of a random robber who happened to be bopping by in the hallway. Once I threw out the suicide idea, the "or else" remark made by Gregory's ex-girlfriend-turned-current-girlfriend suddenly took on new significance.

Doreen Sands must have taken the remark as a direct threat. She was frightened, not thinking rationally. She swiped Turner's gun, but not to kill herself, as Turner believed. Doreen Sands wanted that gun to defend herself from the woman who told her to keep away from Gregory—or else.

It was probably an accident. Ms. Or Else must have gone to see Doreen. They got into an argument. Frightened, Doreen pulled out Turner's gun, they struggled, and the gun went off.

I knew how to find out the identity of Ms. Or Else. As soon as I did, I'd spill all the beans to the cops.

It was four o'clock in the morning when I figured all this out, too early to do anything about it. It was impossible to sleep, so I stayed up the rest of the night and worked on Harriet's hat.

Around seven in the morning, I tied off the last thread. I compared the hat to the sketch. I'd done an excellent job. I didn't like the hat, but it was exactly what Harriet had ordered, her vision, and I was proud of my precise handwork. It seemed really stupid to cover up all that work with the "scads of veiling" she wanted, but this was custom work and my job was not to design, it was to satisfy the customer. Sadly, obscuring my work, I draped veiling over the hat and fastened it with three strategically located stitches.

Done.

I wrapped the finished hat in tissue, eased it down into a large-size Midnight Millinery hatbox, closed the lid, and pulled the cord taut.

I waited until eight to call Ray Marshall.

"I wouldn't have guessed you'd be such an early riser," he said.

"Sometimes I am," I said. "Have you told Gregory yet?"

"No. He wasn't home when I called last night. I can't say I'm in any hurry."

"Good. Do me a favor and hold off for a while. I'd like to do some more checking before you tell him. That information I got was second hand, and it came from a total stranger. It could have been made up for all I know. I wouldn't want to be responsible for spreading hurtful lies. Do you happen to know the name of Gregory's ex? I'd rather hear it from her. I could call on some pretense and—"

"No."

"Oh. Well you could find out, couldn't you? Ask Gregory. I'd really like to talk to that woman."

"You misunderstood," said Ray. "I didn't mean no, I didn't know the name of Gregory's ex. I do know her name. What I meant was no, you're barking up the wrong tree. You see, I already asked her if she told Doreen. And she had. She told her, 'Stay away from Gregory, or else.' "

I was confused. I seriously needed to get some sleep.

Ray continued. "You're probably thinking that maybe this woman who would threaten Doreen Sands, made good on the threat and killed her."

"It's possible."

"You're barking up the other side of the wrong tree."

"Oh."

"And in case you're wondering how I know so god-damn much about it, I regret to say she was with me that morning."

Had I heard right? "Doreen?"

"No, not Doreen. I was with Gregory's so-called ex. Her name, by the way, is Elyse. I guess you could say I'm her alibi."

"Elyse. You mean, you and she . . . you and your friend's . . ." I was floored. This was not the Ray Marshall I knew.

"It's not what you think," said Ray. "Well, it is what you think, but it's probably not as bad as you think. They'd already broken up when I met Elyse. At first, I didn't even know they knew each other. I now believe she engineered meeting me simply because I lived in Gregory's building. She used me to stay close to Gregory, so she could keep tabs on what he was doing and who he was doing it with, which happened to be Doreen. Then, when the time was right, Elyse made her move. She bla-tantly seduced Gregory. He took the bait. But that wasn't enough for Elyse. Oh no. She had to tell Doreen about the affair."

"Including the 'or else' statement?"

"Yes, including that. She told me she didn't mean any-thing by it."

It didn't much matter whether she meant it. She obvi-ously hadn't done it, not if she was with Ray when it happened.

Ray Marshall was a good man. He was brave to admit he'd been duped and used by this Elyse person. I felt bad for him. I even felt a tiny bit bad for Gregory. Most of all I felt bad for Doreen Sands.

So, my new theory of murder was short-lived. Gregory's ex-ex Elyse hadn't killed Doreen Sands. That is, she hadn't pulled the trigger. Doreen Sands had done that herself, just as Turner and McKinley said. Legally, the fact that Elyse had driven Doreen to suicide counted for nothing.

Like it or not, I'd have to get used to the fact that Doreen Sands had killed herself.

Easier said than done. No matter how hard I tried, I could not convince myself that Doreen Sands had committed suicide. Instead, I went back to an earlier possibility, one I liked even less. Fuzzy.

I restructured the scenario. Unfortunately, the facts fit.

In this version Doreen Sands is planning to knock off Fuzzy's new line of hats. Fuzzy somehow finds out. Fuzzy, unarmed and not planning any violence, goes to Doreen Sands's office to confront her. It was easy enough to imagine Fuzzy coming off way too strong in this endeavor. Doreen Sands has Turner's gun to protect herself from Elyse. Fuzzy's aggressive behavior frightens Doreen. Doreen flashes the gun and tells Fuzzy to get out. Fuzzy makes a dive for the gun. It goes off. Doreen Sands dies. Fuzzy flees. Turner finds the gun, sees that it is his.

That's where I and my hatboxes came into the story.

I really hated this.

The time had come to tell the cops everything.

First I called Gundermutter. She wasn't home, nor was she at the precinct. I tried her cell phone, but she didn't answer that either. I hoped she was on her Harley on her way to the precinct. If I still couldn't contact her in an hour, I'd call Turner and McKinley. I couldn't sit on this information much longer.

I locked up the shop and took Jackhammer for a walk over to West Street. I found a stoop to sit on, and stared across the Hudson at New Jersey. While I pondered life and death, Jackhammer frolicked in the rubble.

My stomach was in knots. I was close to tears. I didn't want it to be Fuzzy. Fuzzy was my friend. Fuzzy also had a good motive, and I'd managed to figure out how it had happened.

Now there'd be no Milliners Milling Around the Millennium show. I was saddened to think she'd never get the tale of babushka burnings up on her web page, not unless she could do it from a prison cell.

I thought back, remembering how Fuzzy had said Doreen Sands could have sold purple babushkas—or anything else for that matter—as couture millinery. And what was it Bucky the Third had said when I was buying supplies? He didn't approve of millinery departments that sell everything but the kitchen sink as millinery. He said it was bad for business because it confused the customer. It seemed to me anything that sold was good for business. The Downtown Buyer certainly would have agreed with Bucky though. He had such a bad reaction to my little hatlettes, he denigrated them as hair baubles. Doodads. My ego hadn't been too badly bruised, especially when he placed an order for my real millinery. Still, it kind of irked me. Doreen Sands would have bought them.

That was it, of course. Doreen Sands would have bought the hatlettes, and marked them up, and sold them. I finally realized the significance of this. I now knew whose business Doreen Sands had hurt with her amazing abilities to sell anything as millinery. It was the hair accessories buyer, the woman who'd given Gundermutter a beaded barrette. Her department was losing ground to millinery. That meant she had a motive.

Maybe, just maybe, things were looking up. Maybe it wasn't Fuzzy, after all.

28

I needed to get into Doreen Sands's office. I didn't know how to do it. It was Sunday; Castleberry's wouldn't be open until noon. That gave me about three hours to come up with a plan.

Back in the apartment, I curled up on my banana-shaped couch to think it all through one more time. Jackhammer wedged himself into the triangle of space behind my knees.

I dozed off and found myself in the middle of a complex multimedia dream. There was a of tug of war going on. Instead of rope the opponents yanked at a several-yards-long strip of black lattice-type veiling. Back and forth, they pulled. With every pull, drums sounded, laser lights pulsed to the beat, and a background chorus of milliners cheered and booed. The faces of the two opponents were completely swathed in veiling. I knew one of them was Doreen Sands. I approached the unknown opponent, grabbed onto the veiling, and yanked.

And woke up before the face was revealed.

It didn't matter. First off, it was only a dream. And second, if the killer really was who I thought, I'd never set eyes on the person.

I had a job title, Buyer of Hair Accessories, Castleberry's department store. The motive was simple professional jealousy and self-preservation in the cutthroat

world of fashion retailing. Opportunity? That was easy.
She worked at Castleberry's. She could go anywhere in
the store and no one would give it a second thought.

If I'd stayed in that dream longer, I would have seen
Doreen Sands win the tug of war. And then ultimately
lose.

"I'll call this perfume Veiled Threat," I said.

"That sounds a little too late eighties, don't you
think?" said Elizabeth. "Wicked isn't in any more. This
year, everything's coming up all icky sweetness and light.
Cheerful freckle-faced models with unrealistic healthy
glows and sunlit hair cavort in sweatsuits. Children and
kittens roll around in the background among the flowers."

Elizabeth and I were standing in her bathroom, leaning
over her old-style pedestal sink, draining several old per-
fumes through a funnel into an antique crystal bottle, cre-
ating a new scent. A big-bulbed atomizer with silk tassels
lay on the edge of the sink.

"Exactly," I said. "That means, as we speak, wicked
is trending up. These things go in cycles. What's next is
always a reaction to what's now."

"Speaking of reactions," said Elizabeth. "Mine, when
you told me about Chuck? Remember?"

"Yes. You said you didn't know whether to be flattered
or insulted."

"That's what I said, all right, but I was dead wrong.
The correct reaction, the reaction I had as soon as you
were gone, was angrier than I've ever been. The nerve of
that Chuck Riley to think . . . well, I can't even find words
to describe how I feel. I've got a good mind to tell that
idiot that I *am* his mother. I'll say that on the first day of
his pitiful life I dumped him in front of a church because
I could see he was going to be a frizzy-red-headed gigantic pain in the kazooie. That'd serve him right. I'd love
to see him twist in the wind."

I should never have told her about Chuck's nutty de-
lusion.

"Have you talked to him yet?"

"No."

I opened the last of the old bottles, a square one with a round top, sniffed the unfamiliar perfume, and passed it under Elizabeth's nose.

"Oh my god," she said, "that really takes me back." She got a wistful look on her face. At least for the moment she didn't appear to be thinking about Chuck.

"Scents are like that," I said. "The odor of graphite always gets me going. I remember a drawing class where . . ."

Elizabeth wasn't paying attention. She was somewhere far away. Her eyes were closed and she swayed slightly in a nonexistent breeze.

"Are you all right?" I asked.

She opened her eyes. "Yes. Just remembering. I was wearing this perfume when I got arrested. During the ride to the lockup I kept sniffing my wrist. It covered up the stench of urine and sweat and fear and puke in the paddy wagon."

"You got arrested?"

"Does a bear shit in the woods? Sure I got arrested. Lots of times, overnighters, but this time was the big one. I served three months for refusing to testify against a friend, a charismatic organizer, then the son of a bitch betrayed me. Turned out he really had done everything the government had accused him of, and then some. I fell for his story and then for him, head over heels. I don't want to think about it. It's totally embarrassing." She sniffed the perfume again. "I haven't been the same since."

"Is that when you gave up painting?"

For a moment she got that faraway look again, then snapped out of it. "I don't want to talk about it."

Funny, for a moment she sounded like Chuck.

"Do you want to save this perfume?" I asked.

"No, go ahead and add it to the brew."

When the antique bottle was filled to the top, I took out the funnel, twisted in the atomizer, and gave it a test squirt.

Elizabeth, fully back to the present and herself again, wrinkled her nose and made a face. "Yuck. Smells like bathroom deodorant in a green-tiled gas station in the middle of nowhere and it's midnight and the car with your mattress tied to the roof broke down and the soda machine's on the blink.''

"It'll be perfect."

"Now," said Elizabeth, "please explain to me why you dragged me out of bed on Sunday morning to formulate this atrocious new scent."

"I don't know. Inspiration hit and—"

"Yeah, right. Who do you think you're kidding? Knowing you, I bet it's got something to do with the Doreen Sands murder."

"Well, yes," I admitted. "It sort of does have something to do with that."

"I thought you were off that case for good. If I remember correctly, your exact words were—"

"Whatever I said, much has changed since I said it."

I elaborated, winding up with the story of the babushka burnings. "And that got me thinking about hats that weren't really hats, that were more like hair accessories. Then this idea hit me like a ton of hatblocks and I realized that the Castleberry's hair accessories buyer killed Doreen Sands."

Elizabeth looked at me like I was nuts. "Who is this person?"

"I don't know. That's one of the things I plan to find out when I go to Castleberry's."

"Since when do you believe in guilt by job description? You've been working too hard, Brenda. You could use a vacation."

"It makes perfect sense," I said, defending my theory. "There's opportunity. The person works in the store. And motive. You have to understand that the enormous success of Doreen Sands's millinery department came at the expense of the hair accessories department. As millinery took over more and more floor space, hair accessories shrank. It's like a territorial war, the Barrettes versus the Berets. I figure the last straw was when Doreen started buying hats that weren't true millinery—in other words she bought what many consider to be hair accessories—

and sold them in the millinery department. Where do you think that left the hair accessories department?''

Elizabeth shrugged.

''Out in the cold, that's where. Shoved into a hard-to-find dark crevice of the store. Next stop, a blanket out front on Sixth Avenue. I would have put all the pieces together sooner, except Turner and McKinley threw me for a loop with that suicide bit. That was their world view, not reality.''

Elizabeth rolled her eyes. ''Only Brenda Midnight could come up with a millinery motive for murder.''

''Not murder. Probably manslaughter. I believe it was more or less an accident. Don't forget, Doreen Sands was the person packing the gun. If she hadn't stolen it from Turner to protect herself from her fiancé's ex ex-girlfriend, she'd be alive.''

''What's the deal with the perfume? You still haven't explained why we made that.''

''Veiled Threat is my entrée to the back rooms of Castleberry's. I'm going undercover as a spritzer.''

''Please don't, Brenda. If what you say turns out to be right, then what you're doing is far too dangerous.''

''What could possibly happen? Nobody will ever guess I'm not legit. Spritzers are not part of the regular store staff. They're hired through an outside agency that handles out-of-work actors and models, different ones every day. There's always some new perfume being launched. Who's to say Veiled Threat doesn't really exist? So, you see, I'll be perfectly all right. Besides, immediately afterwards, I'm going straight to the cops, preferably Gundermutter, to tell all.''

''Promise?''

''That's my plan,'' I said. Not quite a promise, but Elizabeth didn't protest.

On my way out of her apartment, I turned to Elizabeth. ''You didn't mean what you said about Chuck twisting in the wind, did you?''

''Of course not, but I am very angry. Smoldering.''

*   *   *

My plan was a bit more vague than I'd led Elizabeth to believe. I wasn't sure what I was after, but was confident I'd know when I found it. Basically my plan was to hang out, poke around, and ask questions of employees—essentially do the job Gundermutter should have done. If I could get into Doreen Sands's office, no telling what I'd come up with.

I figured no one else had searched her office. Not Turner and McKinley. They were positive she'd committed suicide. Not Gundermutter. She was too busy hanging out on the loading dock dreaming up drug conspiracies.

Deep down, I knew I was only grasping at straws in a last-ditch attempt to prove that Fuzzy had not killed Doreen Sands before I had to tell the cops what I knew and cast suspicion on her.

There was a big problem. Say my plan went off without a snag and I found out who'd killed Doreen Sands. What would I do about Turner and McKinley?

Once the hair accessories buyer was caught, the detectives' convoluted stories wouldn't jibe. In order to get off, the guilty party, the hair accessories buyer, would probably claim self-defense, and in describing what had happened, would no doubt mention freaking out and leaving the weapon with the body. As far as the killer knew, the gun belonged to Doreen Sands. How would Turner and McKinley explain that the gun was not found with the body, that it ended up in my hatbox, and then got lost in the system?

To hell with it, I thought. My concern was truth and justice and showing that Fuzzy was innocent before anyone thought she wasn't. Turner and McKinley's problems were just that: Turner and McKinley's problems. Not mine.

For now, I had a new perfume to launch.

29

Any spritzer worth a squirt is dressed head to toe in black. Not a problem for this downtown New Yorker. I put on the catsuit and black patent high heels I'd planned to wear for the Milliners Milling show—that is, if there was a show. I was doing what I could to assure it would go on.

I pouted and postured in front of the mirror, bottle of the about-to-be-launched Veiled Threat held high. I practiced style and attitude, but I didn't let loose with any more test squirts. The fewer whiffs I got of that stuff, the better.

Overall, the look was suitably severe for the product. I threw on a jean jacket, gave Jackhammer a steamed green bean, explained why he couldn't come along, and went over to Midnight Millinery to pick out a hat to complete my perfume-pushing ensemble.

I had lots of veiling left over from Harriet's hat. I cut off a half yard or so, doubled it over, and wrapped it around the perfume bottle. I allowed a seductive peek of the crystal to show through in spots. At the top of the bottle I tied off the veiling with a bow of bright red banding ribbon.

Veiled Threat was now properly packaged and ready for its department store debut.

Next I needed a hat. I carried a length of veiling around the shop, draping it over my display hats, to see which would look best. They all looked equally ridiculous. I don't like veiling; I don't design for veiling. The easy solution was to wear the hat I'd made for Harriet. It was already veiled, and in my opinion, already looked ridiculous.

I lifted Harriet's hat out of the box, and started to put it on when I noticed it didn't have a Midnight Millinery label sewn inside. Amazing. I'd been so careful to get the details absolutely perfect, then I'd forgotten my label. That's what I got for working all night long. I was glad I caught it before Harriet picked up the hat. I'd have been very embarrassed. It was too late to do anything about it now, but I wrote a note to myself, reminding me to take care of it as soon as I got back from Castleberry's.

I put the hat on and looked in the mirror. It worked okay with the rest of my outfit. Harriet would never know it had been worn as long as I was careful to keep the hat upwind of the spritzes of perfume.

I didn't want to attract undue attention on my trek through the Village, so I put Harriet's hat and the Veiled Threat perfume bottle in a generic I LOVE NEW YORK bag. Then I headed over to Sixth Avenue.

I got to Castleberry's not long after it opened. The store was already a madhouse, thanks to a Silly Sunday Sale Daze promotion. Good, I thought. Chaos and crowds would make my job easier. I swooshed through the revolving doors, stepped behind a pillar in the sock department, stuffed my jean jacket into the bag, and put Harriet's hat on my head.

Presto-chango, I was ready to spritz.

Except for the I LOVE NEW YORK bag. I figured it didn't look any too classy hanging down at my side. I'd planned well, but not well enough. I slunk behind another pillar, took my jean jacket out of the bag, stuck the bag into the jacket pocket, and draped the jacket over my arm. Not the ideal situation, but it was better than the dangling plastic bag.

I have to admit, accosting innocent shoppers was an absolute delight, so much fun that I almost forgot my true mission.

My first hit, a lawyer type with a coral-colored cardigan sweater knotted around her neck, pushed a kid in a very expensive, terribly trendy name-brand stroller. As she rolled past me I struck. I held the bottle out, smiled sweetly, and said, "Veiled Threat?"

I got her on the wrist.

She sniffed it and said, "Not half bad."

"Fabulously decadent," was the verdict of my next victim, a farm-fresh blond. "Tell me, where is the Veiled Threat counter?"

"Over there," I said, with a vague sweep of my hand toward the back of the store.

Remembering one of my goals, I spritzed my way over to the hair accessories counter.

"May I help you?" asked the sales clerk. "We recently got in a new shipment of to-die-for rhinestone barrettes." A dozen in various bright colors ran down the left side of her crimped jet-black hair.

"I hope so," I said. "But I'm really not interested in buying barrettes. You see, I work here too, unfortunately just for the day. I thought I'd take a little break from spritzing. I wondered if I might ask you some questions about your job."

"Yeah, sure. It's all right, I guess. But why?"

"You know how it is. The damned rent is due every month. I need a more permanent gig. Spritzing isn't all it's cracked up to be. Hair accessories looks like an interesting spot."

She shrugged. "It's a job."

"Then again," I said, "this Veiled Threat promotion has got me into wearing hats. Maybe I should apply for a job in the millinery department instead."

"Same difference," she said.

"What do you mean?"

"I've heard rumors. We're supposed to get merged with the millinery department."

That was the answer I wanted.

"Thank you," I said. "Thank you very much."

"When you apply for the job, use me as a reference. If they hire you, I'll get a twenty-five-dollar bonus."

* * *

Buoyed up, I spritzed a few more innocents on the first floor, then took the escalator to the second floor where I stationed myself in front of the elevator bank, and merrily spritzed people as they got off. When an up-headed elevator stopped and all the passengers got off, I got on and pushed the button for the top floor. That's where the buying offices, employee lounge, returns, and credit department were located.

Unless someone was putting in overtime, I figured the individual buyers' offices would be closed on Sunday. Everything else should be open and fully functional.

A plan began to take form. First, I'd hang out in the employee lounge for the fifteen-minute break required by law. No one would question that. Then, on the way out, being brand new to the job, I'd simply make a wrong turn and end up in the buyers' corridor, lost, and probably alone. If I got that far, I'd play it by ear.

I stood out too much to poke around on this floor. The Veiled Threat getup had to go. I removed Harriet's hat, put it back in the I LOVE NEW YORK bag along with the perfume bottle, and slipped on my jean jacket.

According to plan, I found the employee lounge, went in, and flopped down in a plastic chair. Three employees sat around a table drinking coffee. They nodded when I came in. I nodded back. They returned to griping about their supervisors.

I took off one of my shoes and began to massage my toes, grimacing occasionally as if they hurt. After I finished with my toes, I picked up a news magazine, stuck it in front of my face, and pretended to read. I was really thinking about how to get into Doreen Sands's office once I located it, and what I might find after I got in. There had to be some clue that would point to the hair accessories buyer as the killer. Or if not, then somebody else. As long as it wasn't Fuzzy, I didn't care.

The office door probably wouldn't have much of a lock. I hoped not, because I wasn't much of a lock picker. In fact, if it took more than a jab with a straightened-out hair pin, it'd be way out of my league.

That's what I meant by playing it by ear. If I got lucky maybe the cleaning crew would be on the job, opening doors, emptying trash, vacuuming floors, and I could sneak into Doreen's office. Or, I could stay in the store overnight, and see if the mannequins came alive and complained about their jobs, and if vicious dogs patrolled the aisles.

I never located Doreen Sands's office, never got to check out what kind of lock it had, never had an opportunity to play it by ear. Deep in thought, I didn't hear the door of the employee lounge open. Nor did I see the other employees make a fast exit.

A firm hand on my shoulder startled me. "You'll have to come along with us, Miss."

It was all that back-and-forth in-and-out action with the I LOVE NEW YORK bag. They were positive I'd shoplifted Harriet's hat.

Under the scrutiny of Castleberry's crack security Rent-A-Cop team, my Veiled Threat cover story fell apart. I had no Castleberry's pass, no ID card from the alleged Veiled Threat distributor, and nobody had ever heard of Veiled Threat, or a Sunday launch. To further complicate matters, Harriet's hat didn't have my Midnight Millinery label in it, so I couldn't prove I'd made it.

They took me into a brightly lighted room and made me sit on a small, hard chair, similar to the one Turner and McKinley used, but without the squeak. Across from me, the man who was to play Good Rent-A-Cop sat in a similar chair, smiling. Standing over me was Bad Rent-A-Cop, hands on his beefy hips, massive frown on his face.

"Where'd you get that hat?" he growled.

"I made it. I'm a milliner."

Blank stare from both Rent-A-Cops.

"That's my profession," I explained. "I make hats."

"I'm afraid, Miss, the only thing you made was a big mistake. A very big mistake. Castleberry's does not take shoplifting lightly. We prosecute criminals like you to the full extent of the law."

Good Rent-A-Cop got into the act. "Let her have her say." He shook his head in mock exasperation at the bullying ways of his mean-spirited colleague. He wanted to give me enough rope to hang myself.

Before I attempted another explanation, a woman opened the door and stepped into the interrogation room.

"She's the one," she said, pointing a long, pink-tipped forefinger at me.

I sneaked a peek at her name tag. Dolores from the return department.

Dolores continued. "I saw her skulking around the hallway, acting suspicious. I recognized the hat as one of ours. She must have worn it up here from the selling floor. Then, when she thought no one was looking, she sneaked it into her I LOVE NEW YORK bag."

I spoke up. "If that's true, how'd I get the anti-theft device off? Search me. I don't have one of those detagging machines."

"We don't put antitheft devices on our hats," said Dolores. "You should have cased the joint better before you made your move."

I'd never noticed. Antitheft tags are the kind of thing that are awfully irritating when they're there, but when they're not, you don't even think about them.

Good Rent-A-Cop did not look happy. "Every item in the store is supposed to be tagged."

"That's not good," said Bad Rent-A-Cop, shaking his head.

"I agree," said Dolores. "Our millinery buyer wouldn't let us tag the hats. She claimed it made them impossible to try on. I suppose that'll all be changing now."

"What do you mean?" asked Good Rent-A-Cop.

"She's the one who got whacked," explained Bad Rent-A-Cop. "Now can we get back to our shoplifter?"

Dolores left the room.

"Am I under arrest?" I directed the question to Good Rent-A-Cop.

Bad Rent-A-Cop answered. "The NYPD will take care

of that. You'll be damned sorry you shoplifted at Castle-berry's.''

"I'd like to make a telephone call.''

No answer from either Rent-A-Cop.

"It's the law,'' I said.

Bad Rent-A-Cop looked at Good Rent-A-Cop. Good Rent-A-Cop shrugged.

"All right. You can use the pay phone in the hallway. Don't you go getting any ideas about escaping.''

Good Rent-A-Cop led me to the phone, leaned up against the wall in hearing range, and watched me.

I dialed Gundermutter's cell phone. Please, please, please, I thought, answer this time.

She did. "Gundermutter,'' she said.

"Are you on duty?''

"Yes.''

I lowered my voice and, using as few words as possible, I explained the situation. "They're gonna call the cops.''

"I'll try to head off the boys in blue,'' she said. "Wish me luck.''

I knew Gundermutter had succeeded when fifteen minutes later she came into the little room where I sat listening to the two Rent-A-Cops tell me how foolish I'd been to mess with Castleberry's.

"Whatcha got for me, boys?'' Gundermutter was either chewing gum or pretending to. Whichever, it added the perfect touch.

"Shoplifter,'' sneered Bad Rent-A-Cop out of the side of his mouth. "Says she works for some perfume outfit.''

"Hmmm,'' said Gundermutter. "Likely story. What'd she boost?''

"Hat,'' said Good Rent-A-Cop.

"A hat?'' Gundermutter gave me a questioning look, caught herself, then turned back to Good Rent-A-Cop, and said, "May I see the alleged stolen item in question?''

Good Rent-A-Cop handed her the hat. "Claims it's hers.''

Gundermutter examined it. "No electronic device at-tached, no price tag. What makes you think the alleged stolen item in question was in fact stolen?''

"Perp acted suspicious. Our return coordinator observed the perp sneak the alleged stolen item in question into an I LOVE NEW YORK bag.'' He went on to explain the lack of antitheft device. "Perp must have yanked off the price tag. That's easy enough.''

"May I speak with the witness of the alleged criminal act?'' asked Gundermutter.

"Of course,'' said Good Rent-A-Cop.

Good Rent-A-Cop and Gundermutter went off to see the return coordinator, leaving me alone with Bad Rent-A-Cop. He crossed his arms and glared down at me.

A few minutes later, Gundermutter returned, carrying the I LOVE NEW YORK bag and a Castleberry's bag. "I'll take the prisoner off your hands now.''

With that, Gundermutter grabbed my arm, a bit harshly I thought, and ushered me onto the elevator and out of the store.

30

Freedom. It was great to be out of Castleberry's or, more precisely, out of that tiny stuffy interrogation room. Really great to be away from the Rent-A-Cops, both Good and Bad.

The sun was out, the day brisk and invigorating. Horns honked, cab drivers cursed, people waited in long lines outside popular brunch spots. Sunday in the city was fully underway.

Gundermutter's patrol car was double parked on Sixth Avenue.

She hadn't said a word. I figured it was up to me to break the ice. "Good job, Gundermutter. How'd you manage to get rid of your partner? How'd you divert the cops who were on their way to Castleberry's to arrest me? You pulled off a major coup. You know that, don't you?"

She unlocked the passenger side door and tossed my bag and the Castleberry's bag into the back seat. "Just get in."

"Front seat?" I asked, only half joking.

She grunted. I took it for a yes and got in. She walked around the front of the vehicle to the driver's side. I leaned over and unlocked her door. Seconds later she peeled out, then turned west onto Fourteenth Street running a red light, flying, and intentionally hitting every pot hole—a skill she'd no doubt picked up from Turner.

Gundermutter was mad at me.

At Ninth Avenue she aimed the vehicle downtown, then

west into the meat district where she pulled up next to an idling truck that had come all the way from somewhere in Kansas. The truck driver was probably asleep in the cab, waiting to unload sides of beef when the meat packers opened up shop in the wee hours of Monday morning.

Gundermutter shut off the engine and turned to me. Her face was red, mouth tense. "Do you have any idea the trouble I could be in because of your stupid stunt? That *you* could be in? That *we* could be in?"

"I'm sorry." I couldn't think of anything better to say.

Gundermutter, however, could.

I didn't take any of it personally.

At the end of her tirade she sucked in a big breath, blew it all out, and came very close to almost cracking a smile.

I think she felt much better having gotten that off her chest.

Unfortunately, she still expected an explanation.

I took a moment to consider where to begin. It would be impossible to begin at the beginning without telling her how Doreen Sands had stolen Turner's gun. I didn't want to do that. Gundermutter wouldn't believe it anyway.

So, I told her little bits and pieces, leaving out big blocks of the story that related to Turner. I also left out the part about how Turner and McKinley had used her, sent her off on what they considered a wild goose chase. I didn't want to be the one to break her heart.

What it finally came down to was this. "It's like I had a hunch about the hair accessories buyer," I said. "I'm pretty sure she killed Doreen Sands. I would have told you, or Turner and McKinley, but I didn't want to bother you guys, know what I mean, not until I knew for sure. So, I went undercover as a spritzer."

"And?"

"And nothing. Veiled Threat went over well with shoppers. Oh yeah, I did hear from a salesperson that the hair accessories department was merging with millinery, so I think I was on the right track, but I never got a look-see into Doreen Sands's office. I'd hoped to find more specific clues to prove my hunch."

"Clues?" repeated Gundermutter. "You were looking for clues?"

"Well, yes. I was. Looking for clues. One or two." I had to admit, said like that, it did sound unrealistic.

Gundermutter didn't think it was unrealistic at all. Brilliant was what she called it, but with lots of sarcasm, raising her eyes skyward as she did so. "So, you were looking for clues, skulking around the employee corridor, acting like a shoplifter."

"All right," I said. "I can see why they might have been suspicious at first. But it was my own hat I put in the bag, a custom job, one of a kind. What made them get the idea it came from Castleberry's?"

"Perhaps this little item might have done the trick." She reached into the back seat and retrieved both bags. She took Harriet's hat out of the I LOVE NEW YORK bag and handed it to me. Then, with a flourish, she took Harriet's hat out of the Castleberry's bag and handed that hat to me.

Two Harriet's hats? I was stunned speechless.

"I thought you'd like to see both of these," she said, "so I told your Rent-A-Cop pals I needed them as evidence to make a case against you," she said. "Pretty clever of me, don't you think?"

I examined both hats carefully. They were virtually the same design, although mine was better made. It was all in the hand stitching. "I made one of these, but not the other."

"Except for the lack of any identifying labels in yours, they look exactly the same to me."

"They're not, but only a milliner can tell." Or Harriet, I thought.

Gundermutter said, "One of these, presumably the one you did not make, was sitting around in the return department waiting to be reshelved. The hat was right there in the room with Dolores when she saw you sneaking your hat into your bag. She is a cautious woman. She didn't jump to conclusions and immediately call security. She didn't want any lawsuits for false arrest. Before taking action, she called down to the millinery department.

The sales associate told her that Castleberry's had an exclusive on that particular design. Do you catch my drift? Do you see where this leads?''

I saw. Very, very clearly.

Gundermutter's radio squawked. "Gotta go," she said. "Take both of these hats with you. I have enough to explain to my partner already."

"Don't you have to arrest me?"

"Nah," she said. "It's a safe bet that Castleberry's security goons won't bother with a followup. That would only complicate their jobs. Besides, they assume a highly skilled NYPD professional such as myself will deal with you appropriately. Justice will be served and you'll never try another stunt like that again, at least not at Castleberry's."

I put both hats back into the bags and got out of the car. "Thanks," I said. "I owe you big."

At last Gundermutter smiled. "I know."

She sped east, leaving me to ponder.

I picked up Jackhammer at the apartment, and took him and both of the hats over to Midnight Millinery. Once there, I placed them side by side on my table and turned on a high-intensity lamp. My workmanship was far superior. That's because I'd not merely knocked off a hat, I'd knocked myself out knocking it off.

I wanted to rip it to shreds. The worst was that Harriet had tricked me into believing the hat was her special vision.

Fuzzy had been absolutely one hundred percent right about Harriet. I wished I'd heeded the many warnings. She was much more than a difficult customer. Thanks to her, I'd not only knocked off someone else's design, I'd almost been arrested, and had blown my one chance to get into Doreen Sands's office to look for clues.

Deep down I knew most of the blame was mine. It had been my stupid idea to wear Harriet's hat as part of my Veiled Threat getup. It's just that Harriet was so damned easy to blame for everything. Next thing I knew, I'd be trying to pin the murder on her too.

*   *   *

Well, why not?

The idea stuck around. The longer it stuck around, the more credibility it gained. Soon I could think of nothing else. When Gundermutter had first showed me the other hat, I'd been too confused, stunned, and angry to pay attention to the details of what she'd been telling me. Now I remembered. The hat, she had said, had been sitting around Castleberry's return department. Obvious conclusion: someone had returned the hat. I now believed that someone was Harriet.

It made sense. Harriet bought lots of hats. I had always thought of her as dealing directly with milliners, but she probably bought any hat she liked, wherever she found it. This particular hat was an exclusive, available only at Castleberry's. I considered for a moment the possibility that Harriet was part of a larger conspiracy to knock off hats. I didn't think so. She was just not in a position to know whatever it was Doreen Sands had been up to.

It was much more simple. Harriet saw the hat at Castleberry's. Harriet wanted the hat. So Harriet bought the hat. Then, Harriet being Harriet, she was dissatisfied with the hat, and took it back to complain.

By having me make the exact same hat, Harriet would still get the style she wanted, only made to her specifications, and if she complained long and loud enough, it was a safe bet I'd throw her and the hat out of Midnight Millinery, and she'd end up with the hat for free. I should have insisted on a deposit. If I was right, there was a lot more at stake than money.

Unlike me, or any other individual milliner, Castleberry's couldn't fix a returned hat. Nor would they ever argue with a customer. They'd smile and refund the money without question. But Harriet lusted after a good argument, thrived on being a pain in the neck, and so she'd forced her way into Doreen Sands's office.

I was assuming quite a bit. I assumed it was Harriet who had bought the hat at Castleberry's. I assumed it was Harriet who had returned the same hat. And, I assumed I could come up with a way to find out.

If it turned out Harriet had returned the hat the morning Doreen Sands had been killed, it meant . . . well, it didn't really mean anything for sure, but it might, and if it did, I had another suspect who wasn't Fuzzy.

Harriet made such a wonderful suspect. She was so much fun to hate.

I resisted the temptation to call Gundermutter. It would be easy for her to get the information I wanted, but I didn't want to explain why I wanted it. I also didn't think it too terribly wise to ask her for another favor so soon.

So I sat down and thought and came up with a way to get the information myself. It would have to wait for tomorrow though. Meanwhile, I would proceed as if nothing unusual had happened.

Customers came in. I sold hats. At the end of the day I sewed my Midnight Millinery label into Harriet's hat.

A little before closing time, I gave Harriet a call. "Your hat will be ready for pickup early tomorrow afternoon."

"I'll be there," she said.

31

I woke to the sound of a car alarm going off in the hallway. It cycled through three distinct patterns—a short rhythmic attention grabber, a haunting wail, and a dynamic, phase-shifting whoop.

A car in the hallway? Getting its radio stolen?

That made no sense. I figured it had to be a dream, and went back to having it.

But then I heard Jackhammer barking. When I told him to stop, he kept right on barking, only louder and more frantically, and I knew it was not a dream. In my dreams Jackhammer always does precisely what he's told. He also does the laundry, irons my clothes, and has a seven-figure income. In my dreams.

The alarm stopped.

Jackhammer didn't.

I got off the mattress and went to investigate. Jackhammer stopped barking and scrambled around my ankles.

"What is it?"

I pushed my ear up against the metal door, which amplified and, at the same time, muddied the sound. Voices. I couldn't make out what was being said, or who was saying it, but it was evident the speakers were angry. I listened for blood-curdling screams. There were none, so I threw on my robe, picked up Jackhammer, and stepped out into the hallway.

Several neighbors stood around taking in the scene. I

didn't see Elizabeth anywhere, but my next-door neighbor Julia was standing halfway down the hall. She looked like a cinderblock wrapped in a tie-dyed muu-muu.

"Well, well, well, look who finally got up," she said.

"What's going on?" I asked. "It sounded like a car alarm."

"It *was* a car alarm."

Julia gestured toward a guy who lived in the apartment directly across from the elevator. He was screaming at a woman from the sixteenth floor. She screamed back at him. Tears streamed down her face.

Julia explained, "The guy claims somebody's been stealing his newspaper every morning. He rigged up a trap to catch the miscreant. Very clever, that man. He got his *Times* the moment it was delivered this morning, and attached a string underneath the paper. The other end of the string led to a car alarm inside his apartment."

"And that lady—"

"When she grabbed the paper, she triggered the alarm. The guy came out into the hallway and sprayed her with some tear gas crap. Now she's talking lawsuit and he's talking citizen's arrest."

The super arrived. "Okay everybody, settle down, unless you want me to get the cops involved."

The newspaper thief snapped sunglasses over her watery, red, tear-gassed eyes and left in a huff. The guy slammed his door. Everybody else went back inside their apartments.

Instead of trying to get back to sleep, I took Jackhammer out for his morning walk. On the way back I picked up a blueberry muffin and large cup of coffee.

I had nothing to do but eat, think, worry, and wait for Castleberry's to open at ten. I actually waited until ten after ten, to give people time to get their coats off and their coffee poured, but by the time I punched my way through Castleberry's voice mail system, most employees were probably already on their second cups.

At last someone came on the line. "Return department."

"May I speak with Dolores please?"

"Afraid not. Dolores takes Mondays off because she works Sundays."

Perfect. Just as I'd hoped.

"Oh no," I said, in an effort to sound distraught. "I thought . . . well, you see, my situation is rather embarrassing. Actually it's more than embarrassing. It's damned serious. I could lose my job over this. I work at Castleberry's too, in the billing department. I think I might have goofed up some paperwork regarding a return. I'd straighten it out myself, but I'm home sick today, and the only person I know in the return department is Dolores."

"Perhaps I can be of help," the woman offered.

"Oh, do you think so? I appreciate that. What happened is I think I screwed up the billing on an item a customer returned."

"No big deal."

"I know, normally it wouldn't be. I mean, mistakes happen, right?"

"You better believe it. The more, the merrier, I always say."

"That's right," I said. "And we've always got the computer to blame."

She laughed. "Love 'em. Don't know what we did before the digital age."

"This time, I'm afraid I won't get away with pinning it on the computer. It's a very good customer, and a special friend—if you know what I mean—of one of our very married VPs, whose name I won't mention. If you could check your return records and see if the lady in question really returned the item, it'd be a big help."

"Sure, that's simple enough."

I gave her the particulars; she put me on hold. When she got back on the phone she told me what I needed to know. Harriet had purchased the hat. And on the morning Doreen Sands had been killed, she returned it.

I called Chuck. Given his recent craziness, I didn't try to engage him in chit-chat. "Is it possible to program one of your spare computers to have it call Midnight Millinery every ten minutes or so?"

"Piece of cake," he said. "I could do nine-minute intervals, ten-minute intervals, ten-minute-plus-two-nanosecond intervals."

"I figured you'd be able to handle it. Thank you."

"Not so freaking fast," he said. "The operative word was 'could.' Notice I didn't say 'would' and I won't until you tell me what you are up to."

"You sound like Turner and McKinley," I said. "Here's the deal: I need the phone to ring, that's all. I want to appear like I'm in demand to impress an important customer."

"That's all?"

"Yep."

"Promise?"

"Er . . ."

"I knew it. You're up to no good."

Chuck knew me too well.

"It's a notoriously difficult customer," I said. "She's so bad Fuzzy featured her in the bad customer alert area of her web page. If you don't believe me, look her up and see what other milliners say about her. She's coming to Midnight Millinery some time today to pick up a hat."

"And you think," said Chuck, "if this tough customer believes you are in demand, maybe she won't be so harsh in her criticism."

"That's right. You read me like a book."

"In that case, I not only can do, I will do."

"I owe you one, Chuck."

I felt guilty saying that. If Chuck knew I'd told Elizabeth he thought he might possibly be her love child, he'd tell me to get lost. I could forget about any more favors. But he didn't know, and so he did program his computer.

Later that day, approximately three and a half minutes after Harriet bustled into Midnight Millinery to pick up her custom-made, one-of-a-kind hat, the phone rang, as it had been doing in ten-minute intervals for the last couple of hours.

"Excuse me," I said, "I'd better get that." Leaving Harriet to frown over her hat, I picked up the phone, listened to the dial tone for a few seconds, then said into the receiver, "Oh no." I said it much louder than necessary.

I turned toward Harriet to make sure she caught the expression of extreme distress on my face. Of course she pretended to be looking intently through her loupe, examining some heinous flaw underneath the head-size band inside the hat, but I could tell from the way her eyebrows raised up that she was on the alert.

Positive I had her rapt attention, I lowered my voice a little and said into the phone, "That's awful." Then, a couple of beats later, "What are we going to do? A replacement? At this late date? You've got to be kidding. We'll never find anyone. Of course, I know the show must go on. All right, I'll see what I can do."

I hung up and sighed loudly.

Meanwhile Harriet, pretending not to have overheard my end of the phone conversation, had pulled out a pair of tiny calipers and was measuring the distance between hand stitches. It was painstaking work. It was probably more difficult to measure than to sew the original stitches. I watched her in wonderment. When I'd read the bit about Harriet's calipers, I had suspected it was only a figure of speech.

"What are you measuring?" I asked.

"Interstitch spacing, of course," she answered, as if it were perfectly normal behavior. "Your stitches exhibit a remarkable regularity of precisely five-point-seven-five per inch. I must say I am quite impressed with the quality of your work."

I smiled. "And I am impressed with how much you know about quality millinery. Few people these days are as knowledgeable."

"You are most certainly correct. It's a shame what some of these milliners think they can get away with."

I slapped the side of my head with my hand. "Ohmygod, I just got the most fabulous idea." If I were a cartoon, there'd have been a picture of a light bulb above my head with rays emanating from it. "You know, that phone call I had?"

"Oh yes, you did receive a call, didn't you?" said Harriet. "I was so absorbed with the inspection of this hat, I barely noticed."

"I'm afraid it was terrible news. A friend of mine is putting on a millinery extravaganza tomorrow, Milliners Milling Around the Millennium, and a very important participant, a quality control expert in the field, has been injured in a terrible millinery accident."

"My goodness," said Harriet, clasping her hand to her chest. "I didn't know there were such things as millinery accidents."

"This accident was of a mechanical nature," I said. "It had to do with a faulty spring-loaded hat block. The victim will be laid up for days. She was to give a little talk on quality in couture."

"An all-too-often neglected subject," said Harriet.

"You are so right. That's why I was thinking maybe you'd like to take the place of our expert."

"Me? I'm not a milliner."

"Perhaps not, but you've demonstrated that you know more about fine millinery than most milliners. Please say you'll do it."

"I must admit, I'm flattered."

"Then you'll do it?"

"I most certainly will."

"Wonderful," I said. "You've saved the show."

I gave her directions to Fuzzy's loft building. "Get there a little early, say seven o'clock. That'll give us a chance to run through your bit, a dress rehearsal. We'll check the sound system, the lights, make sure it all works to your satisfaction."

"I'm very excited. This is quite an opportunity for me."

"I'm excited too. You'll be terrific. I'd be very pleased if you were to wear this hat I made for you as an example of excellent work."

"I believe I will. It's a fine hat."

She hadn't complained. I wondered how she'd get out

of paying. I wrapped the hat in tissue, floated it down into a Midnight Millinery hatbox, closed up the top, and presented it along with a bill to Harriet. It didn't come as too much of a surprise that she'd forgotten her money.

"That's okay," I said. "You can pay me tomorrow at the show."

The phone rang. I picked up and got a dial tone. It was Chuck's computer, calling again, right on schedule. I called Chuck.

"Thanks," I said. "The ringing worked like a charm."

"Did you expect otherwise?" asked Chuck, cranky again.

"Of course not. I knew you could do the technical part, but I wasn't sure of the effect it would have on the customer. That's what I meant. Now, can you stop your computer from calling me?"

Predictably, Chuck said, "Piece of cake."

"Thanks Chuck. I guess I'll see you at Fuzzy's tomorrow."

"I'll be the one with the laser."

"I'll be the one with the hat."

"Very funny, Brenda."

Next I called Fuzzy and told her I'd invited Harriet to participate in the show.

Naturally Fuzzy freaked out. "Girl, are you out of your ever-loving mind? Harriet? Here? My loft? My show? No way. Never. The Milliners Milling Around the Millennium show will be ruined. I don't even want Harriet on the premises, and I would never let her take part in my show."

It would have been so much easier if I could have leveled with Fuzzy and told her it would prove for once and for all that the person who had killed Doreen Sands was not Fuzzy herself. But since Fuzzy didn't have the foggiest idea I knew she had a motive, or that I'd been on the verge of ratting on her to the cops, and was making this one last effort to prove that someone else was the killer, I couldn't say that. Instead I told her, "Trust me. You'll be happy you agreed."

"But I didn't agree."

I switched tactics. "If you go along with this, it will be a service to the millinery community."

"Oh yeah, sure."

"Don't you see? Harriet is bound to make a complete jackass of herself. When all is said and done, she won't dare show her face in any millinery shop anywhere near here. None of us will ever have to worry about her again."

It drove Fuzzy nuts that I refused to elaborate. "Let's just say Harriet will get her due and the media will go wild."

"You positive?"

"Yes. And remember, Fuzzy, it was I who got Johnny Verlane to emcee."

That did it. "This better be good, Brenda."

"Oh it will be. I promise fireworks."

32

I didn't invite Gundermutter to Fuzzy's Milliners Milling Around the Millennium show until two hours before it was to begin. That way, once I talked her into it, she'd have less time to change her mind and try to weasel out of it. I knew she'd be on duty and in Manhattan, so reaching her was no problem. Talking her into it was.

She resisted. "Let me see if I have this straight," she said. "You expect me, while I'm on duty, to ditch my partner and venture out of the precinct to attend a hat show."

"Well, yes."

"Get serious, Brenda."

I was dead serious. However, after yesterday's debacle at Castleberry's, I lacked the credibility to convince Gundermutter. "It's not just any old millinery show. It's an extravaganza. The media will be out in force, Johnny Verlane is the emcee, and my friend Chuck Riley is doing the lights. He's got lasers and—"

"Lasers? I thought lasers were illegal."

Gung-ho Gundermutter, always on the lookout for a crime that would lead to her first arrest.

"These are small lasers, not the kind used by the military. They must be legal," I said. "Remember the seventies? Discos? Polyester bell bottoms and platform shoes? Lasers were all over the place."

"I suppose you're right."

"Now then, getting back to Fuzzy's show, the evening will culminate when I unveil the killer of Doreen Sands. All that, plus free hors d'oeuvres. How can you possibly say no?"

"Easy," said Gundermutter. "No."

"Please."

"I suppose you expect me to snap handcuffs on the villain who, when confronted, will give a teary public confession with all the interested parties conveniently gathered around. Right?"

"That's pretty much what I had in mind," I said.

"In that case, your mind is defective. However, it would be nice to see that handsome Johnny Verlane once again in the flesh. So, tell you what I'll do. You mentioned free food? As a favor—that is, as yet *another* in a long line of increasingly complicated favors—I'll drop by your little hat fest on my dinner break. I'll flirt with Johnny Verlane, sample the hors d'oeuvres, and check out the scene. If I happen to stumble over anybody worth arresting, I'll make the collar." A goofy laugh and she clicked off.

I called Chuck immediately.

"Those lasers you're bringing to Fuzzy's, are they legal?"

"Yep. Why?"

"It's like I kind of invited this cop I know to drop by the show and just wanted to make sure everything was on the up and up."

"Don't worry. I'm properly licensed to operate a laser."

"That's a relief."

"Tell me what's up. Why the cop?"

"She's a friend."

"Somehow I have a sneaking suspicion that this show will end up being more than a light show and bunch of hats. Do you have anything you want to tell me, Brenda?"

"Not that I can think of."

"You didn't get cute and invite Elizabeth, did you?"

"No."

*   *   *

I should have told Chuck "not yet," and I would have too, had I known that early that evening when I was on my way to Fuzzy's I would run into Elizabeth in the hallway outside our apartments.

Elizabeth asked where I was off to, and I had to invite her. It would have been rude not to. What with her painting, and the schedule she'd been keeping, I figured she'd say no.

"That sounds fantastic," she said. "I could use a little break in my routine. I have a couple of errands to do first, then I'll wander on down. Catch you later."

I didn't tell her that Chuck would be manning the light show. It seemed best not to.

Hatbox in hand, I descended into the subway and stepped right onto a downtown-bound Seventh Avenue Express. The train was filled with post-happy-hour midtown workers on their daily commute back home to Brooklyn. They were, for the most part, a jovial bunch.

Wall Street is the last Manhattan stop. As we approached the station, I got up and moved closer to the door. Suddenly the train screeched to a halt. The lights blinked off, on again, then off. With a sigh and a shudder, the motor shut down.

The other passengers rolled their eyes at the indecipherable crackle and electronic noise that signaled the fact that the conductor was making an announcement as to the train's status.

I checked my watch and cursed under my breath. I'm never late.

Never say never.

One hour later, about the time my fellow rail travelers belted out round ninety-nine of a rousing rendition of "Ninety-nine Bottles of Beer on the Wall," the train started up again. After progressing what seemed like no more than thirty feet, we finally rolled into the Wall Street station. The doors parted. I hit the platform running, hightailed it up the steps, out of the station, made a couple of quick turns, and got to Fuzzy's street.

The way real estate ads tout Fuzzy's neighborhood as the hip, trendy new place to live, you'd think the streets would always be teeming with young, new media cyber entrepreneurs, the kind I ran into when I'd visited Fuzzy. Not so. By evening, the streets were deserted and prematurely dark, left in twilight by tall buildings.

I'd almost reached my destination when Harriet stepped out from the shadows and planted herself in front of me on the sidewalk. I was pleased to see she had on the Midnight Millinery hat, less pleased to see the mean-looking scowl that distorted her face.

I could imagine what must have happened. Without me around to smooth things over, some of the milliners had probably ganged up on Harriet and given her a hard time. She must have split, but instead of just going away mad, she waited for me so she could give me a piece of her mind. Thanks to that stalled train, my plan to catch a killer was now totally screwed up.

Tentatively, I smiled at Harriet. "Sorry I'm late. The train stopped between stations. We were stuck in the tunnel for an hour. I should have taken a cab."

"Don't think I don't know about your little plan," she snarled.

"Huh?" I said. How could Harriet know about my plan? If she did, I was in big trouble.

This for sure was not the way I'd planned what I'd planned.

Looking around, I confirmed a frightening fact: I was alone with a killer on one of the loneliest streets in Manhattan. The killer was angry at me and claimed to know of my plan, which was to reveal her guilt. Somehow, the subtlety that I didn't think she was *very* guilty, and would most likely get off with a light sentence or probation, probably didn't matter too much to her at the moment.

I was in way over my head. All I could do was hope somebody else would be late to Fuzzy's show, stumble upon us, and salvage the situation. Somebody like Gundermutter. With her gun.

"You set me up," said Harriet.

I nodded. I could see no advantage in lying.

"I saw right through that fake phone call you took when I was at Midnight Millinery," she said. "And then your perfectly timed brilliant idea that I substitute for your downed quality control expert. A spring-loaded hatblock. You must take me for an idiot."

I didn't think Harriet was an idiot. Not being one myself, I kept my mouth shut.

"I know what you and all those other milliners think about me. The only reason you wanted me here . . ."

I had to say something. Do something. Anything.

". . . was to heckle me."

Heckle? Did Harriet say heckle? She wasn't talking about murder. Or the fact that I was setting her up for a teary confession and subsequent arrest.

While I quickly reanalyzed the situation, Harriet raged on. "I'll have you know I can take whatever you snobby milliners dish out."

I attempted to appease her. "You misunderstood my intentions," I said. "Heckling would never have been a problem."

"Oh, really?"

I thought fast. "Yes, really. You see, Johnny Verlane is the emcee. He's a pro. You better be sure he knows how to stop a heckler. Believe me, milliners listen when Johnny speaks."

"Johnny Verlane? You mean the one from the television show, *Tod Trueman, Urban Detective*?"

"That's him. Johnny is a personal friend of mine. That's why he agreed to do the show."

"That Johnny Verlane is quite a looker."

"And a gentleman."

The situation was definitely turning around. Babbling on about Johnny's level of professionalism and how he could stop a heckler with one look, I gradually edged toward the entrance to Fuzzy's building. If I could make it inside, I'd have a better chance to turn this around.

Harriet inched along with me, not protesting, probably not even noticing our progression.

Little by little we got closer to the doorway. We were almost there when I stubbed my toe on a chunk of busted-up sidewalk and pitched forward. I caught my balance, but in doing so, dropped the hatbox I was carrying.

And watched in horror as it hit the sidewalk.

The impact knocked the lid off; it rolled into the middle of the street. Two hats bounced out. One was the hat I'd made for the show. The other was the hat from Castleberry's—the very same hat Harriet returned the day she killed Doreen Sands, the hat styled exactly like the one she currently had on her head.

Caught by a gust of wind, the Castleberry's hat became airborne. It hovered over the narrow street for a few seconds, then plopped down into the gutter, settling into a pool of unidentifiable viscous liquid.

I looked at Harriet.

Harriet looked at me.

She plucked the hat out of the gutter. "Where'd you get this hat?"

"I uh . . ."

"Don't even try," she said. "I know exactly where you got this hat. It came from Castleberry's. This is the hat I returned."

Like I said, Harriet was no idiot. She put two and two together pretty quickly. If I knew about the hat she'd returned, I must have figured out what she'd done immediately after, which was to burst into Doreen Sands's office to complain about the hat. When Harriet got nasty, Doreen Sands pulled out Turner's gun. In the subsequent struggle, Doreen got killed.

Harriet was no longer concerned about being heckled by a bunch of milliners. She must have surmised I had far more serious plans for her.

"I know you didn't mean to kill Doreen Sands," I said, soothingly. "It was a tragic accident. If you turn yourself in, the cops will go much easier on you. They'll probably see it as self-defense. I know a good lawyer. He can have you back on the street in hours."

Harriet threw down the hat. "You're good at hand-stitching," she snarled, "but you don't know a goddamn thing about murder. The Sands bitch had a lot of nerve, threatened to call security on me. I couldn't let that happen, now could I?"

I didn't see why not, but kept my mouth shut. Harriet wasn't waiting for me to answer anyway.

"I killed Doreen Sands all right. And you, I'm afraid, are next."

Harriet whipped a gun out of her purse and pointed it at me.

Fuzzy's street may have been dark and narrow, but the vacant lot sandwiched between the buildings was much darker and much narrower. And that's where Harriet and I stood, looking at each other, killer and reckless milliner. We were behind a construction trailer, hidden from the street. This had been an incredibly stupid idea. I'd truly outdone myself.

Why did Harriet have a gun? She'd killed Doreen Sands with Turner's gun, right? Very confusing. I didn't dwell. For the moment, it was far more important to focus on the fact that for whatever reason Harriet did in fact have a gun, and that gun was still aimed straight at me.

Should I make a run for it? Scream? Grab her wrist, and try to force her to drop the gun?

"You're making a big mistake," I said.

"Oh yeah?" said Harriet. "Why don't you tell me about it?"

"I'm neither brave nor stupid, and I'm certainly not nuts enough to plan to confront you without letting the cops in on it. In fact, they're watching us right this second."

"Sharpshooters on the rooftops, no doubt."

"Well . . ."

And then I saw it. Out of the corner of my eye. A tiny bright red dot squiggling a pattern on the brick wall.

Chuck. Lasers. Sharpshooters. I didn't know if Chuck was goofing around or if he knew I was in trouble. It didn't matter. I seized the opportunity.

"Funny you should mention the sharpshooters," I said, nodding my head in the direction of the dancing laser dot. "You're already in their laser sights."

Harriet looked at the little laser dot, computed what it meant, and gasped.

"I think you better give me that gun," I said, full of confidence I did not feel.

And she did.

I pointed the gun at her. Frightening, but I dealt with my fear. It was far better than having the gun pointed at me.

"I think we better go inside now," I said.

I marched her out of the lot over to the door to Fuzzy's building. Then, I looked up toward the rooftop and shouted, "Thanks guys. I've got the situation under control. I'm bringing the prisoner in."

The milliners were certainly milling. Among the revelers, I quickly found Gundermutter. I told her what was up. She popped a crab-stuffed mushroom hors d'oeuvre into her mouth and made the collar.

33

To my great and very humbling surprise, the show which must go on, was in fact going on. My time with Harriet had been so personally intense, so all-consuming, I was positive everyone would be aware of what had happened. Yet, it seemed no one knew. Nor had anyone noticed the arrest—Gundermutter's very first—because it happened close to the entrance in the front part of Fuzzy's loft. At the very same moment, at the back of the loft, Johnny Verlane was on stage.

Johnny wore a sexy lush gray fedora with the brim turned down over his left eye. The look was more 1940s private eye than end-of-the-millennium Tod Trueman, Urban Detective of the NYPD, but it was a good look. The milliners were riveted.

I had to give Gundermutter credit for a quick, professional, very subtle arrest. Even Fuzzy, who had a sharp eye, hadn't noticed the disturbance near the entrance of her very own loft. Later, when I spotted her across the room, I made eye contact, and waved.

She hurried over. "Why are you late and where the hell is your hat?"

Both hats were still where they'd landed. The one I'd made for me to wear to Fuzzy's show was on the sidewalk, the hat Harriet had returned to Castleberry's was in the gutter. They'd be long gone by the time I got back outside.

"My train got stuck. As to my hat, in all the excitement—"

"What excitement?"

"Long story. Tell you later."

"Tell me this now: Where is Harriet?"

"Detained. I'm afraid Harriet won't be able to make it after all."

"Well, that's just great," said Fuzzy. "I mean, it's not like I wanted Harriet here, but since you insisted, I rearranged the program to accommodate her. Now I've got a gaping hole to fill."

"How about a tribute to Doreen Sands?" I suggested.

"Great. Fantastic. Why didn't I think of that?"

I wished she had. Since it was my idea, Fuzzy insisted I do it. Because the whole mess was somewhat my fault, I felt obligated.

"Okay, but I don't know what to say."

"Wing it."

I stood off to the side of the stage. In honor of the serious nature of the tribute, Chuck had pulled back on his lighting effects. A single spot lit the center of the stage where Johnny now stood and where I was soon to stand.

Johnny leaned into the microphone and said, in that wonderful broadcast-quality voice of his, "And now, Brenda Midnight will say a few words." He held out his hand to me and guided me up on the stage. We stood together for a moment, then he backed away, leaving me alone in the spotlight.

In the spot, on the spot.

Winging it was not so easy.

My heart pounded. My fingers turned to ice, yet at the same time my palms dripped sweat. This was a whole different kind of scary than out in the vacant lot with Harriet. After that, I should have been able to handle a little bit of stage fright. What was the big deal? I immediately wished I hadn't asked myself that question, because the answer, "people," was so very obvious, and so very frightening. They crowded around—media, milliners, guests, and freeloaders. Every last one of them was looking at me.

I froze. I opened my mouth, but no words came out.

Johnny and I go way back. We've been friends, or more-than-friends, even not-on-speaking-terms friends for such a very long time that I sometimes forget what attracted me to him in the first place. Standing on that stage I refreshed my memory. It had nothing to do with his cheekbones or those smoky gray eyes. Behind all that stuff, deep down Johnny was a good and loyal friend. He could have teased me to get a laugh from the audience. Instead, he saved me. He walked over to me, turned his back to the audience, and brought his voice down low. "Just breathe, Brenda, it'll be okay."

I took that breath, and then another, and it was okay.

I looked out at the audience. "May we have a moment of silence please as we take our hats off to Doreen Sands, a lady who knew good millinery."

After that, I got swallowed up by the show, which was chaotic, and happening not only on the stage, but all over the place, all at the same time. Even I never dreamed there were so many hats in this world.

The media snapped pictures and shot videotape. Fuzzy beamed.

I caught sight of Elizabeth a few times. She seemed to be having a good time, though I noticed she avoided the area off to the side that Chuck had taken over with his lighting equipment.

Chuck made himself scarce. I didn't track him down until after the show. He was cramming his equipment into a sturdy black metal case. He looked mad.

"Hi Chuck."

Before I could thank him for saving my life, he tore into me. "You told me you didn't invite Elizabeth."

"I hadn't when I said I hadn't, but then I did."

"Well, it was a crappy thing to do." For emphasis, he slammed the lid on the case.

"The circumstances were beyond my control," I said.

"Anyway, I'm glad you weren't too angry to save my life."

"What's that crack supposed to mean?"

"It means you saved my life and I came over here to thank you. So, thank you. Thank you very much."

"I didn't save anybody's life."

"Then who pointed the laser out the window?"

"That was me. It's an immutable law, a given. Laser plus window equals laser shining out window. Illegal, of course, also inevitable. It used to be more fun. The little red dot squiggling around drove people crazy. They thought it was from outer space. Then, along came disco and everybody knew what those red dots were. It was no big mystery, no aliens had landed, it was just some nerdy neighbor shining a laser out the window. Again. But now that laser gun sights are standard issue, shining lasers out the window is too dangerous. You could give somebody a heart attack. None of this changed the immutable law. I'd been itching to shine a laser out a window for the longest time. That vacant lot seemed like the perfect place to do it. Nobody was around to freak."

"Wrong," I said. "You didn't look carefully enough. Somebody was around, and they did freak, and it's a damned good thing."

I saved the whole story for later. In fact, holding back turned out to be an effective persuasion to get Chuck and Elizabeth into Angie's at the same time, seated at the same table.

We—Chuck, Elizabeth, Johnny and me—were in the back room, wedged into a booth. We were arranged with girls on one side, boys on the other, me sitting across from Chuck and Elizabeth sitting across from Johnny. We were all a little tense.

Chuck was embarrassed around Elizabeth and still mad at me for inviting her to Fuzzy's, and Elizabeth was embarrassed around Chuck and mad at him. And, as my story unfolded, Johnny, who was never embarrassed, became more and more mad at me for almost getting myself killed.

Since everybody was mad at somebody, nobody interrupted me. I told the entire story from start to finish, leaving out only the part about Turner's gun. "So," I said in conclusion, "Gundermutter made the pinch as planned. Sort of."

I took a big drink of red wine and smiled.

Johnny shook his head. "It's that 'sort of,' Brenda. It sort of bugs the hell out me."

"Sort of bugs me too," said Chuck.

Before Elizabeth chimed in on the subject, I defended myself. "The situation was not supposed to be dangerous. Harriet's gun came as a total surprise."

"Why a surprise?" asked Chuck. "It's like you plan to capture a killer, a killer whom you believed has recently killed with a gun, but now you say you're surprised she had a gun. Something is not right with this picture."

He was wrong. The picture was right, he just didn't have the whole picture, the focal point of which was Turner.

"Harriet must have had more than one gun," said Elizabeth. "It makes sense to me that a killer would have an extra gun or two. She had one gun today, and another gun when she killed Doreen Sands. That's the gun she sneaked into Brenda's hatbox."

Johnny's eyes met mine. He knew about Turner's gun.

I gave my head a tiny shake, enough to let him know to keep mum. "That's right," I said. "She must have." Before anyone demanded a more detailed explanation, I changed the subject. "Nice job by Gundermutter, don't you all think? It was her very first arrest."

"Slick," said Johnny.

"It was hardly like any of the times I got arrested," said Elizabeth. "Of course, I was into passive resistance. I take it Harriet cooperated fully?"

"Yes," I said. "She was afraid of those sharpshooters."

We all laughed at that, even Chuck.

Much later Gundermutter came by the apartment to yell at me. "You should have told me what was going down. You could have gotten yourself killed."

"I did tell you. Remember?"

"Then you should have told me in such a way that I would have believed it. How could you even consider confronting a killer all by yourself? Did you think she'd leave her gun at home?"

"I didn't plan to confront her all by myself. I planned to give Harriet the hat she'd returned to Castleberry's when she was on stage doing her quality control bit. At that moment, she'd know that I knew, and she'd be trapped. I didn't plan for the train to get stuck, or to trip over a chunk of sidewalk, or for the hat to fall out of the box. Besides, I didn't think Harriet would have a gun."

"Why the hell not? Guns. Killers. They frequently go together. Face it, Brenda, basically you weren't thinking."

"You're right," I said. "I acted in haste."

It would have been much easier if I could have told Gundermutter that Doreen Sands had been killed with Turner's gun.

Or was she? I was still mighty confused. My old theory no longer explained the events. Could it be possible that Turner's gun was not the murder weapon?

"I did some checking on your friend Harriet," said Gundermutter. "The lady is a career criminal. The harassment of milliners is merely a hobby. Her real work is armed robbery, knocking over fancy boutiques in Soho and on Madison Avenue. That's quite likely how she discovered fine millinery in the first place."

That explained Harriet's gun. Things were starting to fall into place.

Gundermutter continued. "I think it's gonna shake out like this: Harriet went to Castleberry's to return the hat, got no satisfaction from the return department, and forced her way into Doreen Sands's office to gripe to the big cheese. They argued. You with me so far?"

"Yeah," I said. "Harriet told me Doreen threatened to call security. At the time I wondered why getting thrown out was such a big deal. I get it now. Harriet must have panicked because of her gun. Illegal, I bet."

"Right. She didn't want security to find it. Who knows, maybe she even had stolen goods on her. Guess we'll never know, but we found a shitload of cash and high-class designer duds and jewelry in her apartment.''

"She had good taste.''

Gundermutter chuckled. "So anyway, before Doreen Sands had a chance to make good on her threat to call security, Harriet shot her. Afraid to leave the premises in possession of the smoking gun, she stashed it in your hat-box on her way out.''

Close, I thought, but not quite. Gundermutter had done well, considering she lacked the essential information that Doreen Sands was also armed—with Turner's gun—and that McKinley sneaked a throw-down into my hatbox.

"Too damned bad that gun got lost in the system,'' said Gundermutter. "Lucky for you I found your hats.''

"It sure is,'' I said.

Not long after Gundermutter left, Turner showed up. I figured he would.

"Gundermutter did good,'' he said.

"She certainly did.''

"I'm sorry about that other thing.''

"Sorry enough to answer some questions truthfully?''

"Shoot,'' he said.

When Turner found his gun with the body, he made two wrong assumptions. One, that Doreen Sands had killed herself. And two, that she'd used his gun to do it. He should have known better than to assume.

There was one detail I still didn't understand. "Couldn't you have sniffed your gun or something to see if it had been fired?'' I asked.

Turner gave me one of those looks like I was the stu-pidest person in the world. "Yes, Ms. Midnight, I coulda sniffed it or something. I coulda done that. But I thought it was suicide, and I was worried about keeping my job, so I didn't.''

"I assume Harriet's gun, the one she pointed at me, is the murder weapon.''

"Looks that way,'' said Turner.

"How will you explain that the other gun, the throw-down, the gun McKinley sneaked into my hatbox, the gun that got 'lost in the system' is not the murder weapon?''

"I won't. You see, Ms. Midnight, lots of stuff slips through the cracks. The important thing is, we now have the murder weapon. Sometimes the details don't count.''

Early the next morning Chuck called, waking me up. "Brenda," he said, "I've got great news.''

"Which is?''

"After I got home last night, I started to think about all those times Elizabeth got arrested. I did some research on the web and found a sixties site loaded with data on many well-known radicals and peaceniks. Elizabeth was listed with her dozens of arrests. Did you know she actually served time?''

"She mentioned it.''

"Dig this. I, Chuck Riley, could not possibly be the love child of Elizabeth Franklin Perry. Elizabeth was in the slammer the day I was born.''

"Happy birthday," I said.

34

Chuck went back to being Chuck, weird, but not crazy out of his mind. He was still desperately in love with Elizabeth, who still pretended not to notice, which was probably deep down the way Chuck wanted it.

He never found out that I had broken his confidence and spilled the beans to Elizabeth.

Elizabeth claimed to be on a health food kick. "Had to give up the cookie baking," she said. "Too much sugar. Too much fat."

I knew better. She was applying her creative juices at her secret painting studio down on Spring Street. I frequently ran into her coming or going at odd hours and smelling of turpentine. Once, when she saw me staring at a splotch of alizarin crimson under her fingernails, I think she almost told me.

Fuzzy admitted that she had designed a collection of artistically brilliant, yet wearable hats. She'd planned to show the new line for the first time during Milliners Milling Around the Millennium. "But everything got messed up when Doreen Sands was killed."

"How so?"

"Doreen was helping me on the manufacturing end. We kept it very hush-hush. I didn't want to unveil the hats until the deal was definite."

"I see," I said.

That explained the carefully deconstructed hats at Doreen Sands's apartment. And the matching hats I'd seen at Fuzzy's. It was nice to know Doreen wasn't knocking off hats.

"Then, when Doreen died," said Fuzzy, "I had put the line on hold while I worked out some of the fine points with the manufacturer. It was too late to cancel the show, so I went ahead with it. I figured, why not. It was fun, don't you think?"

"You could call it that."

"It was the perfect venue for the arrest of Harriet. Too bad I didn't get to see you and your cop friend make the bust. Next time, Brenda, try to get the action a little closer to the stage."

When I didn't hear from Ray Marshall, I finally called him. It took awhile to connect, as if the call was forwarded, bounced from here to wherever. Ray could have been half a world away for all I knew. Back on the job, I supposed.

"Brenda," he said. "I've been meaning to get in touch."

"I know how it is. Are you in New York?"

"Uh, not exactly. I'm—"

"That's okay. I wanted you to know they got Doreen's killer."

"I had a feeling the police would come through. Who did it?"

"Some nutcase. Next time I see you I'll give you the details. Did you ever tell Gregory that Doreen knew he was having an affair?"

"Even better. I got Elyse to admit she'd told Doreen herself."

"How'd you get her to do that?"

"Easy. I gave her a dose of her own medicine. 'Do it, or else' I told her."

I settled down and got back to work, finishing the hats for the uptown order and the downtown order slightly ahead of schedule. Just when I got a moment to relax, the uptown buyer reordered. Then, the very next day the downtown buyer reordered. I was swamped.

Turner and McKinley showed up at Midnight Millinery almost every afternoon, leaving their unmarked vehicle double-parked at the curb. They hung out, watched me work, shot the breeze, and played Catch the Chewy Toy with Jackhammer.

Jackhammer loved it, but the detectives got on my nerves.

Finally, I couldn't stand it anymore. I had to comment. "What's the deal? A new doughnut shop open up nearby?"

Turner scowled. "Very funny, Ms. Midnight."

"Well then, why all the attention? You two were never exactly passionate about hats before. Perhaps you are thinking of moonlighting as blockers?"

"Don't be silly, Ms. Midnight."

Who did they think they were kidding? I knew exactly what the detectives were up to. They had to pretend we were great friends to make sure I wouldn't rat on them. If word about Turner's gun and their subsequent coverup ever came to light, they wouldn't be thinking about moonlighting. They'd be thinking about entire new careers.

I wanted to hear them say it, so I kept at them. "What brings you here today, gentlemen?" was my usual question.

Their usual answer. "We were just passing by."

Oh sure.

As a result of their little charade I was kept well informed about Harriet's trip through the system. The prosecutor handling the case was confident she'd spend time behind bars.

Gundermutter also dropped by frequently, often early in the morning on her way to the precinct. For days after her big collar she positively glowed. Apparently it was a very big deal when a cop's first arrest nabs a prosecutable murderer. Whenever either one of us happened to mention Detective Spencer Turner, Gundermutter blushed like a teenager.

*   *   *

I don't believe in interfering or playing cupid. However, when a certain circumstance presented itself, I couldn't resist the opportunity to do a good turn for my friends, the cops.

Lemmy's movie project, the one about the Iowa pig farmer turned sheriff that Johnny so wisely passed up, was due to open. Despite bad feelings, Lemmy gave Johnny two passes for the gala opening night and the party after.

Johnny and I had reached another exciting new plateau in our relationship: we were both so busy—him with his workout-as-you-cook book and me with my reorders—we almost never saw each other. It was like we'd broken up, without all the messy parts, and with the full confidence that someday . . . well, someday. Maybe.

To get to the point, Johnny invited me to the screening and I said sure. Then, the day before, he punked out. "I don't see how I can tear myself away," he said. "I'm at a crucial turning point in my book."

I'd never heard of a crucial turning point in a workout-as-you-cook book. I was sure his backing out was a case of professional jealousy. He'd made the right decision about the movie. Still, it must have been weird for him to think it could have been him.

I couldn't have cared less about seeing one of Lemmy's other clients bigger than life on the silver screen, slopping pigs and speeding down gravel roads in a pickup truck with a cherry on top. I ended up with the two passes anyway. When I noticed the seats were designated by row and aisle, I got an idea.

The next morning when Gundermutter came by, I gave her one of the passes. "They're already talking Academy Award," I said to encourage her to go.

Later that afternoon when Turner and McKinley made their daily visit, I gave Turner the other pass.

I was fully aware that Lemmy Crenshaw would be spitting mad when he saw Turner, his nemesis, in Johnny's seat, which would no doubt be near his own. And, naturally, McKinley was hurt I didn't have a pass for him. They'd get over it.

*   *   *

I had become immune to cops popping into Midnight Millinery, and so was hardly surprised when the two Rent-A-Cops from Castleberry's crack security team darkened my doorway. This time, Good Rent-A-Cop did all the talking. He apologized for rousting me, though not quite in those words. In fact, the words he used were so carefully chosen, and contained so many syllables, and were delivered in such a monotone, I suspected they came straight from Castleberry's legal department. The subtext pretty much said it all: please don't sue our fine department store.

Once he got the canned speech out of the way, Good Rent-A-Cop told me that the "real reason" for their visit was to return my bottle of Veiled Threat, which they had confiscated and which I had forgotten all about. With it was a letter on engraved Castleberry's stationery from an assistant vice president. He cited unprecedented customer demand for the perfume. "Despite the unauthorized and possibly illegal manner in which you launched your new scent, Castleberry's would be proud to add Veiled Threat to our roster."

I scribbled a note back to the assistant vice president. "Sorry. Veiled Threat was a private-label limited edition."

Murder Is on the Menu
at the Hillside Manor Inn
Bed-and-Breakfast Mysteries by
MARY DAHEIM
featuring Judith McMonigle

The Joanna Brady Mysteries by National Bestselling Author

An assassin's bullet shattered Joanna Brady's world, leaving her policeman husband to die in the Arizona desert. But the young widow fought back the only way she knew how: by bringing the killers to justice . . . and winning herself a job as Cochise County Sheriff.

DESERT HEAT
76545-4/$3.99 US/$3.99 Can

TOMBSTONE COURAGE
76546-2/$6.99 US/$8.99 Can

SHOOT/DON'T SHOOT
76548-9/$6.50 US/$8.50 Can

DEAD TO RIGHTS
72432-4/$6.99 US/$8.99 Can

SKELETON CANYON
72433-2/$6.99 US/$8.99 Can

RATTLESNAKE CROSSING
79247-8/$6.99 US/$8.99 Can

———— And in Hardcover ————

OUTLAW MOUNTAIN
97500-9/$24.00 US/$35.00 Can

IRIS HOUSE B & B MYSTERIES

by

JEAN HAGER

Featuring Proprietress and part-time sleuth, Tess Darcy

SEW DEADLY
78638-9/$5.99 US/$7.99 Can

THE LAST NOEL
78637-0/$5.99 US/$7.99 Can

DEATH ON THE DRUNKARD'S PATH
77211-6/$5.50 US/$7.50 Can

DEAD AND BURIED
77210-8/$5.50 US/$7.50 Can

BLOOMING MURDER
77209-4/$5.50 US/$7.50 Can